"Sheriff

At his shout, the [...] rolling and preparing to run.

Eric stepped closer and pinned the suspect with the flashlight beam.

Then the summer night, the achingly familiar sights and sounds pressing in around him and a vision from his past seized him in a moment of déjà vu that rooted him to the spot. Carrinne Wilmington, seventeen years older but somehow exactly the same, dressed from head to toe in burglar black, stared at him, her face a mask of fear and shock.

Eric instinctively adjusted the flashlight's glare out of her eyes.

"Eric?" Carrinne squinted. "What are you doing here?"

Dear Reader,

I've been asked repeatedly where I find the ideas for my stories. And as many writers have said before me, it's not so much that I find my stories and characters, as they find me.

My young family has changed a great deal over the past decade, as my husband and I established our careers and my son raced through preschool and kindergarten. Looking back, it's important to remember the heartache and struggles we've endured. The mistakes and the false starts that showed us what was truly important, and what was best left behind. The decisions that helped us grow into the happy family we are today.

Decisions are powerful things. That's the theme woven into *The Unknown Daughter*. It's through our most difficult choices that we discover who we are and what we believe. I find the process of making life-changing decisions fascinating. Sometimes you succeed. Sometimes you fail. But facing the next challenge, when everything within is screaming at you to run the other way, is the very essence of living.

I wish for you the courage and the determination you need to grow into all that you dream you'll be. And I'd love to hear your thoughts on Carrinne and Eric's story. Visit me at my author Web site, www.annawrites.com, and register for one of my contests.

Sincerely,

Anna DeStefano

The Unknown Daughter

Anna DeStefano

Hope you enjoy!

Anna

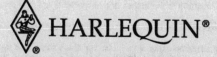

HARLEQUIN®

TORONTO • NEW YORK • LONDON
AMSTERDAM • PARIS • SYDNEY • HAMBURG
STOCKHOLM • ATHENS • TOKYO • MILAN • MADRID
PRAGUE • WARSAW • BUDAPEST • AUCKLAND

ISBN 0-373-71234-0

THE UNKNOWN DAUGHTER

To my father, Walton, whose passing taught me
to cherish all of life, both the ups and the downs.

To my mother, Jane, and her love for the written word,
who never doubted that my name would one day
share space with the countless others on her bookshelves.

To my son, Jimmy, who is a daily reminder
of the perfection of God's miracles.

To my husband, Andrew, who has always wanted for me
every dream I could possibly dream.

And to my critique partners, Tanya, Rachelle, Dorene,
Anna A. and Missy and the countless friends
I've made along my writing journey.

All that's true in this story, all that comes from my heart
wouldn't have been possible
without the blessing of your love.

CHAPTER ONE

CARRINNE WILMINGTON glared through the windshield of her rented Dodge at the stately south Georgia mansion that had been her family's home for as long as they'd kept records in these parts. Ancient oak trees flanked the house, their tops dancing in the balmy July breeze. The moon skimmed a cloud-churned sky, creating midnight shadows that shifted in the changing light.

She fought the urge to peel away from the curb, to keep driving until she reached the airstrip just outside of Oakwood and caught the next flight back to New York. Turning off the ignition, she glanced down at herself, then dropped her head to the steering wheel.

She was a B-movie cliché.

Her city clothes, black on black on black, had seemed a logical choice when she'd left the roadside motel on the outskirts of town. She was sneaking back in the dead of night, for heaven's sake. She needed invisibility, anonymity.

With a groan, she sat back. What she needed was to have her head examined. Who cared what she was wearing, when she was about to walk back into the world that had nearly destroyed her?

Her eyes traveled to the dormer windows her grandfather slept behind. Controlling yet distant, Oliver Wilmington had been the only family she'd ever known after her mother had died giving her life, and he'd let her down when she'd needed him the most. Now, seventeen years later, he couldn't know she was back. No one could. If she was lucky and found what she'd come for, she'd be out of here and back in New York by tomorrow afternoon.

Get on with it, Carrinne.

She pushed open the door and slid out, gritting her teeth against the sick taste of fear.

"Get in, find Mom's diary, then get out," she whispered, creeping through the dimness toward the gray brick house. The diary had to be in the attic, inside the trunk that held her mother's things. "Forget about everything else."

But the past shimmered in every shadow as she skirted landscaped shrubs and flowerbeds that were exactly where they had always been. She turned the corner toward the back terrace and stumbled to a halt at the base of an enormous cypress tree, her childhood refuge where she'd read fairy tales and dreamed girlish dreams.

Her old friend welcomed her home, its phantomlike branches rustling in the night. She turned her back on the memories, on the dreams she'd finally wised up and stopped dreaming years ago.

The solarium's angles came into view. The sight of its glass-and-wooden frame kicked the butterflies in her stomach into a frenzied tap dance. Nostalgia she hadn't expected tugged her lips into a smile even as she panted for breath, winded by the short walk from the car. She struggled against the light-headed, ear-ringing haze, bending at the waist, hands on her knees.

Not now. She straightened and waited for her vision to clear, her lungs to work. *This isn't happening, not now that I'm this close.*

Her equilibrium returning, she took in the sight of the one place in her grandfather's ordered world that had truly belonged to her. Inside the solarium's sanctuary, she'd nurtured tiny buds and seedlings, watching them burst to life year after year. Oliver had called her obsession folly, but the plants had needed her when no one else had. And the solarium had meant freedom in ways her grandfather had never imagined.

She approached the corner windows, willing strength into her legs. Ivy cascaded like a waterfall from a nearby oak, obscuring all but a few inches of the long, opaque panes of glass. She reached for the screwdriver in her back pocket, but a whisper from the past stopped her. The stone was still there, directly beneath the last window, mostly buried now. She knelt and pulled until the rock shifted and she could feel beneath. When her fingers closed around cold steel, her heart nearly beat its way out of her chest.

Pulling the encrusted screwdriver free, she wiped

until streaks of metal gleamed in the pale moonlight. How many nights had she done this, popping the loose latch she'd discovered on the last window and sneaking into a cold, silent house long after curfew? Only, back then she hadn't been alone. Back then there'd been one last kiss to keep her warm until she could escape and once more find heaven in the arms of the boy she'd thought she'd love forever. Her hand clenched around the tool. An overpowering urge to hurl it into the window brought her to her senses.

Standing, she shoved aside the ivy, using the screwdriver to jimmy the latch free. She pushed against the vertical window, strained when it refused to swing inward. The frame stubbornly resisted, then wrenched open with a wood-splitting moan. Staring at the shattered hinge, Carrinne held her breath and waited. Night sounds continued their hypnotic refrain, unperturbed by the commotion.

No alarm sounded, though she hadn't really expected one. Her grandfather abhorred newfangled conveniences, no matter how practical. Changing with the times was a sign of weakness. For once, Oliver's uncompromising certainty that his way was always best would work in her favor.

She pocketed the old screwdriver and slipped through the narrow opening. Back into the one place on earth she'd sworn never to set foot in again.

"WHAT AM I doing here?" Sheriff Eric Rivers cut the headlights and turned into Governor's Square.

"My question exactly," his younger brother, Tony, muttered from the passenger's seat of the squad car. "You could have let me take this one on my own."

"No way are you going solo on a burglary, kid." Eric parked in front of the Wilmington mansion and scanned the grounds for signs of trouble. All he saw was the house he'd managed to avoid for the last seventeen years.

"Unit Fifteen, at 2201 Governor's Square," Tony barked their location through the hands-free radio attached to his uniform near the shoulder—standard equipment Eric had insisted everyone on patrol start carrying. "Give us five to have a look around."

"Roger, Fifteen," Marge replied from dispatch.

Eric walked around the car and waited at the curb for Tony, shaking his head at his brother's scowl. Tony shoved his nightstick into his belt and adjusted his sidearm with a jerk.

"You've been steaming since we left the station. Let it go." Eric rolled the tension from his shoulders and headed up the driveway. It was almost comical, watching his usually easygoing brother chafe at carving out his own place in Oakwood's small-town sheriff's department.

"You treated me like your kid brother in front of the entire station."

"I was the only one *in* the station when this call came in, remember? That's why you're stuck with me."

"But this is the third call out here from that security

company." Tony fell in step beside him. "You know as well as I do it's old man Wilmington's new silent alarm acting up. You coulda let me take it alone."

"Yeah, maybe." Eric paused at the top of the drive, motioning Tony to a stop. Something wasn't right.

He scanned the front of the house, trying to pin down what had his instincts on edge. Nothing out of the ordinary. Everything looked fine. Oliver Wilmington, Oakwood's richest and most influential citizen, had been in the hospital for weeks. None of his staff lived in residence anymore. The house was silent and still, just as it should be. But there was something...

Maybe it was the past tripping all over the present making him nervous as hell. Maybe it was the steamy, night-kissed air rustling the leaves overhead. Maybe he was just stir-crazy and it had been too long since he'd been out on a call.

He rolled his shoulders again and switched on his flashlight.

"Besides—" Tony followed him up the marble steps, shining his own flashlight into the enormous windows fronting the porch. "You're the sheriff now. You never go out on calls anymore."

"I do if backup is needed."

"I don't need backup."

Eric turned from peering through the front door's rectangular glass insets. "Any rookie straight out of the academy needs backup."

"And this has nothing to do with the fact that ten

years ago you were the one paddling my ass for skipping school?"

"No." Eric chuckled and headed back down the steps. Tony had been six when their father died. It had been Eric's job to keep him in line ever since. "This has nothing to do with your ass."

At the same time, they both glimpsed the midsize sedan parked halfway down the block. Not that parking at the curb was so out of the ordinary on downtown streets. But the Wilmington place took up an entire block of the square, and the nondescript car was a little too conveniently out of the home's sight line.

"Run the plates," Eric said. "When you're done, meet me around back."

He didn't wait to see if Tony followed orders. He didn't have to. His brother was a good cop, even if he was too green for his own good.

Heading around the right side of the house, he shined the flashlight on the ground, the shrubs, the shadows on either side of the path. Damn if everything didn't look exactly as it had years ago.

The flashlight's beam picked up a set of footprints in the soft earth beneath the ancient cypress tree. He stopped. It was Carrinne's tree. Their tree. A rattle from behind the house shook the memories from his head.

Moving again, only this time keeping to the shadows, he shined the flashlight at each window, looking for signs of forced entry. He unsnapped the clip that held his gun in its holster and reached for the radio at his shoulder.

"Get over here, Tony," he whispered. "We've got company."

Rounding the back corner of the house, Eric advanced slowly, soundlessly, listening through the darkness. From the direction of the solarium came a crash, followed by another. Sprinting, his hand hovering above his holster, he reached the structure in time to see a blurred figure squeezing out of an all-too-familiar window.

"Freeze!" he barked. "Sheriff's department."

The figure scrambled to the ground, rolling and preparing to run.

"Freeze!" He stepped closer and pinned the suspect with the flashlight beam.

Then the summer night, the achingly familiar sights and sounds pressing in around him, and a vision from his past seized him in a moment of déjà vu that rooted him to the spot. Carrinne Wilmington, seventeen years older, but somehow exactly the same, dressed from head to toe in burglar black, stared back at him, her face a mask of fear and shock.

He instinctively adjusted the flashlight's glare out of her eyes.

"Eric?" She squinted. "What are you doing here?"

Her soft voice had lost some of its southern accent. Still, it swept over his skin like his favorite T-shirt fresh from the dryer. Warm and smooth.

A blink and a deep breath later, she was off. By the time he recovered enough to sprint after her, she'd raced around the side of the house.

He cleared the corner to see Tony grab Carrinne as she flew by. His brother held her arms to her side, subduing her struggles with textbook ease. Carrinne thanked him for his efforts by squealing and fighting even harder to get away.

"Take it easy." Eric raced up to the pair. "She's—"

Before he could finish his sentence, Carrinne went limp and slid to the ground.

"CARRINNE?" came the voice again. "Carrinne. Wake up, darlin'."

A hand patted Carrinne's cheek. Pushed the cap from her head. Moaning, she fought to open her eyes. Where was she? Where was Maggie?

"Who's Maggie?" asked the masculine voice that had called her darlin'.

A voice from her past.

Reality crashed over her in a dizzying wave. After searching the attic as long as she'd dared and finding no sign of her mother's trunk, afraid of waking Oliver if she kept digging, she'd been struggling back out of the solarium window when...

Jerking to full consciousness, she blinked until her vision cleared. She was lying on a carpet of soggy Bermuda grass, and leaning over her was the one man she wanted to see less than her grandfather.

"What...what are you doing here, Eric?" She struggled to sit, flinching when his hand moved to steady her.

With a raised eyebrow, he stepped away. "I could ask you the same question."

"I don't know what you mean." She stood on rubbery legs.

"What are you doing here after all these years?"

"Isn't it obvious?" She inched another few feet away, a nervous cough slipping out before she could stop it. "I'm visiting my grandfather."

"Through the solarium window?"

"It's late," she mumbled, then winced at the feeble excuse. There were so many reasons why this conversation shouldn't be happening. Her gaze fixed on his badge. "You're in uniform."

"It comes with the job."

"You're a cop?"

"He's the new sheriff," a third voice said.

Her attention jumped to the officer who'd stopped her. Something about the younger man made her take a closer look.

T. Rivers, his badge read.

"Tony?" She wrapped her arms around herself, stifling the reflex to give him a hug. Eric's kid brother had been six the last time she'd seen him. "Heavens, you've grown."

Then Tony's words registered. She swung back to Eric. The rebellious teenage boy she'd known was now a severe, responsible-looking man.

"*You're* the sheriff?"

His level stare made her squirm. "Why were you breaking into the solarium, Carrinne?"

To find what I need to protect our daughter.

She bit her lip, bit back the truth she'd never planned to be close enough to tell him or anyone else in this town. Not after he'd dumped her, telling her she'd been nothing more than a mindless distraction. Not after her grandfather had ordered her to have an abortion or get the hell out of his house. A wave of curls fell into her eyes. She pushed them back and reached deep for the nerve she needed to pull this off.

"I wasn't supposed to arrive until the morning," she lied. "And I didn't want to wake Oliver in the middle of the night. All the doors were locked, so I figured I'd give the solarium a try."

"But, Ms. Wilmington—" Tony started to say.

"If your grandfather's expecting you, why was the silent alarm on?" Eric's eyes narrowed. "Are you sure he knows you're coming?"

"Of course." She brushed the dirt from her arms and gave bravado her best shot. "Why don't I just find a motel for the night and come back in the morning?"

"Better yet—" Eric turned toward the front of the house "—why don't we ring the bell and straighten this all out now?"

"No!" She grabbed his arm, then instantly let go. Her fingers tingled from the strong, solid feel of him. "I mean… Can't we wait until morning? Oliver's getting older. He needs his rest."

Eric let out a harsh breath, biting back a curse. He

had no idea what Carrinne was up to, but he knew "guilty as hell" when he heard it.

"Your grandfather's in the hospital," he said, watching her closely. "He had a stroke six weeks ago."

"Oh…I…I haven't spoken with him in over a month." Her face grew paler, even as she squared her shoulders. "We made tentative plans for my visit, and I've been too busy to call him since."

"It's odd that his lawyer didn't contact you about the stroke."

"I've been away on business."

"You don't have an answering machine?"

"I told you, I've been busy. I haven't had time to check my—"

"Lying's only making this worse." They'd be out here all night at this rate. "Are you going to tell me what's really going on, or do I have to take you in?"

"Take me in?" The alarmed expression on her face was the real deal. Not like the casual innocence she'd done such a lousy job of faking a few minutes before.

"Give me one good reason why you were breaking in, and maybe we can end this here."

"I wasn't breaking in. I grew up in this house."

"A technicality that might keep you out of jail. But if you want to avoid coming with me to the station, you'll have to do better than that. Just trust me, okay?"

A battle raged in her green eyes. Then they hardened with a determination that was a chilly reflection of the man who'd raised her.

"The only person I'm talking to is Oliver," she said.

Running a hand through his hair, Eric sighed and turned to Tony. "Radio in. Have Wilmington's lawyer meet us at the station."

When he glanced back, Carrinne was staring at the cypress tree he hadn't realized they'd stopped beneath. Blond and petite, a heart-shaped face he could cup in the palms of his hands. Painfully familiar in so many ways, she was a complete stranger to him.

And why shouldn't she be? He'd cut her out of his life after his father's death. Then she'd left town without saying another word to him. Seventeen years of nothing lay between them.

He'd tried and failed over the years to forget their time together. How he'd thrown away what he never should have let himself want in the first place. But the look of betrayal on her face that last night had made a regular appearance in his dreams, never letting him completely forget.

She clearly didn't want him anywhere near her now. Unfortunately, for both of them, she didn't have a choice. His instincts told him Carrinne Wilmington had more trouble on her hands than she knew what to do with.

No PROBLEM, Carrinne told herself as she rode to the sheriff's department in the back of Eric's squad car. No sweat. She'd tackle the lawyer first, then her grandfather. She was a pro at talking her way out of tough situations. She'd built her small New York accounting firm from the ground up. Whatever it took to get the job done, that's what she did.

Getting what she needed without Oliver's help was no longer an option. She'd come up empty-handed at the house, and she needed more time in the attic to look for her mother's things. But would her grandfather be willing to help? That was a question she hadn't let herself worry about until now, because she was afraid she already knew the answer.

At the age of ten, she'd found the stash of diaries in her mother's closet and had read cover-to-cover each precious link to the woman she'd never known. There'd been a diary for every year after her mother turned seven, except the last. Angelica Wilmington's sixteenth year. The year she'd become pregnant with Carrinne.

Finding the missing book had become Carrinne's obsession. But each time she'd hunted for it, Oliver had demanded she stop digging up the past. She'd told him about her nanny Matilda's stories. About how her mother had kept her diary with her always, up until the day she died delivering Carrinne. But he'd refused to listen. Discussing his daughter or anything about their lives before Carrinne's birth was an unpardonable sin in the Wilmington house.

Finally, he'd ordered all her mother's things packed into an enormous trunk and sent to the attic. He'd decreed her mother's memory off-limits, and by God that's the way things were going to be. And, because she'd longed for her grandfather's approval back then, even more than she'd wanted to read her mother's final hopes and dreams for her unborn baby, Carrinne had forced herself to stop looking. Eventually, she'd forgotten about that last diary all together.

Until now, when finding it had become a matter of life and death.

She cleared her throat against a cough, not quite succeeding in stopping it.

"You okay?" Eric asked from behind the wheel as he parked.

Her gaze collided with concerned brown eyes reflecting back from the rearview mirror, eyes the exact same shade of chocolate as their daughter's. When he glanced over his shoulder, she bit the inside of her cheek to keep from staring. Seventeen years hadn't made the least bit of difference. Seventy years wouldn't.

His thick brown hair, now sprinkled with slivers of distinguished gray, made a woman want to tame it with her fingers. The angles and planes of his face were just as strong as she remembered, arranged as if by a force of nature into cheekbones and lips that looked as though they were carved from granite. At least until he smiled. Eric's smile had melted straight through her heart the first time she'd coaxed it out of him. He didn't appear to smile any more now than he had when they were kids.

"Carrinne?" he prompted.

She cleared her throat and her mind at the same time. "I'm fine."

He shot her a look of disbelief.

"Are we just going to sit here?" She unfastened her seat belt and stared out the window at the thoroughly captivating view of the almost-empty parking lot. Her door couldn't be opened from the inside, or she'd already be out of the car.

"Fifteen," a woman's voice said over the radio. "The Wilmington lawyer's here."

"We just pulled up. I'll meet with him in room one." Eric took the keys out of the ignition.

He planned to meet with Oliver's lawyer alone? Was Clifford Brimsley still working for her grandfather? "But—"

"Tony." Eric's eyes met hers in the mirror. "Show Ms. Wilmington to my office."

"But, I want to—"

Ignoring her, Eric stepped out of the car and strode away. Despite the mantle of responsibility he wore with such ease now, Oakwood's sheriff still sauntered like a rebellious James Dean. Too cool and confident to hurry, no matter who was looking. Exactly the way Maggie swaggered when it was important that everyone around her knew just how much she didn't care what they thought.

"Ms. Wilmington?" Tony had opened her door and was watching her watch Eric.

Unfolding her legs and pushing herself off the seat, she stumbled.

"Careful." Tony caught her with both hands as her knees buckled. "Maybe you should sit back down."

"No. I'm fine."

She had to be.

She straightened and gave him a reassuring smile she didn't feel.

"Maybe I could find you some juice or something." Tony hovered at her side as they walked, opening the door to the sprawling, single-story building so she could enter in front of him. "I'll check the vending machine."

"Thanks," she replied, barely hearing a word. Looking for any sign of Eric, she let Tony lead her past the officer at the front desk and into the partitioned squad room.

Was Brimsley still the Wilmington family lawyer? Would he know about her reasons for leaving Oakwood seventeen years ago? Her stomach churned at the thought of what he could be telling Eric at that very moment.

The sound of typing tapped faintly from somewhere to her left. They passed a row of desks deserted for the night. When they'd reached another hallway, Tony ushered her to the right. At the same time, Eric's voice rumbled from one of the closed rooms behind them. She turned toward the sound, jumping at Tony's firm grasp on her elbow.

"The sheriff's office is this way." His expression left no room for discussion.

She did the math quickly. Tony was twenty-three now. A very mature twenty-three, and on his way to being as formidable as his big brother. They reached the end of the hall, and he released her arm beside a door with a sign that read simply, Sheriff.

"If you'll promise to wait here, I'll try to find you something to eat," he offered.

Her stomach growled in encouragement. Skipping meals had become a bad habit since she'd flown out of New York.

"I'll stay put." She stepped into the office and sank into a chair opposite the cluttered mess that passed as Eric's desk. She caught Tony's dubious expression. "Really. I don't have the energy to stray."

Nodding, he turned to leave.

"Tony?"

He raised one eyebrow in a gesture so much like his brother, something inside her began to hurt.

"Thanks," she said through the lump in her throat.

"You bet." He winked and shut the door, leaving her alone.

In spite of the disaster the last hour had made of her plans, she smiled.

Life was just too weird. The kid who'd spat bubble gum into her hair the last time she'd baby-sat for him was all grown up now, and off to find her something to eat so she wouldn't pass out. Meanwhile her grandfather's attorney and her high-school-flame-turned sheriff were down the hall somewhere, chatting about her rookie crack at breaking and entering. It had been quite a night.

Her cell phone chirped. She fumbled it from her jeans pocket and recognized her daughter's number on the display. She finally managed to flip it open.

"Maggie?"

"Mom!" Maggie sighed with relief. "Where have you been?"

Carrinne was out of the chair in an instant, glancing toward the still-closed door. "I need to call you back later, sweetheart."

"You were supposed to call hours ago," her daughter replied with the kind of I'm-the-mother-now attitude only a sixteen-year-old could pull off.

"This isn't a good time. I'll call you in the morning." Carrinne walked to the farthest corner of the office. Chills shook her from the inside out, persisting despite the cloying humidity the station's central air-conditioning couldn't keep up with. She hugged her free arm across her chest, furious with her body's betrayal.

"Mom, I...I went to the clinic today for the blood tests."

"What?" Ringing filled Carrinne's ears. She'd left Maggie in her best friend's care, with specific instructions that her daughter was not to go anywhere near the hospital. "Put Kim on the phone."

"It's one-thirty in the morning, Mom. She's asleep."

"I don't care. Put her on the phone."

"She doesn't know I went. I forged your signature on the consent form." Emotion shook her daughter's voice. Her beautiful, brave daughter. The only light in Carrinne's life. "I had to go. I have to know."

"No, you don't." She tried her best to sound understanding, not scared out of her mind. "Because it doesn't matter. I'm not letting you have the procedure, regardless."

"But if I'm a match—"

"It doesn't matter."

"I'm sixteen. It should be my choice to make. If we're lucky enough that I can help you, I want to do it."

Lucky. That's what the doctors kept saying. Carrinne was very lucky.

They'd congratulated themselves on catching her rare form of liver disease early. She was at such an early stage, her symptoms were almost nonexistent. Her prognosis was a full recovery once she received a transplant, and they had a year, maybe two, to locate a donor. She was so lucky, it was possible the surgeons might be able to harvest half of her sixteen-year-old daughter's healthy liver, if the tests showed Maggie was a match. The living donor procedure was delicate and brutally invasive, but *luckily* it was considered safe.

What mother, faced with the choice of risking her child's health in order to save her own, wouldn't feel lucky?

"No," was all Carrinne could manage. She'd been the cause of her own mother's death. Nothing on this earth could persuade her to risk her daughter's life, too.

"They're putting a rush on the tests," Maggie pressed. "Because it's Friday, they said we won't hear anything until early next week. We may know something Monday—"

"No, Maggie. I told you. There have to be other options. I'm trying to find one right now."

God, please let me find my mother's last diary. There had to be something in it to lead her to the father her mother had never named. *Please let him be a match and be willing to be a donor.*

"Mom, I want to help."

"I know you do, baby." The hurt in Maggie's voice sliced into Carrinne's heart. "You do help me. By caring. By worrying when you should be in bed getting some rest. But you've got to let me go, so I can do what I have to here. It looks like I'll need to stay a few more days. I'll call tomorrow when I know something more. I promise."

"You need to rest, too. You need help with whatever you're doing there." Maggie's reply was watery, with a tinge of exasperation.

Carrinne hadn't shared many details about this trip, and her daughter never liked being in the dark. Carrinne had told her they still had family in Oakwood, family she'd avoided like the plague for years. Beyond that, she'd only said she was tracking down a possible donor.

"I'm diving into bed," she reassured Maggie. "Just as soon as I can. Tell Kim I'll call tomorrow afternoon, okay?"

"Okay," was her daughter's less-than-enthusiastic reply.

"I love you, baby."

"I love you, too."

Carrinne stared at the phone long after the connection went dead. Then she flipped it closed and shoved it back into her pocket, hating that she wasn't any closer to the answers she needed. She paced across the room and back, trying to focus past the panicked feeling that time was running out.

She couldn't just wait here, doing nothing, wondering what Eric and that attorney were talking about. What if Eric found out about Maggie? What would she tell him?

Heading toward the back wall once more, she paused before the eight-by-ten plaque hanging behind the desk. Her vision blurred as she confronted yet another piece of the past she remembered as if it was yesterday.

Sheriff, 1965–1985, simple gold letters proclaimed beneath a picture of Gerald Rivers, Eric's father. *Killed in the line of duty, protecting his fellow officers.*

She'd been at Eric's house that awful night the call had come in. It had been just a few short weeks after his high school graduation. She'd rushed with him to the hospital, even though his father had already been declared dead on arrival. It was the one and only time she'd ever seen Eric cry. And after that night, everything between them had changed.

The sound of the door opening dragged her away from the memory. She wiped at her eyes, preparing to thank Tony again for finding her something to eat. Only, when she turned, it was Eric standing in the doorway.

"You've been lying to me from the start, haven't you?" He pinned her with a look that made her instinctive denial shrivel in her throat.

CHAPTER TWO

ERIC'S GAZE skipped from Carrinne's guilty expression to his father's plaque behind her. It must be inconceivable to her that he'd turned out exactly the way his by-the-book father had wanted.

Responsible. Stable. Dependable.

Some days, Eric barely believed it himself.

Leaning against the door frame, he crossed his arms and marveled at the almost two decades that had passed since he'd last been alone with this woman.

"Eric, I...I can explain." She brushed at her eyes. She'd been crying, and he'd bet a week's salary that didn't happen often.

"We already tried that, remember?" The impulse to reassure her almost got the best of him. Glancing once more at his father's picture, he moved into the room. "It's probably a good time for you to start doing some serious listening instead."

He inched closer, and she skirted around the side of the desk. He stared as she inched a few more steps away.

"What's the matter with you? You're acting like I'm going to attack you or something."

Her chin shot up. "Just say whatever it is you have to say. I'd like to settle things and get out of here."

"Well, you see, that's the problem." He removed his sidearm and locked it in the top drawer of his desk. Settling into his beaten-up leather chair, he motioned for her to take a seat. She didn't budge. "I'm afraid it won't be that easy."

She hugged her arms close, like someone who'd forgotten her jacket on a windy day. "Was it Brimsley you were talking to? What did he tell you?"

"What should he have told me?" The chair's wooden frame creaked as he leaned back and stared.

She opened her mouth, then closed it. The shape of that mouth had him remembering things that would only make his job more difficult.

Focus, Rivers. You're the only thing standing between her and a night in jail.

"You'll have to talk eventually," he continued. "Brimsley's out for blood. He doesn't know anything about you contacting Oliver for a visit, and he wants you booked for the break-in."

"Oh." Carrinne's hands slipped to her side, her pinched expression relaxing. "Is that all?"

Eric blinked at her reaction. "I've tried to talk him out of pressing charges, but he won't agree to anything until he's met with you himself."

She stumbled toward the guest chair and slid into it.

"What's going on, Carrinne?"

The controlled way she straightened was a decent attempt at nonchalance. A knock jerked their attention to the open door.

Tony stepped in, juggling a can of juice and a handful of snacks.

"What?" Eric barked.

"I offered to get Ms. Wilmington something to eat. She still wasn't feeling well when we got out of the car."

Eric waited for Tony to lay his bounty on the table. "Go see if Wilmington's lawyer needs anything," he said. He'd left Clifford Brimsley cooling his heels down the hall.

Tony hovered at Carrinne's shoulder, glancing between Eric and their suspect, who had already pounced on a packet of crackers as if she hadn't eaten in days.

Putting all his impatience into a glare, Eric waited until Tony looked back his way.

"Um, right." Tony backpedaled out of the room. "I'll go check on Brimsley."

The door shut, leaving them alone. Carrinne struggled to open the juice, her fingers shaking.

Resigned, Eric took the can, popped it, and returned it to the desk with a thump. "Let me know when you're done with your picnic."

Carrinne gave him a narrow look as she took a long sip. She polished off the last of the crackers in silence, color creeping into her cheeks with each bite. When she sat back and folded her hands in her lap, confidence swam in her expressive eyes. "What now?"

Any other time, any other place, any other woman,

and he might enjoy puzzling out why she was challenging him at every turn. The possibilities were downright intriguing. Only with this woman, he'd be messing with dynamite.

The Carrinne of his youth had tunneled her way into his teenage heart, getting close enough for it to hurt like hell when he'd walked away. And he'd deserved the pain. He'd learned from an early age not to trust, but somehow he'd convinced himself he deserved to keep the soft-hearted angel Carrinne had been back then. He'd let himself believe she was a little piece of good in the world, created just for him.

But the tough package sitting across from him now was no longer the sheltered girl who'd begged him to show her how to live. Puzzling out *anything* about this woman would be an open invitation for disaster.

"Ready to face the music?" he asked both himself and Carrinne as he stood. "Brimsley's waiting."

"So, YOU SEE? I meant no harm. I just wanted my mother's diary." Carrinne smiled at the scowling lawyer sitting on the other side of the interview room, forcing herself to ignore Eric hovering somewhere behind her.

Her game face firmly in place, she was playing the role of unconcerned innocent. The diary story was a convincing enough reason for what she'd done. She'd have to tell her grandfather more, but she could only deal with one unpleasant reality at a time.

"And breaking in was your solution to getting my client to cooperate with your needs?" Clifford Brimsley was just as creepy and unapproachable as ever.

His hair was cut short in the same style, complete now with a receding hairline. And as far as she could tell, he'd worn the exact same mortician-drab suit since the first day he'd started working for Oliver almost thirty years ago.

"Your *client's* never stooped to cooperating with anyone, counselor." She clenched her hands in her lap. She'd negotiated fees with uptown Manhattan businessmen who, one and all, thought choosing a small, private firm meant bargain-basement rates. She could handle one past-his-prime country attorney. "Let's just say I preempted the inevitable argument and tried to save everyone a lot of time."

"Let's just say you were breaking and entering and trespassing, and move on to discussing whether or not you should be charged with a misdemeanor or a felony."

"Now, Cliff," Eric spoke up for the first time since leading her into the room. While she scrambled to think of a way to finesse felony into something less disturbing, he stepped away from his post at the door and relaxed into the vinyl chair beside hers. "There was minimal property damage. You'd be lucky to make a misdemeanor stick. Do you really think Oliver would want to waste his time and money taking this to court?"

"She knowingly and willingly broke the law, defacing Mr. Wilmington's property in the process," Brimsley argued.

"She was avoiding contact with an old man who we all know makes Frank Capra's Mr. Potter look like Captain Kangaroo. At worst, she made a stupid choice."

"Stupid!" A part of Carrinne knew she should let Eric handle this. Just not the part that itched to tell him exactly where he could shove his colorful observations.

"It's a safe bet," Eric continued as if she'd never spoken, "that any jury from Oakwood would be full of people who've been burned at one time or another by old man Wilmington. Either them or someone in their family. The only reason the town still does business with him is because he has more money and influence than God. You'll be hard-pressed to find anyone willing to put his granddaughter in jail for breaking a windowsill so she could avoid confronting the old goat. This is a family matter between Carrinne and her grandfather."

"I—" she began.

"My job is to protect my client's best interests in this situation," Brimsley said over her. "Don't think just because she's Mr. Wilmington's granddaughter, or because you two had some kind of teenage fling, that you can talk me into dropping the charges."

"I—" she tried again.

"Your client's interests would be better served in this situation," Eric cut in, "if we settled everything here tonight, instead of dragging things out."

"I am *not* a situation," Carrinne bit out. "And I'm right here, in case either of you is interested."

Two stunned pairs of eyes swung in her direction.

"Ms. Wilmington." Brimsley's gaze shifted to Eric then back to her. "These are very serious charges. Before I'll consider dropping them, I'll need some assurances on my client's behalf."

"Such as?" She gave Eric a look to keep him quiet, which induced a bemused smile.

"Such as you paying to repair the damage to the solarium window. And you'll have to agree to meet with your grandfather in the morning as soon as he's able. He'll be beside himself when he hears about this. Plus, I'll need to know what you were really doing at the house." He pointed an accusing finger. "I don't believe for a second you're back after all this time for some silly old journal."

"Nothing about my mother or anything that belonged to her is silly, Mr. Brimsley. I'll thank you to remember that."

Dead silence choked the momentum out of whatever the man had been about to say next.

So much for her people skills.

"Spit it out, Cliff." Eric's voice sliced through the silence, efficient and calm in an unfair way. "You said you were willing to drop the charges. What else is it going to take to get us out of here? It's after two in the morning, and we've all had a long night."

"Well...I..." Brimsley made a production out of straightening his tie. "I'd settle for an explanation of why she wants this diary."

"I'm looking for my father, all right?" Carrinne kept her voice level as she fed them one more detail she'd hoped to keep to herself. They'd know by morning anyway, once she'd met with Oliver. In a town as small as Oakwood, privacy had gone out the window with the arrival of the first telephone. "I came back to find my father, and I'm looking for my mother's final diary, hoping there will be some clue to point me in the right direction."

"Why the hell are you looking for your old man after all these years?" Eric's stunned question gave Carrinne a jolt of satisfaction. She'd finally ruffled his composure. But when she turned, she found his control replaced with something worse—concern. Disbelief and concern.

"Because I need to find him. And the sooner I do—" horrified by the uneven break in her voice, she cleared her throat "—the sooner I can put this town and every memory I have of it behind me once and for all."

"Cliff?" Eric continued to study Carrinne. His face was a mask of calm again, except for a muscle twitching along his jaw.

"Will she meet with her grandfather in the morning?" Brimsley asked.

"Yes." Carrinne gave the lawyer her full attention. Looking at Eric made breathing hurt. He was every reason she'd never trust her heart to any man again.

"Then I have no problem with dropping the charges," Brimsley said. "For now."

"CAN I GET YOU anything, Ms. Wilmington?" Tony asked from the door of the interview room.

Carrinne was resting her head on her crossed arms. Pushing away from the table, she tried to stretch the kinks out of her neck. Eric had left with a disgruntled but marginally more cooperative Brimsley over half an hour ago.

"You used to call me Carrinne, Tony." She rubbed her eyes with the heels of her hands, realizing too late that she was smearing what was left of the mascara she'd applied almost twenty hours before. She wiped away the residue on her hands, then rubbed at what she knew must have collected beneath her eyes. "Is *Ms. Wilmington* your way of pointing out how much older I am now?"

"Oh, no, ma'am." His laugh was pure good-ol'-boy charm. "I was just being polite."

She stood, massaging muscles in her lower back that were threatening never to straighten again. "Well, I guess Ms. and ma'am just aren't my style anymore."

"No, ma'am." Tony gave her body and her form-fitting city clothes an appreciative once-over. "I don't suppose they are."

"Am I intruding?" Eric appeared behind his brother.

"Just trying to make myself useful while you finished working over that crotchety old lawyer," Tony replied with unabashed innocence.

"You've been useful enough for one night." Eric jerked his head in the direction of the squad room. "Don't you have some call reports to file?"

"Right." Tony smiled, raising that eyebrow again. "It was nice to run into you, Carrinne. Enjoy your visit to Oakwood, and try to stay out of trouble."

He'd disappeared around the corner before Eric spoke. "So, it's Carrinne now?"

"That's my name." She ignored the urge to sink back into the uncomfortable chair. Lord, she was tired. "I don't have much use for Southern formality these days."

"I guess in a place like New York, manners might make you an easy target."

"I've learned to take care of myself—" She stopped short. "How did you know I live in New York?"

"We ran the plates on your rental car. The leasing company faxed a copy of your agreement. It says you're a corporate accountant. Must have been hard to get away from a high-pressure job like that."

"I've set aside a few days of vacation." Tiny hairs stood on end up and down her arms. A man in Eric's position could get his hands on whatever information he wanted. "If the charges are dropped, I'd like to go."

Eric's respect for how far Carrinne had come grew as he watched her swallow her fear and stare him down. He liked this gutsy new version of the girl he'd known.

"You know—" he intentionally closed the distance between them "—you'd be rid of me a lot quicker if you just came right out and owned up to the truth, whatever it is. What are you doing back in Oakwood?"

She held her ground, her features a blank canvas of New York confidence. "I told you why I'm back."

"You want to find your father."

"Yes."

"After all these years." He snapped his fingers. "Just like that."

"Yes." Her eyes narrowed. "It's important to me."

"Why would you care? You've clearly managed to build a good life for yourself." He studied her outfit with the same thoroughness he'd seen Tony enjoy. Her jeans were no doubt from some high-end New York boutique. And he'd felt the softness of silk when his hands had brushed her top as he'd revived her at the Wilmington place. "Digging up old wounds after all this time, I'd think that would be the last thing you'd want. I know there's nothing short of a bullet that would get me to hunt down my lousy excuse for a mother."

And just that easily, a part of the past he never thought of anymore slipped into the present.

The topic of his mother had been off-limits for him from the moment she'd abandoned his family a year after Tony was born. Off-limits, that was, until he'd met Carrinne, and she'd seen straight through the rebellious hatred that had ruled his life back then.

He'd told himself he didn't need family or friends. That he wanted nothing more to do with anyone saying that they loved him. Love meant pain and loss, and he was determined to live without it. By the time Carrinne came into the picture, he'd done a good enough job of being a hard-ass that most everyone in Oakwood, except his father, had written him off. But Carrinne's sweetness had wormed through his anger, straight to the pain he was fighting to forget. She hadn't been afraid of the darkness driving him to hurt himself and everyone who cared about him.

An orphan raised by a cold-hearted old man, she'd survived her own version of rejection and emotional abandonment. And she'd been determined that Eric would, too. She hadn't left him alone until he'd opened up about his mother and shared what he'd never discussed before or since, not even with his brother. He'd begun to trust that the future could be different than the past, that not everyone who loved him was going to leave him.

Then his dad had died, abandoning Eric all over again. And the shaky belief in love that Carrinne had helped him build hadn't stood a chance. Eighteen, alone, and saddled with the responsibility of raising Tony, the last thing he'd been able to handle was Carrinne's unshakable hope that tomorrow would be better. He'd needed to be angry until he'd burned out the rage and no longer felt any of the pain.

So he'd pushed her away. And when she'd left, she'd taken her sweetness and his last taste of love with her.

Eric blinked back to the present. Carrinne's puzzled expression shimmered into focus. He made himself step away.

Carrinne's eyes, pools of green that still haunted his dreams, softened with the very empathy he'd run from. "It's easier for me not to hate my father the way you do your mom. I never knew him."

"Lucky you." His lips wouldn't smile, so he gave up trying. "But I still don't buy it."

"What?"

"The break-in. I backed you up with Lurch." He caught her smirk at his use of the nickname they'd shared for Brimsley. "But his suspicions were dead on. Maybe if you'd called first and the old man had refused to cooperate, it might make more sense."

She crossed her arms. "Are you having a good time?"

"Trying to get you to come clean?"

"Playing detective because there's nothing better to do in this backwater town than butt in where you don't belong."

"I want to help."

"I stopped needing anyone's help forever ago."

"Well, unless you're itching to end up in jail, I suggest you find a more legal means of going after whatever you're really looking for."

"Thanks for the advice, but I figured that one out on my own."

Eric bit back his next retort and ran a hand through his hair. This wasn't getting them anywhere. "You can go. But don't do anything I can't get you out of, Carrinne. I'd hate to have you arrested, but I'll do what I have to do."

"Haven't you always?" Her eyes were suddenly moist. She pushed past him to leave.

Stricken by the hint of weakness beneath all that grit, he grabbed her arm. "Wait. I'm just trying to be a friend."

"Let me go." She yanked away, her hand rubbing where he'd touched her. "You're not my friend, and I don't want your help. I don't want anything from you."

"If this is about how I ended things when we were teenagers—"

"This is about me being dead on my feet and needing some sleep," she said calmly. Sparks still smoldered in her eyes. "You were very helpful with Brimsley. Thank you. And I'll sort things out with Oliver in the morning. I can handle the rest on my own."

Eric scrubbed his hand across his face. The idea that she might still carry scars from their breakup made him feel like the class-A jerk he'd been to her. He had no idea if he could help her with whatever she was up to, but he was sure as hell going to try. She was in trouble, and it would take a lot more than a handful of uncomfortable memories to turn him away. He had to make sure she was okay.

Besides, she'd pegged his life right on the nose. It wasn't like he had much else but paperwork and small-town bureaucracy pressing for his attention these days.

"I'll have Tony meet you out front," he finally said. "He'll drive you back to your car."

"Thanks." She turned with a sigh and headed toward the front of the building.

Tomorrow, he promised himself as he went to search for Tony. Tomorrow was soon enough to help the last person in Oakwood who wanted his help.

"WHAT DO YOU MEAN I can't go in?" Carrinne asked the elderly woman dressed in starched pink cotton.

It was early Saturday afternoon. She'd meant to get

to the hospital hours ago. But after collapsing into bed around four that morning, thoughts of Eric and Maggie had kept her tossing and turning for hours. Once she'd nodded off, she'd slept like the dead until after eleven.

Nurse Able, according to her name badge, stepped around the nurses' station and attempted to lead Carrinne into the visitors' lounge. "I'm sorry, Ms. Wilmington, but we only allow one visitor at a time. If you'll just wait over here."

"But I'm his granddaughter." Carrinne evaded the nurse's grasp.

"Oh, I know who you are, dear." The nurse clasped her hands in front of her and smiled. "I'm sure you don't remember, but I used to change your diapers every Sunday when I worked in the church nursery. You're just as beautiful now as you were then."

Carrinne fought to keep her eyes from rolling heavenward. Hadn't anyone else moved away from this place in the last seventeen years?

First, the clerk at the motel had been one of the varsity football players all the cheerleaders had fawned over back in high school. Then the volunteer at the welcome desk downstairs had turned out to be the lunchroom lady who'd sneaked Carrinne extra pudding in elementary school. Now Nurse Able.

"When can I see my grandfather?" She tried to smile, she really did.

"Oh, call me Glinda. It sure has been a long—"

"It's really important that I see him as soon as possible." Carrinne let her voice roughen, shamelessly harnessing the emotion swimming ever closer to the surface of what used to be her composure. "It's been so long, I don't want to waste another moment."

"Of course you don't," Glinda replied. She took Carrinne's hand. "Tragedy brings us together in the most difficult way."

"It would really mean a lot if you could get me in to see him now."

"I'm sure you have a lot to talk about." She squeezed Carrinne's fingers. "Let me go see what's keeping Mr. Brimsley."

"Brimsley?"

"Why, yes. He usually stops by on his lunch break. He has your grandfather's power of attorney, you know. Sometimes they meet for hours, going over all kinds of paperwork and whatnot. I can't tell you how many times the doctors have warned your grandfather to slow down, but he says he wants to stay up-to-date—"

"You said you could check on what was keeping Mr. Brimsley?" Every minute that man was with her grandfather was a minute too long.

"Of course, dear. Let me see what I can do."

Carrinne watched her go, clenching her fists and trying not to stomp with impatience as she stared down the brightly lit hallway. The reality of her surroundings seeped through her frustration. The antiseptic smell. The beige and green tiles on the floor. The hum of hushed voices and whirring medical equipment. This could just as easily be a hallway at Mount Sinai Hospital in New York, her home away from home for the last few months.

Her need for Oliver's assistance was the only thing short of a medical emergency that could have coaxed her into yet another hospital. And running into Eric had red-lined the necessity to get what she'd come for and get the heck out of Oakwood. She needed her grandfather's help now. Whatever it took.

Glinda returned, her affronted scowl dampening what Carrinne had assumed was chronic perkiness. "That man! He—"

"I'll take it from here, nurse." Brimsley appeared behind Glinda, his stern frown directed at Carrinne.

"You let me know if you need anything," Glinda said to Carrinne as she marched to her station. Her eyes shot daggers at Brimsley the entire way.

"You do have a way with people, don't you?" Carrinne's skin crawled as the lawyer sized her up. He could still make her feel like the six-year-old he'd once caught doodling all over some important business contracts he'd laid out for Oliver.

"I want to know what you're going to say to him." Brimsley pointed a finger for emphasis. "Your grandfather's a very sick man, and he doesn't need you unsettling things even more."

"Unsettling things? This meeting was your idea."

"Because I want whatever you've got to say out of the way with the least amount of stress to Oliver. The first thing he heard when he woke this morning was that you were back in town. He was in a frenzy when I got here, demanding that I track you down and bring you over. Though why he cares after all these years, I can't imagine."

Oh, but she could. It was too much to ask that her grandfather would dismiss her out of hand as Brimsley had. A cold, disinterested Oliver Wilmington would have been so much easier to handle. But true to form, as soon as he'd heard she was in town, he'd expected her to present herself upon demand.

And here she was.

"What I have to say won't take long." She reined in the urge to run and moved to pass Brimsley. "So if you don't mind—"

He grabbed her arm. "Why are you back?"

Yanking away, she looked him up and down. "Maybe I'm here to remind myself why I fled this insufferable place and everything connected to it. Maybe I needed a good dose of Southern bad manners to remind me how good I have it up north."

A giggle to her right caught Carrinne's attention. Glinda smothered another laugh as she straightened the files scattered across the station counter. With a wink to Carrinne, the nurse answered the phone that never seemed to stop ringing.

Carrinne turned on her heels and headed down the hall, mentally pulling herself together. Her steps slowed as she neared her grandfather's room. She'd left Oliver

Wilmington's warped brand of control and manipulation behind years ago. Since then, she'd proven that she had the nerve and the brains to succeed when he'd been so sure she would fail without him. She was successful and sophisticated, where she'd once been painfully timid and shy. She'd earned the right to face him with confidence.

Instead, she felt only dread.

She needed Oliver's help. And that gave him far more leverage than good sense told her was wise.

"I WANT TO SEE my great-grandchild," Carrinne's grandfather repeated from his hospital bed.

In the five minutes since she'd stepped into his room, Oliver Wilmington had refused to talk about anything else. His imperious tone was everything she remembered, though time and illness had done their dirty work on his diminished frame. He struggled for every breath.

"And I've already told you," she repeated. "That's not possible."

"I'm an old man. I'm paralyzed down one side, and my heart's giving out. I'm dying." He pushed himself up and yanked at the sheet, as impatient with his infirmities as he'd always been with anything he couldn't bend to his will. "I think I'm entitled to meet my only great-grandchild before I go."

"Well, I'm thirty-three, and *I'm* dying." She threw her purse into the guest chair, watching her revelation sink in as she played the only ace up her sleeve. Oliver lapsed into silence for the first time since she'd gotten there. "Does that mean I win?"

CHAPTER THREE

"WHAT ARE YOU talking about?" No longer fussing with the sheet, Oliver grew unnaturally still.

"Primary sclerosing cholangitis." A chill raced down Carrinne's spine as she said the full diagnosis out loud. "It's chronic, and it's degenerative. And if I don't find a liver donor in the next year or two, it'll most likely be fatal. They've put me on the national transplant registry, but my rare blood factors make the chance of finding a match outside of the immediate family minuscule. I'm hoping my father will agree to be a living donor."

"Is that what this is all about?"

Carrinne stared at her shoes. *This* was about so many things, things she had no intention of discussing.

"Carrinne Louise, look at me."

When she did, her heart lurched with the same appalling spasm of emotion that had struck when she'd first walked into the room. Medical equipment surrounded his bed, beeping and whirring, creating a symphony of life support.

She'd thought hatred was all she'd feel when she saw Oliver Wilmington again. Yet what consumed her now was sadness and regret. He'd lost his wife to cancer when he was far too young. They'd both lost her mother. They'd been all the family either of them had left, yet the only way he'd been able to deal with her had been to control every aspect of her life. And she'd needed so much more.

"It's not just your illness that's brought you home after all these years, is it?" he asked. His eyes narrowed. "If you wanted to find your father, why not hire a detective?"

"Hiring a detective is my next step," she explained. "But someone wandering around Oakwood asking a lot of questions might have made you suspicious. I came for the diary myself, hoping I could get in and out without you ever knowing I was here. I hadn't planned on being even a blip on this insufferable town's radar."

"Oakwood is your home, Carrinne. This town and the people you've cut out of your life, they're a part of you."

"This place was never a home for me." She gripped the bedrail. "You made sure of that. I'm back because I have no other choice. The question is, can you put someone else's needs before your own for just once in your life? Tell me what you know about my mother's last diary. Tell me who you think my father might be."

With a look of grudging respect, Oliver pushed himself higher on the pillows. "It seems we're at an impasse. We both want something very badly, something we can't get without the other one's help. I want to meet my great-grandchild, and you want to meet your father."

"Do you know who my father is?"

"No." He looked away. "I never could get your mother to tell me, and once she was gone… It just didn't seem to matter."

"It mattered to me. It always mattered to me. And you wouldn't lift a finger to help me look for him. You forbade me from even trying, and now it may be too late. Mother's diary is probably the only shot I've got."

"Yes, Angelica's diary." He cleared his throat. "Brimsley mentioned that's what you were looking for at the house. I told you when you were a child—I don't know anything about her diary. She was sixteen years old when you were born. That seems a little old to be keeping a diary, I don't care what your nanny said. What makes you so sure you can find it now, or that your father is even mentioned in it?"

"I'm not sure. But if there's even the slightest chance it exists, I have to look."

"I'd like to help." A shocking warmth laced his statement. *Compassion* wasn't the right word for the expression on his face, but there was something close to yearning there. Something she'd never seen before. Then his gaze hardened. "Provided…"

"Provided what?"

"I want to see my great-grandchild."

She dropped her hands from the rail and stepped away to make sure she wasn't close enough to wring his neck. "You don't know how to do anything but control people, do you? You make them bend until they break, and you don't even bat an eye. Not as long as you get what you want."

"One man's manipulation is another man's just cause," Oliver said in a pained whisper. Then he cleared his throat again. "I'm not asking you for anything that dire. Your child is a Wilmington. As your grandfather, I have a right to know him."

Of course he'd assume his grandchild was a boy. The male heir to the great Wilmington legacy, no doubt. What did it say that a man of his power and influence hadn't cared enough to bother finding out the gender of his only great-grandchild?

"This is the child you wanted destroyed," she reminded him.

"That was a mistake." A grimace of shame flashed across his face. "I've always regretted how I overreacted. After losing your mother the way I did, I was afraid something might happen to you, too…"

"If that's your way of reminding me that it's my fault my mother's dead, don't bother. You made it perfectly clear when I was a child how much you blamed me."

"That's not true. I never blamed—"

"Save it." She held up her hand. "It doesn't matter now."

After a moment, he nodded. "You're right. That's all in the past. I made my share of mistakes, but haven't I paid enough of a price? The child's almost grown, and I've never seen him. Would it be so terrible, granting me this one request?"

It would be a disaster.

Maggie couldn't come to Oakwood, not as long as Eric was here. Maggie thought her father was dead. Carrinne had charmed her with stories about how much he'd cared for them both, how he would have loved watching his daughter grow up. Maggie kept Carrinne's only picture of Eric with her everywhere she went. She was the perfect female reflection of her father.

Carrinne had never dreamed they might one day meet.

"So, what will it be?" Oliver smiled. He was clearly enjoying his status as the only person Carrinne could turn to in town. "I'll make sure you have unlimited use of the house, that you have anything you need as you search for your father. Whatever I can do. All I ask is this one small thing in return."

"I'll consider bringing her back—"

"Her? It's a girl?"

"I'll *consider* bringing her back." She studied the parking deck below his window, making him wait. "But only after I find my father. Totally contingent on your cooperation while I'm here, as well as your silence."

"My silence?" Her grandfather's confusion lasted less than a second. "Ah. You mean about why you ran away."

"Tell me you haven't told anyone."

"Why would I? It was a family matter."

"You mean I was an embarrassment, and you were thankful no one had to know."

"I mean I won't have more of our family problems become fodder for small-town gossip. No one knows you were pregnant."

"Good." She took her first deep breath since seeing Eric last night. "I want to keep it that way."

"I assume you're worried about our illustrious Sheriff Rivers. It would prove inconvenient for him to find out about his child after all these years, wouldn't it?"

"That's none of your business."

"You made it my business. Everyone in Oakwood knew you were going with that young man. Skipping class together, sneaking out all hours of the night. To this day, I'll never understand why you felt it necessary to pick the one person in town I thought was least suitable for you."

"Not everything is about you." She reached for her purse and slung the strap over her shoulder. "Do I have your word or not?"

"I get to see my great-granddaughter?"

"Help me with what I need, and I'll find a way to make it happen." Just *how* she'd make it happen while keeping Eric and Maggie apart, she had no idea. But that was a worry that could wait. There were so many others in line before it.

"Then you have my full support. Whatever I can do to help. Although, I don't know anything more about your mother's diaries than you do." There was that look of almost longing again, the hint that there was something more he wanted to say. Then he gave a wry chuckle. "I'd offer you my liver, but I don't suppose a wasted old body like mine would be much use to you."

"No." She swallowed the *but thank you* that almost

slipped out. "The donor needs to be healthy, and preferably under the age of sixty."

"What about your daughter? Could she be a donor?"

"Not an alternative." She made herself walk slowly toward the door, when what she really wanted was to bolt from her grandfather's penetrating gaze.

"Carrinne?"

"What?" She didn't turn back.

"I'll alert Robert that you'll be moving back home."

Robert had been the Wilmington butler since before she was born. The man must be almost as old as Oliver.

"My *home* is in New York. And I'm staying at a motel while I'm here. Tell Robert I'll be by first thing in the morning. I need to get back into the attic."

"When will I see you again?" he asked, his voice gravelly. She looked over her shoulder, and the reality of the lonely, fragile old man in the hospital bed slid past her defenses once more.

"I'll be in touch," she finally managed to say.

"It's good to see you." His mouth curved upward, but smiling still didn't sit well on his face. "You're so beautiful, just like your mother."

"I'll be in touch," she repeated. She jerked the door open and stepped into the silent hallway, horrified by the emotion stinging her eyes.

Striding away, grateful that Brimsley was nowhere in sight, she ignored the buzzing that filled her ears. It shouldn't matter that her grandfather thought she was beautiful now. Why should she care? But damn it, unbelievably, something inside her did.

As a child, she'd done anything and everything to earn Oliver's approval, to grab just one crumb of praise to go along with his never-ending stream of rules and regulations. But whatever capacity the man had had to love had died along with first his wife and then Carrinne's mother. All that had remained for Carrinne was a rigid shell of a man and the hollow pretense of a happy family.

She hadn't been allowed to wear makeup, because he wasn't raising one of *those* girls. No pants, either, because she was a young lady. No skirts shorter than a certain length. No dating, no dances. And the list went on. But regardless of how hard she tried, no matter how many hoops she jumped through, he hadn't doled out the first smidgen of love. Instead, she became a disappointment, a constant reminder of all he'd lost with her mother. Until finally, she'd stopped trying and had gone to look for someone else to love her. The worst possible person, in her grandfather's opinion.

She wiped at her eyes, furious at the unwanted emotion controlling her. First Eric, now Oliver. People didn't push her buttons like this. Not anymore.

She rode the elevator to the second level of the hospital's parking garage, forcing her mind to clear. By the time she'd reached her rental car, deep breathing and determination had returned some measure of control. Starting the engine and cranking the barely adequate air conditioner, she secured her seat belt and headed for the nearest exit. She should be planning her next move, but forming a coherent thought was light years beyond her at the moment.

She left the parking garage, driving down the steep hill to Crabapple Street. The light at the bottom turned yellow, and the urge to run it nagged her. She applied the brakes with a growl, the thought of bottoming out on the uneven pavement below and damaging the car— the thought of spending one more minute at the hospital while she waited for a tow—overruling her impulse.

As she slowed, a large shadow in the rearview mirror drew her attention away from the road. The vehicle behind her seemed to be accelerating. She checked the light, now red, and rolled to a stop. Then she glanced over her shoulder to make sure the driver behind her had followed suit.

The other vehicle's front bumper slammed into her car a split second before her scream rent the air. The car and her body pitched forward. Her seat belt caught, but not soon enough. The side of her head snapped against the steering wheel. Through the fuzziness that followed and the painful echo of bells ringing, some disengaged part of her brain had the capacity to curse her small-town rental. It was clearly so old it predated the standard issue of airbags.

Feeling as though she was moving in slow motion, she roused herself and stomped on the brake pedal for all she was worth. Tires squealed against asphalt. The smell of burnt rubber would have choked her if she'd been able to breathe. The engine of the vehicle behind her revved even louder, and with another jolt, she was hurtled into oncoming traffic. What was this nut's problem?

Anger seared through Carrinne's panic. Maggie's face flashed before her eyes. No way was it going to end like this, with some hick turning her into roadkill when she finally had a legitimate shot at getting her second chance.

Remembering the emergency brake at the last minute, she pulled the lever at her elbow, wincing as the car spun sideways. She watched in horror at the sight of a red pickup barreling down Crabapple, headed straight toward the intersection and her passenger door. She braced for impact, lifting her arms to protect her face.

The roar of metal shredding metal drowned out her cry. Then everything blessedly faded to black.

ERIC CHECKED the wall clock again. Ten minutes after three.

He pushed back from his desk and the stack of paperwork he'd been mulling over since noon. Reaching for his coffee mug, he found it empty and growled. He'd already filled the thing twice. When was the jarring brew going to clear his head?

Normally he'd be anywhere but the office on a Saturday afternoon. Since winning his bid for sheriff a little over a year ago, he'd fought tooth and nail to keep his weekends free. His appearance this morning had been so rare, you'd have thought from the looks on the faces of the officers he'd passed that they'd seen a ghost.

Maybe they had. This was exactly where his father had spent every single Saturday. And Eric had sworn he'd do it differently. That he'd have a life outside this place.

He shouldn't have come in.

Where he should be was home in bed, since focusing on anything for longer than five minutes was impossible. But his attempts to sleep after finally leaving Carrinne in Tony's capable hands last night had met with one dead end after another. First by his neighbor's dog, which had barked all night. Then a telemarketer had called just after nine, offering him the opportunity of a lifetime to buy into a fabulous Gulf Shore timeshare. And each time he'd drifted off, his thoughts had returned to Carrinne and all the reasons he should leave her alone as she'd asked—regardless of his need to help. So he'd thrown on jeans and a T-shirt and headed in.

Staring with disgust at the overdue reports his chief deputy, Angie Carter, had been after him for days to complete, he shoved himself out of his chair and headed for the coffee machine in the break room.

A few more years of this, he reminded himself. Just a few more years. He'd make sure Tony was settled, that he could handle himself on the force, then Eric was out of this town. Just like he'd always wanted to be. He'd stuck it out, had been there for his little brother every day of the last seventeen years. He'd used his dad's contacts in the department to secure training and a spot on the force, and he'd done his best to become a good cop. And maybe, just maybe, he'd done right by Tony along the way.

He'd even run for the position of sheriff so he could keep a closer eye on his kid brother. Plus the salary increase was putting a sizable dent in what was left of their mortgage. But nothing could erase his need to feel a motorcycle between his legs again. The need to put a few hundred miles between himself and everything this town could never be for him. He just wasn't cut out for small-town community and friendships. He was better off alone.

"Worked it all out of your system?" Tony asked, catching up to Eric at the break room. He was dressed in wrinkled jeans and a T-shirt—one of Eric's favorite T-shirts, as a matter of fact.

"You're not on 'til five." Eric poured his brother a cup of coffee after refilling his own.

"You're not on at all." Tony looked into the mug Eric held out and pulled a face. He shook his head to pass.

"Didn't you know living in this place was one of the perks of being the top dog?" Eric sipped a burning mouthful of, hands-down, the worst coffee ever brewed in the town of Oakwood.

"Angie caught me on my way to the batting cages. Said you were holed up in your office, pretending to get your paperwork done. It's so out of character, you've got her worried you're going postal or something."

Eric trudged out of the break room. "This town is so

small, it's a wonder I can take a piss without someone phoning you about it."

"I told her you were just cranky 'cause you have the hots for an old girlfriend who's giving you the cold shoulder."

Eric turned back, swallowing his curse. Anyone in the station could pass them in the hall, so he nixed the instinct to vent his sleepless night right then and there. He headed for his office, motioning for Tony to follow. Once inside, Eric slammed the door and rounded on his brother. "Why the hell would you say something like that?"

Tony held up his hands in mock surrender. "Hey, I just call them like I see them. You were in rare form last night. One minute you were a jealous hound dog because a woman you haven't seen since high school was smiling at me, the next you were hunting me down to drive the very lovely but elusive Ms. Wilmington back to her car."

"If you said one word about Carrinne and me to Angie, the ass-whipping I gave you when you kept skipping school in sixth grade will seem like a tickle. Carrinne's got enough trouble without having to deal with rumors flying all over town about—"

"Relax." Tony sat in a guest chair, his grin now ear-to-ear. "I didn't say a thing. I wouldn't do that to Carrinne. Now you, on the other hand…"

"You can still be a brat, you know that?" Resisting the urge to paddle his kid brother, just to see if he still could, Eric settled in his own chair. Coffee spilled over the edge of his mug and burned his hand. "Damn."

"You should get some sleep."

"I tried that." He sipped coffee from his thumb. "Cuddles had different ideas."

Tony chuckled. "I'm glad that rat lives next to your bedroom window and not mine. Who knew a miniature poodle could make so much noise?"

"Clearly, Mrs. Davis chose the pick of the litter."

They sat silently while Eric contemplated throwing his weight around at the pound and having Cuddles picked up for disturbing the peace.

"So." Tony slouched deeper into the chair Eric was pretty sure predated their father's term as sheriff. "Are you having her tailed?"

"Mrs. Davis?"

A stare was Tony's only response.

"No, I'm not having Carrinne Wilmington tailed. Why would I?" Eric pushed the coffee aside and tried to focus on the report in front of him. "Brimsley's agreed not to press charges, so there's no reason for the department to be involved."

"Unless, of course, you didn't buy her story and wanted to help out an old friend before she got herself into even more trouble."

"Carrinne and I haven't been friends for a long time." And that hurt more than it should. "Not since I told her to get out of my life and she obliged."

"If memory serves, she's the only female you ever stuck with for longer than two months at a clip. That's got to count for something."

Eric dropped the report to the desk. "I offered to help last night. She declined. She's determined to handle whatever she's come back to do on her own."

"And that's okay with you?"

No, it definitely wasn't okay.

When had his brother grown up and become so good at reading people? It used to be that the only things Tony paid any attention to were motorcycles and pretty girls. Time was, that was all Eric had cared about, too.

"Hey, Eric?" Angie said over the intercom. "Didn't you take the call out to the Wilmington place last night?"

"Yeah," was his monotone reply. He glowered at his brother. Didn't anyone have anything better to talk about?

"Thought you might like to know. Dispatch got a call. Your break-in suspect just did a three-sixty into oncoming traffic in front of the hospital."

CHAPTER FOUR

"WILL SHE BE all right?"

"… mild concussion."

"Why isn't she waking up?"

"…running some blood tests…under observation until her condition improves…should be coming out of it by now…"

The voices kept pulling at Carrinne, disturbing the peaceful numbness she had no desire to come back from. One of the voices, the deeper one, sounded so familiar. It floated in and out of the disjointed dream playing in her mind.

It had been so long since she'd let herself dream…

The man's voice belonged to a rugged teenager who had melting brown eyes and could drive a motorcycle like an avenging angel. She was sitting behind him as he raced his Harley down a country highway. Her arms wrapped around his muscled body, she leaned close and let the wind and the rush of danger take her. She was sixteen again, and with him she was wanted and safe. Closing her eyes and resting her cheek against his leather-covered back, she whispered words of love into the wind, knowing he'd never want to hear them, but yearning to say them anyway. He needed her, when no one had ever needed her. And though he didn't know it yet, he'd given her the most precious gift of all.

They were going to love each other always.

"Carrinne?" He called to her from somewhere that wasn't the dream. "Carrinne, it's time to wake up. Can you hear me, darlin'? Wake up for me."

He wanted her to wake up. And what he wanted became what she wanted, too, just as it had when she was sixteen. Swimming up from her dream, she looked back one last time, down that endless country road. But he was already driving away, the motorcycle just a speck on the horizon.

A sickening throb behind her eyes kept her from running after him. Grounded more firmly in the present with each passing second, she realized she hadn't really been dreaming at all. Instead, she'd been remembering her first taste of how cruel dreams could be when they crashed head-first into reality.

Pain hit her full-out, yanking her away from the memory of the last ride she and Eric had taken on his motorcycle. The ride on which she'd planned to tell him she was pregnant. But before she could, he'd destroyed everything. He couldn't deal with having a kid like her in his life anymore, he'd said. He wanted her to stay away from him. Then he'd driven away, taking everything that she'd cared about with him. Everything except Maggie.

Through her closed eyelids, an overhead light shot daggers into her skull. She tried to shade her eyes with her hand.

"Open your eyes, Carrinne." The voice really *did* belong to Eric. A very grown-up Eric. "Doctor, I think she's coming to."

"What's going on?" She struggled to make sense of the confusing signals her brain couldn't seem to process.

A hand pressed her down as she tried to sit up. "You've been in an accident. Hold still until the doctor can take another look."

Blinking, groaning as nausea rolled in her stomach, she'd barely managed to focus on Eric before a man in a white coat appeared.

"I'm Dr. Burns." He shined a blast of light into each of her eyes. "Can you tell me your name?"

"Carrinne." She winced. "Carrinne Wilmington."

"And the day?"

"It's…um…it's July…thirteenth or fourteenth."

"Uh-huh." He checked her pulse while he studied the display on the machine attached to the pressure cuff on her arm. "Good. Now can you tell me what you remember from this morning?"

Her gaze strayed to Eric. He was dressed in a black T-shirt and jeans rather than his sheriff's uniform. What had happened? What on earth was he doing here?

His reassuring smile was as unexpected as the touch of his hand, the slight squeeze he gave her fingers.

"Um," she stuttered, her mind still too full of the past to focus on the doctor's questions. "This morning…"

"What's the last thing you remember?" Eric prompted. He soothed the inside of her palm with his thumb, something he'd done when they were teenagers.

"I…" Pulling her hand away was nearly impossible, but she managed it. She focused on the doctor. "I was visiting my grandfather… Then I rode the elevator down to the parking deck."

"And after that?" the doctor asked.

"Nothing…I…I don't know what happened next." Concentrating made the throbbing in her head worse. "I was driving out of the deck, and… Someone said something about an accident?"

"At the light turning onto Crabapple." Eric's expression darkened. "You ran it and pulled in front of a pickup truck."

"I…" She rubbed her temple. "I remember a red truck… But that's not right… There was a van, or a bigger truck behind me…" Why couldn't she remember? "Was anyone hurt?"

The doctor jotted notes onto a chart. "I hear your car and the truck that hit you are both a mess, but the other driver was unharmed, and you seem to have suffered only a mild concussion—"

"What do you mean a bigger truck?" Eric asked over the doctor. When she only stared, her thoughts still a jumble of mixed images, he took her hand again. "You said there was a van or a bigger truck involved in the accident."

"I don't know... I don't remember..."

"Short-term memory loss is very common with a concussed brain," the doctor offered.

"It's just that I know there's something more." She hated the way she was clinging to Eric's hand, but her fingers had a mind of their own and had no interest in letting go. "I wouldn't have run that light. I know how busy Crabapple is this time of day. And there was—"

She coughed, her breath catching on a light-headed feeling she knew all too well.

"There was a van behind me, or a dark truck—" Another series of coughs worked to clear her lungs as her mind filled with the image of a large vehicle barreling up behind her rental car. "I think someone hit me from behind when I stopped at the light."

"This other vehicle—" Both of Eric's hands held hers now. His grip was firm. "What exactly did it look like?"

She tried to answer, if only to ease the awful expression on Eric's face. But the tightness in her chest had other ideas. Another coughing fit stripped her breath away.

"Excuse me, Sheriff." The doctor stepped between them to listen to her chest through his stethoscope. Eric dropped her hands and moved away.

"Tell me, Ms. Wilmington," the doctor said. "Have you been fighting off a flu bug or some other kind of infection?"

"No. Why?" Having a good idea why, she glanced at Eric. His scowl deepened as the doctor started probing the lymph nodes behind her ears.

"Because you're running a midgrade fever, and your pulse and blood pressure are unusually low," the doctor replied. "Your lungs are clear, but that cough's concerning me. Your body's under some kind of stress that may or may not be connected with the accident."

She raised a hand to the ache at her temple, fingering the bandage she found there. The nightmare she'd stumbled into last night kept getting worse and worse. "Can I have a word with you alone, Doctor?"

Dr. Burns hesitated for only a second before turning to face a looming Eric.

"Will you excuse us, Sheriff?" He nodded toward the partially closed curtain that separated Carrinne's alcove from the rest of the ER floor.

"I need more information about the accident," Eric countered. "If another car was involved—"

"I understand, Sheriff. But that can wait."

"Not if—"

"The longer we stand here—" the doctor's hands found the pockets of his lab coat "—the longer it'll be before we both find the answers we need."

"Eric, please," she added. No way could he be here for the conversation she knew was coming.

Eric pinned the doctor with an unblinking, bad-boy stare. To Dr. Burns's credit, he didn't budge. With a worried look at Carrinne, Eric turned and left.

Closing the curtain, Dr. Burns returned to the bed. "Better?"

"Yes, thank you." She continued to toy with the edge

of the bandage, the list of disasters playing havoc with her plans growing by second. "I'm only visiting Oakwood. No one but my grandfather knows about my condition, and I'd like to keep it that way."

"It's important that I know what we're dealing with, if I'm going to help you."

Glancing at the curtain, she sighed. "I was diagnosed with primary sclerosing cholangitis about six months ago. That may be what's causing some of the symptoms you mentioned."

"I see." After a slight pause and a professional nod, he scribbled even more notes onto the chart. "Have you had a liver biopsy?"

"A few months ago. I'm in the very early stages, so my symptoms have been mild so far. The doctors wouldn't have diagnosed it this early if it weren't for the battery of blood tests they ran at my yearly physical. I'd felt run-down for a few months. At first, they thought it was just stress."

"Okay. We'll do some additional lab work to test your enzyme levels. I'll need your doctor's name and number so we can compare them to his baseline." Dr. Burns looked up from the chart. "Have there been any recurring symptoms?"

"The fever you mentioned, and I tire more easily than I used to. The cough only happens every now and then, when I can't catch my breath."

"Any weight loss?"

"A little, but I'm working with a nutritionist to design a better diet. I've skipped several meals lately, so I'm not exactly where I should be."

"You must be aware that with your condition, your system absorbs fat less efficiently. Your abnormally low blood pressure and heart rate are symptoms that your body's not getting the energy it needs. Even though you're in the early stages of the disease, your stamina will deteriorate without regular meals and rest. The fever's probably a sign of infection, and the more run-down your body is, the less able it will be to fight off illness."

"I understand. It's just been a difficult few days."

"I'm going to prescribe some antibiotics for the infection." More notes on the chart. "Are you taking vitamins?"

"Yes. Every morning."

"Good. Leave the nurse a list. Maybe there's something more we can suggest to help." He set the chart aside. Crossing his arms across his chest, he gave her the kind of look doctors always give you when they're about to say something they know you don't want to hear. "I'm recommending several days of bed rest until we have the infection cleared up."

"Here?"

"No. We'll release you as soon as you're cleared for the concussion. But I want you doing as little as possible once you're home. You need to rebuild your strength before things go from bad to worse."

"But I'm only in town for a few days, and there's something critical I need to be doing."

"Then I'd suggest you find someone who can help you with whatever it is. Keep going at the pace you are, and you'll wind up right back here."

Carrinne knew he was right. If she pushed her body, she'd only get sicker. But she couldn't stop looking for her father. Even with Oliver's help, she might never find the diary, and then her search would only become harder. And the only other person in town she knew well enough to ask for help was—

"Sheriff Rivers seems like a good friend," the doctor suggested. "He's been here for over an hour, came as soon as he heard we'd brought you in. Perhaps he could be of assistance."

"Perhaps," she managed to say, still not fully recovered from waking to find Eric beside her, all concern and support.

Having Oakwood's sheriff helping her dig into the past might be an asset, except she'd learned a long time ago what trusting Eric could cost her. Then there was the daughter he had no idea they'd made together. Maggie's very existence lay like a coiled snake between her parents, waiting for the right time to strike and cause the most damage.

Eric couldn't know about Maggie, and Maggie couldn't know about him. Not right now, maybe not ever. Carrinne had come back to Oakwood to protect Maggie from pain. Finding out about Eric would hurt her in the worst way, and that was out of the question.

Dr. Burns's beeper chirped.

"I've got to take this call," he said as he checked the display. He gave her a harried frown. "I'll be back in a while. Think about what I said, okay?"

When he opened the curtain, Eric was leaning against the opposite wall. He was a solid, immovable presence, even though he'd given her the privacy she'd needed with the doctor.

"Sheriff," Dr. Burns said as he headed down the hall.

Eric couldn't take his eyes off Carrinne. His knees were still weak from the panic that had sent him sprinting from the office after Angie's page.

He wasn't in uniform and he'd been driving his truck, but he'd broken every speed limit in town to get here regardless. And somewhere during the ride, he'd dropped the pretense about helping Carrinne out of obligation. No weak excuse about owing her could explain the knot of worry still twisting inside him.

Carrinne's wary glance as he approached the bed wished him a thousand miles away. She was wearing black again, a black knit pantsuit and dainty black sandals. Cinderella sandals, he mused. Only she wasn't a fairy-tale princess waiting to be rescued. And heaven knew he was no one's Prince Charming.

She looked so small and scared lying there on the exam table, and more beautiful every time he saw her.

"I called Brimsley to let him know what's happened." He buried his hands in his back pockets to stop himself from touching her again.

"Thank you," she said calmly. Any calmer, and she

might actually make him believe his presence wasn't driving her nuts.

"I figured it was better your grandfather didn't hear about it through the rumor mill."

"Why are you here, Eric?" she asked with an exhausted sigh. "Why do you even care about any of this?"

"Why do I—" He shook his head, not sure he'd heard right. "I came here to make sure you were okay. Is it so terrible that I care?"

"I'd say inconceivable would be more like it." Her wariness hardened to sarcasm.

"What have I ever done to make you think I wouldn't care whether you lived or died?"

"Try telling me I was little more than a pest, and that you'd had enough—" she choked, then cleared her throat "that you'd had enough of me."

"That was a long time ago, Carrinne. And you were never a pest. I never should have said that, and I didn't mean it." He closed his eyes against the reality of the pain he'd caused her. "I know I hurt you, but I was a mixed-up kid. I was going through hell, and I—"

"I know all about what you were going through." She swallowed against what must be a killer headache. "I was there, remember? You'd lost your dad, and you had Tony to take care of. You suddenly had to be a grown-up, and you hated the world for it. Somehow, I guess that meant you had to hate me, too. No matter that you'd made me believe you needed me. I was just a kid to you. One more burden you had to get off your back."

"No, you weren't a burden. You were…it was just…" The words wouldn't stumble out. Nothing could make up for his blind need back then to destroy what he'd felt for her. "It wasn't you. It was me. I was angry at the choices that were no longer mine. And there you were, trying to make everything better. I figured if I leaned on you, you'd get smart eventually and want out, too. So I cut and ran before you had the chance. I'm sorry. Really."

She wouldn't look at him, just when he'd give everything he owned to see forgiveness in her beautiful green eyes.

"Carrinne—"

"It doesn't matter now."

"Carrinne—"

"Drop it, Eric." Those green eyes were spitting fire now.

She fingered her bandaged temple. The gesture was just the slap of reality Eric needed.

"I've got a call into Tony about the accident," he said. *Business. Stick with business.* "Can you remember anything else about the vehicle you saw behind—"

"Ah," Dr. Burns said as he walked back in. "Have you gotten around to asking our good sheriff for the help you need?"

Carrinne shot the doctor a narrowed look, then Eric a warning.

"No." She crossed her arms. "I haven't decided exactly what to do yet. When can I get out of here?"

The doctor checked beneath the bandage then felt her

pulse. "The nurse is going to take some blood and start an IV. I've ordered a round of antibiotics. Once that's done, assuming you have no further complications from the concussion, I'll consider releasing you. That is, if I have some assurances that you'll be sensible and follow the course of treatment I've prescribed."

Carrinne's expression turned positively mutinous. "I don't—"

"You need rest. And you're going to need some help for a few days." Dr. Burns glanced pointedly at Eric. "I suggest you bite the bullet and get the inevitable over with."

As soon as the other man was gone, Eric stepped closer. "What are the antibiotics and the blood tests for? What wouldn't you discuss with the doctor until I left the room?"

"I'm going to be fine." She turned her head away. "You don't have to worry."

"Well, I am worried." He touched a finger to her chin and turned her face back. "He said you needed rest. That you needed help. Let me help you, damn it. Don't let stubbornness and the mistakes I made when we were kids keep you from getting the care you need now."

She jerked away. He watched her weigh her options.

"It's the only logical choice," he prompted. "I'm the only person in town you know well enough, except for Oliver."

Hostility flashed across her face, quickly overridden by the calm acceptance of someone who'd learned not to let emotions rule her. She took a deep breath. "The antibiotic is for a recurring infection. It's a side effect of a liver condition that's weakening my immune system. A condition I'd prefer Oakwood's gossip chain didn't know about right now."

"A liver condition?" Eric felt as if a gaping hole had opened in the floor directly beneath him. He leaned a hand on the bed to keep his knees from buckling. "How bad is this condition?"

"Right now—" she wouldn't meet his eyes "—it just tires me out. Particularly when I'm not eating or sleeping right. That's why the doctor wants me to rest for a few days."

"But?"

"But." When she made eye contact, her expression was completely open for the first time since he'd caught her shimmying out of her grandfather's solarium. She watched him with a mixture of fear and determination that clawed at his gut. "My condition will slowly deteriorate to the point that I'll need a new liver to survive. That's the real reason I'm looking for my father. I'm hoping he'll be a match to be a living donor."

"But there must be other options."

There had to be.

She gave her head a tiny shake, wincing at the motion. "I have some pretty rare stuff in my blood. I'll probably win the lottery before they find a donor on the general transplant list."

"God, Carrinne." Eric wanted to take her in his arms. To comfort her, or comfort himself, he wasn't quite sure which. But his body was completely numb. It refused to move. She wouldn't want him to hold her anyway. "I don't know what to say."

"Say you'll help me." The vulnerability of her statement was at direct odds with the anger that colored each word. "I might not be able to find my father on my own. Say I can depend on you this time."

"I'LL BE FINE at the motel." Carrinne signed the last of the hospital release forms. She needed out of the ER and away from Eric.

"You'd be more comfortable at my house," he argued, just as he had the entire half hour it had taken for the IV to push a broad-spectrum antibiotic into her bloodstream. "And you'd have someone to look out for you until you completely recover."

"I've been looking out for myself since I was a teenager. I'm calling a cab." She stood too fast and had to lean into the examination table.

Shrugging off the dizziness, she walked to the small table beside the bed. She rifled through the bag that held her purse and jewelry, finding and pulling out her cell phone. She wasn't supposed to have the thing on in the hospital, but she had to check her messages. Damn. There were two from Maggie. She flipped the phone closed and tossed it back in her bag, making a mental note to call her daughter when she got back to the motel.

"Someone has to check you every couple of hours, Ms. Wilmington." Dr. Burns stood beside the wheelchair he'd had a nurse bring in. "I can't release you until I know that's going to happen."

"I'll check on her." Eric's reassurance was loaded with aggravation. "If I have to, I'll call her motel room every two hours. If she doesn't answer, I live only ten minutes away."

"Everyone in this town lives only ten minutes away." Carrinne longed for the sanctuary of her Manhattan apartment. In the city, constantly surrounded by a thriving sea of people, you became a master at creating privacy and solitude, no matter how few square feet you had to yourself. In lazy, sprawling Oakwood, where she'd never felt she belonged, she was suddenly at the suffocating center of too many people's attention.

Dr. Burns glanced between Eric and Carrinne. "I guess that'll have to do. You're just a wheelchair ride from being rid of me, Ms. Wilmington."

"Thank you, Doctor. For everything." She barely glanced at the chair as she stepped into the hall. "But I'd rather walk."

"Ms. Wilmington—"

"Get in the wheelchair, Carrinne." Eric caught her arm, his touch nowhere near gentle. The bewitching concern swirling in his eyes kicked her heartbeat into a crazy tap-tap-tap. "It's after five, and I haven't eaten since breakfast. I'm betting you haven't either. Go one more round with hospital regulations, and we'll both starve."

Why couldn't his stunned reaction to learning about her

liver condition have been an act? Why did he have to be committed to helping her in a way she'd never expected?

Why did she have to be hurting so badly she couldn't think straight?

"I need to walk out of this hospital," she explained, looking down. "It's important that I do for myself for as long as I can."

"And you will." He moved infinitesimally closer, his aftershave hinting of a winter campfire and skin-warmed flannel. "But tomorrow's soon enough. Today you need help."

She forced herself to turn back to the chair and, more to the point, away from Eric's unwanted concern.

"Come in tomorrow afternoon for a recheck." Dr. Burns moved aside as she sat and Eric stepped behind her. The doctor handed Eric the antibiotic prescription he'd had filled in the hospital pharmacy. "I'm on call after three."

"I'll be here," she replied.

After the doctor left, Carrinne folded her hands. "What now?"

"I'm parked at the curb out front." Eric released the wheelchair's brakes and pushed her into the hall.

"And then?"

"Then we get you settled somewhere, and you can tell me everything you remember about the accident."

He was all business again. Good for him. Good for her. She let his use of the word *somewhere* slide. It's not like he could force her to move out of her motel.

It felt wonderful to walk out—okay, roll out—into the warm July air. If only the sun wasn't so bright. She blocked the glare with her hand.

"Do you have any sunglasses?" Eric stopped beside a large black truck, not the squad car she'd expected. "The doctor said you'd be sensitive to light for several more hours."

"Yes. I…" She tried to open the small backpack she used as a purse, but her shaking fingers were useless.

"Here." He deftly loosened the clasp and reached inside. He'd handed her the glasses and resecured the bag before she could blast him for invading her privacy. His overly patient expression said he hadn't missed her annoyance. "I'll get your door."

He did more than that. He lifted her from the chair and gently settled her in the front seat of the truck. She bit back a groan as the world spun, then settled around her. The ache in her head had migrated down her neck and beyond. Her entire body throbbed. She fought to remain perfectly still as Eric closed her door and walked around to the driver's side.

"You okay?" Seated behind the wheel, he reached behind him and handed her a blanket from the back of the cab.

"Fine. Just take me to my motel."

"Carrinne—"

"Take me to my motel, or I'm calling a taxi."

A curse was his only response as he fired the powerful engine and put the truck in reverse. When they

stopped for the light at Crabapple Street, Carrinne
averted her gaze from the intersection that had been the
lowest point of her negative karma since coming back
to town.

She hugged the blanket and stared out her window.
Had it been a truck or a van behind her when she slowed
for the light? Her thundering headache made it difficult
to care, but enduring the pain splitting her skull in two
was exactly what she needed to keep her mind off the
man sitting beside her. She was okay as long as she
didn't look at Eric. One more of his exasperated, troubled expressions, and she was either going to scream or
burst into tears.

In no time, they reached the heart of Oakwood.
Quaint, historic homes and shops flanked either side of
the street, announcing the center of town. Wide side-
walks invited passersby to amble and linger, to chat
with neighbors or perhaps stop in at Buddy's Five and
Dime for a root-beer float. A line of oak trees still
flanked either side of the street. They'd been planted at
the town's founding over a hundred years ago, and as
they'd grown, their stately, moss-dripping branches had
stretched to meet each other across the street. A half-
mile of dense green canopy now sheltered the cars that
drove beneath.

Carrinne eyed the town of her youth with a detach-
ment she resented to her soul. Oakwood's Norman
Rockwell facade was only a brittle shell to her. Instead
of filling her with warm nostalgia, the passing blur of

familiar sights brought back the isolation of her childhood, the years of being different, set apart, when she'd
desperately wanted to belong. Other kids had roamed
Oakwood's picturesque streets, first on bikes, then with
groups of friends in cars on Friday and Saturday nights.
But not Oliver Wilmington's granddaughter.

No, her activities had been planned from the cradle
to appropriately complement her family's heritage and
lofty station. To keep her busy and out of her grandfather's way.

She'd never lacked for anything his money could
buy her. She'd attended functions at the country club,
formal dance classes and balls, riding lessons. She'd
been allowed to accept invitations to the *right* kinds of
parties. Oliver had arranged friendships with girls
whose snobbery and disdain for those outside what they
saw as their class had turned Carrinne's stomach. The
same girls had whispered behind her back, gossiping
that, rich or not, she was still an everyday, garden-vari-
ety bastard. She was the girl who'd killed her own
mother by coming into the world.

Finally, burned by shallow relationships once too
often, Carrinne had stopped going to the parties and the
club altogether. Instead, she'd retreated into a world of
fantasy, reading the days and nights away, burying herself in the endless volumes of classic poetry and litera-
ture she'd found in Oliver's study. Under her favorite
cypress tree, she'd lost herself in fascinating cities and
worlds beyond the narrow confines of her life. And

she'd dreamed of the romantic knight who would one day carry her away to a paradise where she would finally belong. Where someone would want and need her at last.

When at fifteen she'd literally stumbled across Eric one afternoon, the knight she'd been waiting for had roared into her life. Walking home from school, her nose in a book as usual, she'd been crossing Crabapple to buy a Coke at Buddy's and hadn't seen a sixteen-year-old Eric approaching on his motorcycle until he'd almost run her down. He'd slid to a stop less than an inch away, cursing as she'd shrieked and dropped her books.

He'd gotten off his bike to make sure she was all right. Then he'd touched her, just her hand, but something in his dangerous expression had shifted, and for the first time in her life she'd found herself face-to-face with a man who was completely, blatantly aware of her as a woman. Her knight, her savior, had arrived. He'd only been a year older, but he'd been light years ahead of her in life. And she'd known that from that moment on, her sheltered, solitary world would never be the same.

Electronic ringing sliced through the truck's silence and Carrinne's memories. Dazed, she was still fumbling with the dratted clasp on her bag when she realized Eric had answered his phone.

"Rivers here." He turned onto Juniper Street as he listened. "Away from the point of impact? Are you sure, Tony? What about her brakes?"

The worry in Eric's voice captured her attention. His

solid, six-foot-plus frame consumed the small space behind the steering wheel, the strength of his presence
making a joke of the few feet separating them. One
large hand controlled the wheel. The other held the
phone to his ear as he glanced from her to the road and
back. Any other woman in Oakwood would likely think
herself lucky to have the honorable Sheriff Rivers' help.
But all Carrinne felt was trapped.

"…Carrinne?" His voice intruded on her thoughts.
"Where did you park at the hospital?"

"What?" She realized he'd asked the question several times.

"Your parking spot at the hospital. Do you remember where you parked?" He balanced the phone between his ear and shoulder and reached to tuck the
meandering blanket more snugly around her.

She stared at his hand until he removed it, the gen-
tleness of his gesture more of a shock than the heat of
his touch through the blanket. Gentle and Eric she didn't
want to think about.

"Carrinne?"

"I…" Her eyes flicked to his face.

"Where did you park?"

Swallowing, she fought to focus. "I…in the last spot
beside the second-level elevators."

"Beside the level two elevators, Tony. Check and see
if there's any video of the deck, and let me know what
you come up with. We're making a stop, so keep trying
to reach me on the cell."

He ended the call and gave her another quick glance, his attention dropping to where she clutched the blanket to her chest. "You can breathe now. I promise not to touch you again. Making you angrier isn't high on my list of smart moves right now."

"Thank you." Let him think what she was feeling was as simple as anger. Please God, don't let him see the weakness that still drew her to him.

"Why was Tony asking about my parking spot?" she asked as he turned into the lot beside Builda Burger, a local fast-food restaurant that had been an Oakwood mainstay since long before they'd gotten a McDonalds. "What's this?"

"Dinner." Eric pulled into the drive-through lane and braked beside a rusted microphone shaped like a cartoon French fry. "What do you want?"

"What did Tony say?" She matched his emotionless stare until she wanted to slap both herself and him for being so childish. She sighed. "I'll have a cheeseburger."

Eric shouted their order into the staticky French fry and pulled behind the car waiting in front of them.

"I asked Tony to look into your accident." He gazed out the windshield. "Your brakes are still in working order, even after the pounding your rental took, so we know it wasn't a mechanical malfunction. And you pulled the emergency brake lever, which eliminates the theory that you intentionally ran the light. Plus, your rear bumper shows definite signs you were hit from behind. A witness saw a dark gray van follow you down the hill leading from the parking deck to Crabapple. She said it looked like he waited until you were slowing for the light, then he gunned his motor and hit you. Twice. That means we have a problem."

"A problem?" she repeated, too caught up in the stream of information he'd dumped on her to really know what she was saying. An image of a large shadow looming in her car's rearview mirror flashed through Carrinne's mind. "But… Maybe they didn't see me stopped at the light until it was too late."

"From the eyewitness account, I'd say there's a better chance someone deliberately caused the accident. Tony's checking for video surveillance cameras in the parking deck between where you parked and the exit. Maybe we can get a better look at the van the witness saw. Do you have any idea who might want to see you hurt?"

Eric watched Carrinne swallow her shock. He didn't like the way her already pale complexion was blanching even whiter. She fumbled with the blanket, sifting through all he'd told her. The cop in him hoped the hard-as-nails resolve that had kept her going so far would hold up a little bit longer. The rest of him despised his instinct to push her for answers.

Actually, she looked a hell of a lot calmer than he felt. Her bombshell about her liver condition still had his heart hammering. While a nurse had started Carrinne's IV, he'd calmly relayed the details of her concussion to Tony. But he hadn't revealed her disease or the real reason she needed to find her father. He'd keep her secrets, if for no other reason than to prove to Carrinne that she could trust him.

When it was their turn at the drive-through window, a familiar face peered out at them. Just what they needed.

"Well, hi, Sheriff." Even though he was now in his thirties with kids of his own, Tommy Linders, son of the Builda Burger's founder, was still as gangly as a teen-ager. He took Eric's money and stretched to see farther into the truck. "And Carrinne Wilmington. I heard you were back in Oakwood."

"Hey, Tommy." Carrinne gave him a pitiful excuse for a smile. She was the most interesting thing Oakwood had had to gossip about in years. Clearly the distinction wasn't sitting well.

Eric collected their meals, waving his thanks to a smiling Tommy as he pulled away. Carrinne was once again staring out her window, doing a bang-up job of ignoring his existence. Did she honestly expect he'd let her handle this on her own, too?

She might not want to need him, but that didn't change the reality of her situation. She was sick, and someone might have deliberately tried to hurt her. There was a fine line between tough and careless, and Carrinne had crossed it nearly twenty-four hours ago. He pulled into one of the parking spaces rather than driving out of the lot.

"Talk to me about the accident, Carrinne."

"I can't remember anything more."

"You've been in town less than twenty-four hours, and someone may have tried to hurt you. Any idea why?"

"Is Tony sure?" She twisted the blanket's hem. "I mean, couldn't there be some mistake? Maybe someone was just being careless. Not paying attention to what they were doing."

"The witness saw the van accelerate into your car, rev its motor, and hit you a second time. Then it sped away after the pickup hit you. Tony's looking into it some more, but until he calls me back, one assumption has to be that someone in Oakwood might not be too happy to have you home."

"Who could have known I was back in town this morning?"

Eric waited until she looked his way. "It's a small town. You've left a stream of so-good-to-see-you-agains behind you all over the place. Did you burn any bridges before you left seventeen years ago?"

"You know I was never that close to anyone here." The memories clouding her eyes made him desperate to hold her. "You're the only person I ever let in enough to hurt me."

Memories charged through Eric's mind, too. Memories of just how close he and Carrinne had been. He'd buried his rebelliousness inside her sweet, receptive body. And her passion had blossomed, then raged right along with his.

Carrinne rubbed her injured temple and continued.

"I can't think of anyone who'd care one way or another that I'm back."

"What about this search for your father?" He almost didn't ask, but the possibility was riding him hard.

Her eyes narrowed. "My father?"

"You came back to track the man down. Someone may not want you to find him."

"Oh my God. That means he might actually be here." Elated relief transformed her features.

"Carrinne—"

"He really might be right here in Oakwood."

"And searching for him might just get you killed."

For a second she was speechless. Then she fired back, "Or the accident could be nothing more than a coincidence."

"I don't believe in coincidences." He refused to sugarcoat it. This was too damn serious.

Her frown deepened as she ran out of arguments. "But why? Why would anyone want to hurt me?"

"That's what I was hoping you could tell me."

She shook her head in response, hugging her arms in an uncoordinated kind of slow motion. She covered her mouth to stifle a sob, and the tough New York businesswoman disappeared before his eyes.

With a curse, he drew her tense body close, crushing the bags of food he'd placed between them as he rubbed warmth into her chilled skin. He had no way of knowing if she could even hear the array of nonsense he was muttering, but he kept talking in low tones, kept reassuring her that he wouldn't let anyone hurt her again.

His cell phone rang, causing them both to stiffen. Almost immediately, she began to struggle in his grasp, recoiling from his closeness. Reasserting at least the pretense of control.

Reluctantly, Eric let her pull away and answered the phone.

CHAPTER FIVE

"WHAT HAVE YOU GOT?" Eric barked into the phone as the world around Carrinne continued to shimmer in and out of focus.

She tried to follow his end of the conversation. But his "okay"s and "uh-huh"s sounded as if they were coming through an endless tunnel. His suspicions were ridiculous. They couldn't be true. If someone wanted to stop her search badly enough to harm her, then this whole thing was over before it even began. And that simply wasn't an option.

"No." The frustration in that one word had her looking up. Eric was studying her with a protective warmth that made her want to run to him and away from him at the same time. "We haven't settled that yet. Just find out as much as you can, and I'll work things out here."

He ended the call and put the truck into gear. Then he exited the parking lot, his face a mask of determination.

"What did Tony say?" she asked.

"The parking deck has 'round-the-clock security cameras. The tape shows a dark van trailing you down the ramp to the ground level."

"And…?"

Eric took Juniper the few short blocks to the turn onto Route 60. From there, it was a straight two-mile shot to the motel. "And, the van had no tags. The driver was wearing a hat and dark glasses—in the deck, where there's only artificial lighting. Someone followed you after you left your grandfather, Carrinne, and he deliberately caused the collision that spun you into Crabapple."

"You don't know that for sure." Eric's words settled in the middle of her diaphragm, squeezing off her breath. "It still could have been an accident."

"Not a chance." His hands clenched around the steering wheel. "Someone intentionally tried to hurt you."

Silence filled the truck for the few minutes it took them to reach the motel.

"Which room?" he asked when they arrived.

"Ten."

He pulled into a spot. "Let me have your key, and I'll get you packed."

"What are you talking about?" She threw open the truck door and pushed herself to her feet.

She hadn't taken two steps before he'd blocked her path, her bag in his hand. "There's no way in hell you're staying here by yourself. Not now."

She snatched the bag away and shot him a drop-dead look that made her head hurt. Sidestepping him, she stopped in front of the door, fumbling for her key. She lost her grip, and her backpack tumbled to the ground.

When she almost fell on her face trying to grab it, he caught her arm.

"Get out of my way," she breathed through clenched teeth.

Her balance chose that moment to completely desert her.

"And watch you pass out at my feet?" Catching her and reclaiming her bag at the same time, he effortlessly located her traitorous key and lifted her into his arms. The solid feel of him set sirens clamoring through her aching head, but she was too dizzy to push him away.

Once inside, he placed her on the first of the two double beds and handed back her purse. All she wanted to do was collapse onto the overly firm mattress and close her eyes. Somehow she managed to stay upright.

Eric stepped to the other bed and began packing the clothes spilling from her open suitcase, stacking them until he could zipper the case shut.

"Is there anything in the bathroom?" he asked.

When she didn't answer, he crossed his arms and stared. He was a stubborn, take-no-prisoners cop once more, content to wait all night if he had to.

"There are a few things on the vanity, nothing in the bathroom," she mumbled.

He stepped to the sink to pack her toiletries and meager supply of makeup.

She rallied the last speck of strength within her. "I'm not going home with you."

"You're fresh out of alternatives." The insensitive

words gave way to concern as his troubled gaze slid over her. He stuffed her cosmetic bag in with her clothes and crouched in front of her. "You could be in very real danger until we find out who was driving that van, and you can barely stand on your own two feet. You need help, and it looks like I'm all you've got."

"You're overreacting."

"And you're being naive."

"I…" Lord, how did she say this without saying too much? "Going home with you is a mistake."

"Mistake or not, you know I'm right. You'll have your privacy at the house. I'll keep my distance, if that's what you're worried about. Besides, Tony still lives with me. He'll be a built-in chaperone."

"But—"

"We need to take precautions, Carrinne. Alone, in an isolated motel room, you're a sitting duck."

And living in your house, I'm not?

"I can stay at my grandfather's," she argued.

Why wouldn't her ears stop ringing?

"None of the staff lives there anymore." He shook his head. "You're not staying alone. Not after today."

"But you're the sheriff." Knowing she'd already lost the argument was no reason to give up fighting. There had to be a way out of this. "You don't have time to babysit me all day."

"It's Saturday, and my chief deputy is in charge for the rest of the weekend." He smiled their daughter's smile, wry and confident. The similarity tugged at Carrinne's heart. "Besides, my job's a farce of paperwork and staff meetings. I think I can fit in protecting an irritating, self-destructive damsel in distress. No one's going to miss me."

His words echoed the teenage Eric she'd known almost two decades ago, the one who'd wanted nothing to do with his dad's small-town sense of community. As if realizing he'd revealed too much, Eric rose to his feet, plucked her suitcase from the other bed, and headed across the room.

"Let's go." He yanked the door open and waited as she pulled herself together and off the bed.

The thought of spending the night under his roof made everything inside her shake. But if some nut had set his sights on hurting her, he was a threat to her finding what she needed to protect Maggie's happiness. Add in the extreme effort it took just to keep her eyes open, and she found herself once again accepting the inevitable. She'd do things Eric's way.

For now.

"YOUR BURGER is cold. I can warm it up, or we could pull something else together in the kitchen." Eric shifted Carrinne's suitcase and unlocked his front door.

"The burger's fine the way it is." Carrinne stepped around him and into the Rivers' house, too tired to eat more than a few bites anyway. "I'll just take it up to my room."

She clutched the fast-food bags and stepped into the foyer, coming to a halt as the past washed over her in waves of unwanted longing. She'd fallen in love with this place the very first time Eric had invited her over for dinner. She'd known instantly this was a home in every way that mattered, regardless of how much Eric had wanted to get out of here.

It had been a noisy place, filled with mismatched furniture and the wall-to-wall knickknacks Eric had made throughout grade school, Scouts and junior high shop. And unlike her grandfather's monstrous estate, it had been filled with people who cared about each other. Eric and his dad had had their differences. They'd lost both wife and mother, leaving Sheriff Rivers a workaholic and Eric an angry kid who was terrified of being emotionally tied to anyone or anything again. But Gerald Rivers had loved his son with the same single-minded determination that had driven Eric to act out. And Carrinne had been beside herself with envy.

Eric had had a family to come home to each night, whether he wanted it or not. He'd known how very much he'd meant to his father. And even though he couldn't stand to be in the same room with the man half the time, his bond with his family had never been in doubt. He'd had a home; her grandfather's house and the rest of Oakwood had never been anything more to her than the place where she lived.

She wandered through the den and beyond, past comfortable pieces of furniture that announced that lives were still being lived there. Stepping around an enormous, surprisingly modern, sofa, she nearly tripped over what looked like a three- or four-day pile of newspapers. She stopped in the doorway to the kitchen, flipped on the overhead lights, and gasped.

Her gaze skipped from the homey blue-checked wallpaper to the enormous white stove where Mr. Rivers had dished up his one and only specialty—pancakes for dinner. The refrigerator, as ancient as the stove, sported the same rainbow of magnets that had always been there. There was still no dishwasher, and the same battered table dominated the center of the room.

"It's exactly the same," she said with wonder.

"No point changing things when you like them the way they are." Eric, who'd trailed her through the house, dropped her suitcase and purse just outside the kitchen door.

He took the Builda Burger bags from her and set them on the kitchen table before opening the fridge. He pulled out two bottles of Coke. Glass bottles, she noted with a double take, when she could have sworn they'd stopped packaging soda in anything but plastic and cans decades ago.

Her chuckle surprised them both. She dropped her head to study her sandals in hopes he'd let the moment pass.

"What's so funny?" He fished an opener from the drawer beside the stove and popped the caps, handing her a bottle.

"Nothing." She swallowed a frosty mouthful. "It just takes a little getting used to. You, reveling in hearth and home, happy with the way things have always been."

He downed half his soda in one gulp. His eyes narrowed, whether from the sting of the carbonation or an attempt to stare straight through her, she had no idea. Setting his drink aside, he strode past her and back out of the kitchen. "I'll take your bags up. You'll be in the first bedroom at the top of the stairs."

Kicking herself for getting caught up in nonsense that didn't matter anymore, she grabbed her burger and followed him up the paneled stairs. But she hadn't taken two steps before the gallery of photographs running at a diagonal up the stairwell walls stopped her. Picture after picture showed Tony from early childhood, snaggle-toothed and freckle-faced, growing up right before her eyes. Eric was there, too, hamming it up with his kid brother, stepping in where their dad should have been.

Her feet climbed upward. Her fingertips traced image after image. Pictures of ball games, Scout camping trips, birthday parties and trips to Disney World. A montage of Christmas snapshots: Tony getting his first bike, opening a policeman's costume complete with cap guns, hugging his first record player. Another captured years of Halloween costumes: Batman, Spiderman, a policeman, a fireman. Tony had worked his way through every boyhood hero.

Each precious moment of childhood had been magically recorded by the hand of someone totally entrenched in the life of a little boy growing up. Eric's hand. The realization shook her, when after the events of the last twenty-four hours she should have been shock-proof.

In her wildest imagination, the few times she'd allowed herself to look back and think of this world she'd left behind, Eric being a father to Tony had never entered her mind. For her sake, for the sake of her daughter, Carrinne hadn't let herself dwell on what was happening here without her.

The Eric who'd left her by the side of that dusty road had been running, determined to need no one but himself. And she'd always assumed he had run, riding off into every sunset they'd dreamed of together. That's how she'd found the strength not to look back. How she'd convinced herself that their daughter was better off thinking her father was dead.

She absorbed the reality in front of her, felt the enormity of what it represented drain every last ounce of the denial which had protected her for seventeen years. She cataloged each sacrifice Eric had made, every hour of hard work. Personal experience filled in the gaps. The colds and teacher conferences and teenage arguments that must have occurred along the way. Eric had been a hands-on, dedicated father. And from everything she'd seen, Tony had grown into a fine man.

"Something wrong?" Eric stood at the top of the stairs, her small suitcase and pocketbook held easily in one hand.

"I…" She struggled not to drop her Coke and the bag of fast food. Of course something was wrong. Her entire world turned inside out each time she looked at him, with each new detail she learned about his life.

"You've done an amazing job with Tony. You've been a wonderful father."

He set her bags on the landing and retraced the steps to her side. He glanced from her to a picture of what looked like Tony's high school graduation. In the photo, Eric held a diploma-bearing Tony in a hug that was more like a wrestling headlock.

"I did what anyone would have done," he mumbled as he ambled back up the steps. His hip and thigh brushed her side as he went, shooting warmth through her even as he stepped away. At the landing, he grabbed her things and continued to the right.

With one last glance at the photos, at Eric's eyes, shining with pride and affection for his brother, she followed.

Let this drop, Carrinne.

But she couldn't. There were too many missing pieces in what she thought she knew. Too many clues adding up to a truth she didn't want to see but loved her daughter too much to ignore.

"What anyone would do?" She entered the bedroom Eric had disappeared into and laid her food on a small table beside the door. "But you weren't anyone. The last thing you said to me was that you didn't care about anything. Not me. Not Tony. Not anyone. And you weren't going to throw your life away hanging around this backwater town pretending that you did. You wanted to drive away and never look back."

He dumped her bags on a quilt-covered four-poster bed. He kept his back to her, his hands on his hips, and studied the oval rug covering the center of the hard-wood floor. Several deep breaths stretched the seams of his shirt.

When he turned, a shrug shifted those rock-solid shoulders. "I told you at the hospital. I regret everything I said to you that night. I was crazy after losing my dad, and I hated the world for being beyond anyone's control, especially mine. My choices for the future were made the second my dad died, the day my mom left us for some easy lay who'd promised her better than she could ever get in a small town like Oakwood. I was trapped, and I resented the hell out of everyone because of it. What you heard was the last part of me wanting to get out of here. Even though I knew I couldn't."

"But you could have left, if you'd really wanted to." She stepped to the bed and sat on the edge of the feather mattress. "I always assumed you had."

"No." He gave his head a tight shake, his eyes frosting with the anger and pain of that night long ago. "Leaving would have made me no better than my mother. Tony had no one. He needed me. And when someone needs me, I stay."

"I... I never thought..."

When someone needs me, I stay.

All these years.

The sickness shaking her suddenly had very little to do with her concussion. What if she'd told Eric about Maggie that night? What if *she'd* stayed instead of running?

"I had no idea," she whispered.

"How could you have?" His stormy expression faded into a wisp of a smile. It was like watching the clouds part for the sun on a winter day. "You got out, and I'm glad you did. Leaving this place was the best decision you ever made."

The conviction in his voice as he spoke of leaving Oakwood underscored just how much he'd given up to stay. Pride for him filled Carrinne's eyes with tears.

He'd clipped his rebel's wings and accepted a life he'd never wanted—the same small life his father had lived, with the same responsibility and ties to the people he'd fought so hard to distance himself from. She thought of the pictures in the stairwell. Frame after frame of commitment that had nothing to do with the simple duty of caring for his brother. The man who hadn't wanted to need anybody had sacrificed everything, and somewhere along the way he'd learned how to love.

"Oh my God." She covered her face with her hands, a million might-have-beens she'd never let herself imagine now all too real. "I had no idea."

Eric dropped to one knee and drew her hands from her face. His worried gaze caressed her, open and honest and tempered with a bone-deep resolve that stole her breath. "Forget about it, Carrinne. You were right to hate me for how I treated you. To assume I'd blow out of town like the useless drifter I was so determined to become."

"I… I didn't hate you." She gripped his hands. She

couldn't think when he was this close, yet somehow she couldn't let go. "No matter how hard I tried, I couldn't hate you."

"Well, that's something at least." His eyes dropped to her mouth and lingered. She felt his breath stop. The room around them grew still, except for the sound of her heartbeat keeping time with his. He was too close. Everything was just too close.

With one last squeeze, one last glance, he was the one who moved away. He headed for the closet, opening the door and pulling the chain to turn on the light. All business again. All broad shoulders and detached efficiency.

"You've got a life waiting for you back in New York." He set her suitcase inside the closet. "The sooner we figure out who hit your car and find your father, the sooner you'll be able to get back there."

Back to her life. Back to the daughter she could no longer make herself believe Eric didn't deserve to know.

She had to tell him. God help her, she had to find some way to tell them both.

Her purse chirped from its place at the foot of the bed. She glanced at her watch and winced. It was no doubt Maggie, wondering why Carrinne hadn't called all day again. She grabbed her bag, then all she could do was stare at it. Eric's daughter was on the other end of the line.

"Expecting a call?" he asked

She dropped the bag. His gaze shifted from her frozen expression to the floor. She looked down, too. The bag's clasp had come loose on its own. The contents lay spread at her feet, her phone ringing like a bad dream that wouldn't let her wake.

Pick it up.

But, for the life of her, she couldn't move.

"Here you go." He laid the cell phone in her hand, unvoiced questions in his eyes. "Looks like you need some space. We can talk more in the morning."

Space? The other end of the world wouldn't be enough space. She had to find a way to tell him about their daughter and still protect Maggie. Soon. Before one too many close calls like this helped him figure it out for himself.

"I'll talk to you in the morning," she mumbled, the phone's ringing adding to the symphony of pain in her head.

His eyes flicked to the phone. He felt her forehead with the back of his hand.

"Get some sleep," he said, turning away.

The door shut behind him.

She rubbed the skin that tingled from his touch, then she answered the phone with a stab of her thumb.

"Maggie?" she whispered, not sure how far out of earshot Eric was.

"Mom. Are you okay?"

"I… I'm fine." She gritted her teeth, trying to slow her galloping heart so she could talk. "I just couldn't get to the phone."

"You sound horrible." Fear weighted her daughter's voice. "Has something happened? Are you okay?"

"I'm just a little tired, sweetie. That's all."

Tired and bruised and maybe being stalked by someone who's not thrilled that I'm back in town. Oh, and you're father's still alive.

That's all.

MAGGIE WILMINGTON didn't believe a word of her mom's fake assurances. She could tell her mother was exhausted. And *she* was tired of sitting in New York doing nothing. Tired of her mother treating her like she was just a kid.

"You need help, Mom. I hate the thought of you staying in that motel all alone, exhausting yourself, when I could be there helping you."

"Where you need to be right now is home focusing on school. Summer semester is the only second chance you're going to get. You only have a month to make up your incompletes," Maggie's mom added, as if anything as monotonous as summer school could be Maggie's number-one concern right now.

"This *is* an emergency," she replied. "Don't they make allowances for stuff like that? Can't I serve my sentence when you get back home?"

"It's not a sentence, Maggie. And don't start with the attitude." Tired or not, her mom still managed that voice that always boded ill for Maggie or whatever client was jerking her around at the moment. "You're the one who chose to cut so much class last year. The only way you're going to graduate on time is to make it up over the summer."

"I know I messed up, okay? Geez, do we have to go through this again?" Maggie paced back and forth across Kim's small guest room. Kim, their across-the-hall neighbor and one of her mom's few friends outside of work, was Maggie's warden for the foreseeable future. "It just sucks. As usual, you're trying to take care of everything yourself. Well, this time you can't. And I could help."

"No, you can't."

"Mom."

"No, Maggie. This is something you have to let me do myself. And that's final." Her mom's voice rang with desperation.

It scared Maggie to hear her sounding anything but confident. Nothing ever rattled the woman. Not when she'd worked three jobs to pay for day care and put herself through a bachelor's program and graduate school. Not when the first accounting firm she'd worked for had dissolved and she'd decided to start her own with nothing more than her reputation and a few contacts to her name. Not even when Maggie had messed up big-time last year and let a crowd she'd desperately wanted to be part of talk her into skipping classes at Stuyvesant every afternoon for over a month.

Cool and collected, her mom had handled it all. But

even though she insisted her liver condition was no-where near life-threatening at this stage, even though she said they had years to find a donor, something in her voice hadn't sounded right since she'd first talked about making this trip to Oakwood.

For the first time in Maggie's life, she was certain her mom was lying to her.

"Whatever's going on," Maggie said, "please, let me help you. You always said we could tell each other anything."

"Oh, Maggie." Her mom sounded closer to tears than Maggie had ever heard her. "This is hard for me, too. I'd rather be there with you, but I can't be. And the most important thing you can do for me is to make things right at school. You can't throw away all your hard work. Stuyvesant is one of the top high schools in the country. Graduating from there with your GPA will be your ticket into whatever college you choose."

"I don't care about that right now."

"Well, I do. You're not going to make the same mistake I did and ruin the opportunities you have to start your life in the right direction." Her mom's voice was at its I-know-what's-best hardest. "And I don't want to discuss this anymore."

Maggie yanked the cell phone from her ear, every muscle in her arm coiling to hurl it across the room. She almost hated her mom for not listening, and the emotion made Maggie sick. Her mother might be dying, and Maggie wanted to scream at her. Scream all the words she could use with her friends but not her mom. Scream until the frustration and the worry and the…fear went away.

"Maggie?" her mom said faintly. "Maggie, honey. Are you still there?"

"I'm here." She brought the phone back to her ear. "I'm sorry. I didn't meant to upset you."

"I know you didn't." Her mom's sigh made silent tears form in Maggie's eyes. Tears she was determined to keep to herself, even as they trickled down. "You're right. This sucks, and I'm sorry. I shouldn't be away from you right now."

"Just promise me you'll get some sleep tonight."

"I will. And you promise not to drive Kim crazy while I'm away."

"I won't."

"Good. Now let me go. I'll check back in with you tomorrow morning."

"Where have I heard that before?"

"I will this time. And you can reach me on the cell if you need anything before then."

"I know."

"Okay. I'll talk to you later. I love you, Maggie."

"I love you, too."

Maggie cut the line while she kept pacing.

Her mom was hiding something, probably because she thought she had to. Why did parents always think they had to protect their kids? She sat on the edge of the twin bed that took up half of Kim's tiny guest room.

With a sigh, she grabbed her backpack and rummaged for the one possession she took with her everywhere she went. Pulling out the laminated photo, she studied the faded image of the father she'd never met.

Eyes and hair the same dark color as her own, his face was so familiar. And not just because she stared at his picture every day. She saw so much of her dad every time she looked in the mirror. Her mom had commented on the resemblance more and more the last few years, in that sad way that told Maggie just how much she'd loved him. In the picture, the dark-haired man was leaning against a kick-ass motorcycle and refusing to smile into the camera.

Maggie had dreamed of him her whole life, inspired by her mom's stories of a rebel with a heart of gold. Her dad had made up his own mind and lived his life his own way, but he'd have done anything for her or her mom. He'd never have let her mother face something like this on her own. Well, Maggie wasn't going to either. No way in hell.

Something had her mom spooked. She'd give it one more day, and if things didn't start sounding better, then tomorrow afternoon she was headed for Oakwood.

CHAPTER SIX

AFTER LEAVING Carrinne and their painful foray into honesty behind, Eric had taken a quick shower and changed into a loose T-shirt and gym shorts.

Still wired, he listened to his stomach growl for the dinner he should have eaten hours ago. He headed downstairs, dreading the cold bag of burgers that was the only edible option in the house at the moment.

The sound of rustling in the kitchen quickened his steps. Tony was home. It was about time.

"Where the hell have you be—" Eric skidded to a halt, registering too late the graying head of his neighbor bent over the open door of the refrigerator. "Mrs. Davis? Is there something I can do for you?"

"Just as I expected. Nothing for that poor girl to eat but beer and cocktail olives."

He inhaled. Held it. Exhaled. All the time counting to ten. The stove clock read nine-fifteen. Didn't most self-respecting women over the age of sixty spend their Saturday evenings watching reruns of *Lawrence Welk* or *Murder, She Wrote*?

"This really isn't a good time, Mrs. Davis. Perhaps you could come back in the morning."

"And let you feed Miss Wilmington toast and olives for breakfast? What kind of neighbor would I be then?"

Neighbor. A loaded distinction in a place like Oakwood. Eric's blood began a slow boil.

This town was too small. He'd been living here too long. He'd never been given a choice. The litany of useless complaints was as familiar as the wallpaper Carrinne had so admired when she'd seen this room again for the first time.

There was no point wondering how Mrs. Davis knew Carrinne was here. He'd pushed Carrinne's wheelchair when she'd left Emergency. He'd checked her out of that motel himself. Given Mrs. Davis's family connections, church connections, garden club connections… It didn't take anywhere near six degrees of separation for her to put two and two together and determine this was an ideal situation, ripe for some juicy meddling. Why hadn't he asked her to return that key his dad had given her years ago?

Mrs. Davis and his dad had become single parents within a year of each other, Mrs. Davis when her husband died of a sudden heart attack. They had banded together and leaned on each other up until the day his dad had died. Since then, Eric hadn't had it in him to refuse her good-hearted, if overexuberant, offers of help. Though he did from time to time consider removing the wind-up noisemaker she passed off as a poodle from the face of the earth.

He willed patience into his voice. "I was planning to run to the grocery first thing in the morning, Mrs. Davis."

"That's not necessary." She plucked a plastic container from the refrigerator's top shelf, carrying it to the sink using only her fingertips. She pried the lid loose and peered at the science experiment he expected covered the three-week-old leftovers inside. "I just stocked up at the Piggly Wiggly. Be a dear and go grab the shopping bags I left on my kitchen counter while I wash up a few of these…" she dropped the container and turned on the hot water "…things. And grab the fresh carton of milk from the refrigerator."

"Really, I appreciate your help. But—"

"Eric Rivers." She rounded on him, wrinkled hands on ample, apron-covered hips. "I've known Carrinne Wilmington since she was in diapers and that recluse of a millionaire grandfather of hers let her wander off during the Founders' Day parade. The whole town is buzzing about her being back, looking for her father. And that awful accident she was in. Heavens! That poor child's been through enough today without you and your brother starving her half to death. Has she even had dinner?"

"Yes, ma'am. We picked up a few things on the way home."

"Fast food?" At his nod, she shook her head and resumed rummaging through the refrigerator. "Just as I thought. Now be a dear and go fetch those groceries for me."

"Yes, ma'am." He headed for the back door. Trying to change Mrs. Davis's mind would only keep her there longer.

"And mind you don't let Cuddles out. He's exhausted, the little dear. Wore himself out this morning, barking at something or other. Never can figure out what gets him going like that."

"No, ma'am." Maybe the toy-sized demon would be sleeping it off inside tonight, instead of serenading Eric's bedroom window.

Two steps beyond the illuminated circle of the porch light, Eric stopped and squinted into the glare of Tony's headlights. His brother parked his Chevy 4X4 in the driveway that separated their house from the Davis place.

"Where have you been?" Eric snapped.

"You said you were bringing Carrinne home. I stopped at the grocery for a few things." Tony stepped from the pickup and pulled two sacks from the cab. "The cupboards always look like we've been hit by a swarm of locusts, and it's your week to clean out the fridge. We both know what that means."

"Yeah, and it's your week to clean the bathrooms. Wanna flip for which scares Carrinne first, the kitchen or the shower?" Eric trudged to Mrs. Davis's door, images of Carrinne in his shower nipping at his heels. The fit of his jeans grew uncomfortably tight a split second before he forced the images away.

Hell.

Her staying here had seemed a logical choice, right

up until he'd watched her fall back in love with his home. Right up until she'd told him what a wonderful father he'd been to his brother. The look on her face as she'd gazed at their wall of memories was a sight he'd never forget. How was he supposed to keep things on a professional level now, when all he could think about was what the last seventeen years would have been like if she'd remained a part of his life?

Like that would have happened.

"Hey." Tony stepped into their neighbor's kitchen behind him. "Where you going?"

"Mrs. Davis went shopping, too. Probably as soon as Freddy at the Econo Motel alerted the entire county that I'd driven away with Carrinne and all her belongings."

"Is Mrs. Davis over at our place scouring the refrigerator?" A grin spread across Tony's face.

"You don't have to be so damn tickled about all this. The woman could teach a SWAT team a few things about infiltrating enemy territory." Eric added the bags from the counter to the ones his brother already held, just as Cuddles emerged from the laundry room. Growling, the white miniature poodle locked onto his pants cuff and dragged behind as Eric headed for the refrigerator. "Did you pick up milk?"

"No." Tony's chuckle at least sounded as if he'd tried to stifle it. "Knew I forgot something."

"Never mind." Eric pulled the half-gallon container from the door. Shaking off the yapping house slipper still snacking on his ankles, he grabbed a bag from his brother and walked back out the door. "Let's get this over with."

Slowing before he reached their house, Eric turned to Tony.

"Carrinne's still lying to me." That cell phone call had scared her to death. "There's something she's doesn't want me to know. If she's in some kind of trouble, if someone's threatening her, why wouldn't she tell me?"

Tony juggled his bags, every trace of humor gone from his face. "I'd bet a month's salary that van ran her down on purpose. We don't have enough even to know where to start looking for the guy, but my gut's telling me Carrinne's got a stalker. Has she given you any idea who this asshole might be?"

"No. She was more concerned with convincing me to leave her in a roadside stop-and-sleep hours after someone tried to kill her."

"So much for staying out of the lady's way because that's the way she wants it."

"I'm not sure she knows what she wants right now. And even if she did, there's a limit to how much I can sit back and watch. She's vulnerable, no matter how much she hates to admit it."

Tony raised an eyebrow. "She didn't take kindly to your generous offer to have her stay with us."

"If she'd had the strength, I'm sure she'd have told me to go to hell." She was too weak to get away from him, but she was still fighting him every step of the way.

Which made him admire her more.

She had rocked his world from the first moment he'd seen her last night. He had vowed to steer clear of commitment. He couldn't make commitment work, he reminded himself. He'd tried and failed in the most painful way, watching joy fade from Carrinne's eyes with every word he'd shouted at her.

With every other woman since, he'd kept things casual and light, enjoying and cherishing until deeper feelings began to threaten. With every other woman, he'd had no trouble walking away.

But one day back with Carrinne, and every feeling he thought he'd banished a lifetime ago had come roaring back.

It doesn't matter, Rivers. You have a job to do. Help her find her liver donor, keep her safe and get her out of Oakwood while you can still stand to let her go.

"We need to figure this out fast," he said to Tony. "Start a full background check on her in the morning. Find out if there's anyone in her life who would benefit from something happening to her."

"Anything else?" His brother's expression said he knew he was only getting about half the story. Less than a year on the force, and the kid was already scary-good at reading people. Just like their old man.

"Not yet." Eric owed it to Carrinne to protect her secrets for as long as he could. "Just look into her life in New York for me. Let's take this one step at a time."

"You got it." Tony walked ahead and up their porch

steps. "Because from what I saw of what was left of her car, there's one mean son of a bitch after her."

THE NEXT MORNING, Carrinne slipped from between age-worn cotton sheets, regretting the loss of her heavenly cocoon. Her head still ached, though a timpani band no longer beat its rumba behind her eyes. And thanks to Dr. Burns's antibiotics, her fever had broken during the night.

She pulled the bandage from her temple, wincing as the tape caught her eyebrow. It wasn't quite 6:00 a.m. But someone's dog had been barking for over half an hour.

Abandoning all hope of dozing off again, she padded as silently as possible across the rug-covered floor. She wrapped her arms around herself, shivering in the summer morning dampness. It was mid-July in Georgia, and she was chilled to the bone. Before she'd gotten sick, her internal thermostat had been stuck on subtropical.

She rummaged inside her suitcase for the winter-weight clothes she'd packed at the bottom. Searching for her trusty black sweater and leggings, a flash of fire-engine red caught her eye. Digging deeper, she uncovered a rainbow of familiar items, none of which were hers.

Maggie was forever on Carrinne's case, needling her to spice up her disgustingly New York professional wardrobe of complementary black separates. It looked as though her daughter had taken matters into her own hands, replacing much of what Carrinne had packed with more colorful pieces from her own closet.

Carrinne pulled a cropped red sweatshirt from the pile and smiled. She slipped out of her gown and pulled on a bra and the cotton top. Her daughter's spirit wrapped itself around her.

I love you, Maggie. Everything's going to be okay. I promise.

She didn't know how yet, but everything had to be okay.

She'd tossed and turned most of the night, worried that Maggie was worried so much. Searching for some way to let Eric know about the daughter he never should have been denied. Some way for all of this not to rip Maggie's life to pieces even more.

No answers had come.

It didn't help that Eric had knocked on the door at two-hour intervals, checking on her concussion. She'd answered from the bed, saying she was all right, no longer trusting herself to look him in the eye. And then she'd tossed and turned some more.

She needed to get back to her grandfather's house. Dr. Burns's warning to slow down barely made a dent as she threw on the rest of her clothes and her shoes. It didn't take much energy to look through a musty old attic. And if she slipped away before anyone else woke, she'd earn herself a few Eric-free hours in the bargain.

Dressed and stalked by troubling memories of how it had once felt to have Eric's strength wrapped around her, she marched to the table beside the bed and plucked her cell phone and electronic palm pro from her purse. Dialing 411, she spoke with the operator, asking for and recording Brimsley's home number.

Time to put her grandfather's commitment to help her to the test.

She placed the call.

"What…hello?" Brimsley grumbled into the phone. "Who is this? Do you have any idea what time it is?"

"It's Carrinne. I need Oliver's car. Would you have someone pick me up in a half hour?"

"I work for Oliver Wilmington, not you," the lawyer hissed, all traces of sleep gone. "If you think I'm going to—"

"You're going to make sure I have whatever I need while I'm here." Check off one of the daily goals on her Oakwood to-do list. She'd irritated Brimsley, and it wasn't even time for breakfast yet. "Or haven't you talked with Oliver since I met with him?"

"I've talked with him." Rustling heralded the lawyer kicking his way out of bed. "It's the crack of dawn, Carrinne. Didn't you almost die yesterday or something?"

"I'm fine, thanks for your concern." She ignored the callousness of his remark. The man was nothing to her. "When can you have someone here?"

A sigh was his response, then a grunt. Another sigh. "You want Calvin to pick you up at your motel?"

Now that was one question she should have seen coming. "No…I'm not… Actually, I checked out of the motel last night."

"And?" Silence filled the line as he waited for Carrinne to continue. "It's too early in the morning for guessing games. Tell me where you are, or let me get back to sleep."

"I'm staying at the Rivers' place for a few days. Ask Calvin to pick me up at the end of the drive."

"Well, now. You're with Sheriff Rivers. Why doesn't that surprise me?"

"I'm not *with* anyone. The doctor wouldn't release me unless I had someone to help me for the next few days. So I agreed to stay here temporarily. Not that any of this concerns you. I'll be out front in half an hour."

ERIC STUMBLED into the kitchen, feeding and starting the coffeemaker out of instinct, because he could barely keep his eyes open long enough to see what he was doing.

He'd set the alarm to rouse him every two hours throughout the night, so he could check on Carrinne. Not that he'd managed to sleep much in between. Instead, he'd lain there, two rooms down from her, staring at the ceiling, listening into the night in case she needed anything, working through the gaping holes in what he knew about her accident and her reasons for being home.

Somewhere around dawn, Cuddles's ritual greeting of the new day had pulled him from his latest doze, and he'd headed to the kitchen for his first hit of caffeine. Maybe eating one of Mrs. Davis's English muffins would curb his appetite for poodle-hunting. Maybe if he got enough coffee into his system, he'd think of a way to get Carrinne to trust him so she'd stop doling out the truth one scrap at a time.

He heard the warped step creak on the stairs. Catching himself, he managed not to turn around. He didn't have to look to know it was Carrinne. No way would Tony be up at this ungodly hour on a Sunday. And neither should Carrinne. She hadn't slept much more than he had, and she'd tangoed with a van and a pickup truck yesterday afternoon.

When she didn't join him in the kitchen, he turned toward the stairs. No one was there. The faint scrape of a dead bolt drew him into the den. Sure enough, Carrinne was halfway out the front door. He folded his arms and leaned against the bookshelves he and Tony had made for one of his brother's last Boy Scout projects.

"Give me a minute to dress, and I'll be right with you," he said.

She jumped and spun around. "Eric. I didn't know you were up."

"Cuddles is an equal-opportunity pest."

"Cuddles?"

"The barking machine that lives below our bedroom windows."

"Oh."

That seemed to Eric like a pretty good place to kill the polite chit-chat.

"The doctor wanted you in bed for the next few days, Carrinne. You look like hell." Hell on wheels, he added to himself. The red sweatshirt she'd opted for this morning was simple, almost collegiate looking, and it didn't quite meet the waistband of her black sweatpants. His fingers itched to drag it over her head and discover if she was wearing black underneath, too.

"I feel like hell, but that doesn't change a thing." She shut the door and dropped her backpack onto a nearby table. "I've arranged for a ride to my grandfather's. I need to find a trunk of my mother's things."

"I'm your ride." Stepping away from the bookshelves, he advanced slowly.

"There's no point in ruining your entire Sunday. I'll be fine on my own for a few hours."

"Are you forgetting someone knocked you into oncoming traffic yesterday?"

"No, I haven't forgotten."

"Then we're agreed. I'm your ride wherever you want to go." He felt her forehead. "Fever's gone."

She flinched away.

Annoyed with them both, he took her arm and led her away from the door. "Come have some coffee while I get washed up."

She dug in her heels. "I already have someone coming. You can meet me at Oliver's later—"

"You're not leaving this house without me." Beneath his hands, soft cotton covered delicate, toned flesh.

Carrinne's flesh.

Damn it, he had to stop touching her.

"I don't know what this is all about, darlin'. But you're not going to shake me. Save yourself the effort."

She pressed her lips together and stepped beyond his reach. "You said there was coffee?"

He followed as she headed for the kitchen and settled into one of the worn chairs.

"Did you call Gordon?" he reached for the phone. Gordon Willis was the only taxi in town. "I'll let him know you don't need him."

"No, I called Brimsley."

"Brimsley?" She'd called a man she despised for help rather than asking him.

Eric turned without further comment and filled two mugs with coffee. He was pretty good at reading handwriting on the wall, and it was too early in the morning to play cat and mouse.

"Still take it black?" he asked.

Their eyes locked as he handed her the mug. He'd taught her to drink coffee, and she'd insisted on liking it the way he did, strong and black as midnight.

"I'll take some milk, please." She reached for the sugar dish. After spooning in the sweetener, she added the milk he'd retrieved from the refrigerator.

"Want something to eat? An English muffin?"

That earned him a disbelieving look. "You and Tony have English muffins for breakfast?"

"No, but my meddlesome neighbor graciously

shopped for you yesterday afternoon, as soon as she heard you'd be staying with us."

Carrinne rolled her eyes, then squeezed them shut as a green cast tinted her cheeks. She cleared her throat. "Mrs. Davis, wasn't that your neighbor's name?"

"One and the same."

"Mrs. Davis brought me English muffins because…?"

"Tony and I are cavemen bachelors who would let you starve without her expert intervention."

"Of course." Carrinne saluted him with her coffee. "How can I refuse such a ladylike slam to your commitment to protect and serve. English muffins it is."

He popped them into the toaster oven, playing along. She might be stalling, but at least she was eating. When he returned to the table with a toasted pastry for each of them, she took a tentative bite. She swallowed. With a sigh, she settled deeper into the chair to nibble a little more.

Home.

The first word that jumped into Eric's mind as he watched from across the table was *home*. She looked like she belonged here. It *felt* like she belonged here.

Well, get over it, Rivers. This is the last place either one of you wants her to be. She's out of this tiny town just as soon as she gets what she came for, and watching her leave is going to be hard enough without getting any more attached than you already are.

He rubbed his hand across the Sunday-morning stubble covering his chin and let her finish her breakfast. When she started stirring her coffee again, he made his move.

"Wanna tell me why you're all of a sudden asking Brimsley for help? And why he's so willing to be of service?"

Her spoon stilled. She tapped it on the brim of her mug and set it on the table. "Simple. Oliver agreed to make sure I have whatever I need while I'm home."

"Oliver did."

"Yes. At the hospital yesterday. Before the accident."

"Why would he be so cooperative all of a sudden? We both know he never does anything unless he gets something in return."

"He wants to help me find my mother's diary."

"Sure he does. He's never lifted a finger to help you learn anything about your mother."

Her chin rose in a mutinous slant that made him itch to know just what a tough New York woman tasted like. All that sweetness he remembered, flavored with a tinge of spice. His mouth watered. His next bite of muffin tasted like sawdust.

He swallowed and refocused on the business at hand. "Two days ago, you were so sure he wouldn't help, you broke into his house rather than waste your time asking first."

Her eyes narrowed. "Maybe learning about my terminal condition changed things."

The air in the room, the air in Eric's lungs, was suddenly too thick to breathe. It made him sick, what she was facing completely on her own.

The doorbell chimed.

Carrinne pushed back from the table and headed for the den, hating herself because she was running from Eric again. But being a coward was better than sitting across from the man one more aching second.

"I'll let Calvin know I don't need a ride after all," she said over her shoulder.

Within two strides, Eric had reached her. "I don't want you answering the door. Too many people already know you're here."

"It's just Calvin." She tried to move away, only to stop as he stepped in front of her.

"You're not answering the door." The determination in his voice had nothing on the conviction hardening his dark-brown eyes. "Independence may have made you a success in New York, but at the rate you're going, you'll be lucky if it doesn't get you killed here."

He checked the peephole first, then ushered in her grandfather's elderly driver.

"Thanks for coming, Calvin," he said. "But I'll bring her over myself later this morning."

Calvin's weathered brown face broke into a smile when he saw Carrinne. "Ms. Wilmington, aren't you a sight for sore eyes."

Carrinne stepped into his embrace, returning his hug with gusto. "Calvin, how have you been? How's your family?"

"Well, Nina," he said, speaking of his wife, "she's the same as ever. Still your grandfather's housekeeper and cook. She's just dying to get a look at you. Said she's all set to cook you all your favorites. Just tell her when."

Carrinne made a mental note to find her appetite somewhere between here and Governor's Square. Nina's calling in life was to feed everyone in sight until the seams popped in their clothing. "And your kids?"

"Michael graduated from UGA last fall. Went on to law school at Emory. Trish is a junior this year. Dean's list every semester. She wants to be a doctor."

"That's wonderful." Neither Calvin nor his wife had finished high school, but they'd raised a doctor and a lawyer.

Her grandfather might be a tyrant, but he took care of his own. As long as she'd known the man, he'd been better at throwing his money around than loving people. He spared no expense providing for those for whom he felt responsible. And in some old-fashioned, Southern way, that included making sure the families within the circle of his employ were well cared for financially.

He was a world-class benefactor, as long as he didn't have to get emotionally involved in the lives of those he was helping.

Her cell phone rang in her purse.

"Excuse me a minute." She grabbed her bag and walked to the other end of the room. Something must be wrong for Maggie to be calling this early in the morning. Only it wasn't a New York number on the display.

"I'll get goin'," she heard Calvin say behind her. "We'll see you two later at the house."

"Hello," she said into the phone. She waved a quick goodbye as Eric shut the door behind the elderly man.

"Get out of town, bitch," a distorted masculine voice rasped back. "Get out of Oakwood, or you'll wish you had."

"What?"

"Get out now, or next time I'll do more than wreck your car." The line went dead with an ominous click.

She stared at the phone, tried to find her voice.

"Carrinne?" Eric materialized beside her.

"Oh, God." Her hands were shaking.

"Carrinne? Damn it. Who was it? What's going on?"

Tony shuffled into the den, wearing hole-riddled jeans and an ancient T-shirt that read I Do It On My Harley.

He stumbled to a stop, glancing between Eric and Carrinne with eyes that were only half-open. "Everyone sleep all right last night?"

CHAPTER SEVEN

"OH MY GOD." Carrinne dropped the phone to the couch and bolted into the kitchen, needing to move. The caller's voice, his threats, wouldn't stop echoing through her head.

"Who was it, Carrinne?" Eric dogged her every step. "Damn it, who keeps calling and upsetting you?"

"I don't know… He said—"

"Is someone threatening her?" Tony was right behind them, his concerned expression only a shade less furious than his brother's.

"Does this have anything to do with that call last night?" Eric pressed. "The one you didn't want to answer when I was in the room."

"What? No. I mean, yes, I just got a threatening phone call. But, no. This has nothing to do with last night."

Eric turned to Tony. "Put a trace on her cell records. Incoming and outgoing."

"Don't you dare. My phone calls are my business." She couldn't feel her legs. Standing was suddenly not a good idea.

She dropped into one of the kitchen chairs and leaned her head into her hand, shielding her eyes from the morning sunlight now streaming through the window.

Eric cursed and crossed to the counter. A few seconds later, he placed a fresh cup of coffee in front of her. "Take it easy, darlin'. Take your time and tell us what's going on."

"There've been other calls?" Tony took a seat across the table.

"No." Carrinne cradled the cup, willing its warmth to seep into her numb fingers. "He…he's never called before."

"You're sure it was a *he?*" Tony probed.

"He…it was so distorted, but it was a man. He said to get out of town before he did worse than wreck my car." She shuddered.

"I guess we can stop wondering if the accident was really an accident." Tony rubbed his hand across his neck.

"Who knows your cell-phone number?" Eric asked.

"No one. No one in Oakwood."

"And that call last night?" Eric pressed, his voice tight.

"It was a business associate. I had a client emergency in New York." Maggie's phone was registered under Carrinne's name. It was plausible that Carrinne would provide company phones to her staff—at least that would be her story if Eric checked.

"Well whoever it was, the call scared the shit out of you." He crouched on one knee, crowding her. "Just like that call a few minutes ago. You expect me to believe the two aren't related? What kind of business emergency was it?"

"My business, Eric. Not yours."

He stood and dropped into the chair beside her. "Whatever you're not telling me, it's only making things worse. This guy's not messing around. You've got to give us something to go on."

"I…I wish I could tell you more. I really do." She clenched her teeth to stop their chattering. A light-headed rush flooded through her. As if on cue, Eric's face faded to white. Hot and cold waves shook her, even as she fought to keep them at bay. She swayed forward. "I—"

"Carrinne!" He caught her. "Tony, call the hospital. I'm taking her back in."

He smelled delicious, she thought vaguely as he stood with her in his arms. Like laundry detergent and English muffins. Then his words registered.

"No. No hospital." She pushed her head off his shoulder. He'd carried her back into the den. "Just let me rest for a few minutes. It'll pass. It never lasts for long. Eric, please. I need to get to my grandfather's."

"Carrinne." His mouth was just inches away, and his eyes, his arms, belonged to the boy in her dreams. Eyes filled with longing and strength, caring and a protective desire. "I'm not going to let you get sicker—"

"I'm fine," she said. "I just get light-headed sometimes first thing in the morning. Trust me."

For a second she was sure he was going to kiss her. For a second she was sure she'd let him. Then he settled her onto the couch and gave her the distance she so desperately needed.

"Tony," he called into the kitchen. "Hold off on the hospital."

Tony popped his head into the den, portable phone in hand. "She's okay?"

"For now." Eric never took his eyes off Carrinne. "We'll see."

Tony plucked Carrinne's phone from the couch. He pressed a few buttons, then lifted the phone to his ear. He gave her an apologetic glance. After several seconds, he pushed a few more buttons while he studied the display.

"We've got the number of the caller," he said. "But no one's answering my call-back. We should be able to trace it. It's definitely a local number."

"Light a fire under the search for the van that hit Carrinne, too," Eric added as Tony headed out of the room. "And while you're at it, get in touch with Gus Crain."

Tony turned back. "Gus retired last year."

"He's still the best detective in three counties, and he was dad's best man. He did about ten years as a department detective before going private, so he knows his way around our investigative procedures. Besides, we need answers as fast as we can get them, and he's probably the only one we have a prayer of snagging on the weekend."

"It may take him a while to get here. Didn't he move back to his family place in Pineview?"

"Just see if you can track him down."

Nodding, Tony disappeared into the kitchen.

"I was going to hire a detective to help me look for my father," Carrinne said.

"This isn't just about your father anymore. The people in my department are good, but I don't want to wait any longer than I have to for answers. Gus is an old family friend." Eric's eyes traced her features. An electric moment later, he sat beside her on the couch. "Can you tell me anything that will save us time?"

"About?"

"About that call last night, for one thing."

Shivering, she struggled for the right words. "I can't. Not yet. It's… My life is complicated."

"Complicated? Carrinne, you're a grown woman. Your life is your business. But someone or something scared you when that phone rang last night. It might have some bearing on your case, something you're not aware of. I have to know what you know, before this maniac makes good on his threats and really hurts you."

"Last night's call was personal," she whispered. "This guy, whoever he is, he's after me because of something here. He doesn't want me to stay in Oakwood. He—"

"He wants you out of town badly enough to keep coming after you, even though everyone knows by now that you're under my protection. Someone that determined will find a way sooner or later to get what he wants."

Get out now, or next time I'll do more than wreck your car.

Panic and the ever-present weakness leaching her

strength spun the room in circles around Carrinne. She covered her ears and squeezed her eyes shut, blocking out the sound of the caller's voice.

"Easy, darlin'." Eric pulled her against his chest. "I'm not going to let him anywhere near you."

Carrinne let herself lean into the hero from her dreams. Letting herself need Eric's help was a mistake. But God help her, she needed him.

"Help me find my mother's trunk and her diary," she said. "Help me find my father. Finding him means everything to me."

"So you're agreeing to trust me, just a little?" He smoothed his hand up and down her back, his all-too-familiar touch undoing her in a million different ways. "Does this mean we have a truce, that we can be friends now?"

"Friends," she forced herself to repeat as she nodded against his chest.

There was so much more coursing between them than friendship. Too much more. And the half frown on his face when she glanced up told her he'd felt it, too.

ERIC WATCHED Carrinne from across Oliver Wilmington's blazing hot attic. Her cropped sweatshirt might have looked ridiculous on another woman her age. But Carrinne wore the middle-baring top with the same confidence she faced everything else in her life, and she looked amazing. He almost wished she'd worn black again. In the dimness of the attic, the top's bright color drew his attention every time she moved. Or maybe it was Carrinne's calm determination that kept him mesmerized. He could stand there and watch her for hours.

Friends, he'd said. He shrugged aside the urge to laugh. Holding Carrinne on his couch had ended all chance of him ignoring his body's growing hunger for her. Each second they were in the same room together, the need to feel her body against his burned higher and higher.

He wiped at the sweat running down his face and resumed looking through a box of dust-covered children's books. Damn it. Where was Gus? Right about now, Eric would take whatever distraction he could get.

Tony had left a message on the detective's cell, and Gus had called back almost immediately. As luck would have it, he was in Oakwood for the weekend on other business, and he'd promised to stop by the Wilmington place on his way to the station.

Carrinne grew unnaturally still. Eric was beside her in two strides.

"Are you okay?" he asked.

"This is it. I found my mother's trunk." She was shivering, even though there was no way she could be chilled in the attic's stifling heat. "It was buried under all these old drapes. That's why I missed it when I was up here Friday night."

He shoved the pile of crimson velvet aside. Angelica Wilmington's name was stenciled across the top of the enormous trunk. Getting a quick nod from Carrinne, he released the catch and opened the lid. The smell of cedar and yesterday wafted up to them. Jumbled inside was a childhood full of memories. Stuffed animals and dolls, scrapbooks and an endless parade of the kind of treasures that only meant something to the person saving them.

"Oliver caught me going through my mother's closet when I was a child." Carrinne sank to her knees, her hand reaching inside with reverence. "I told him that I wanted to know everything I could about her. I demanded he tell me who my father was, that he help me find my mother's last diary in case she'd left some clue. But Oliver just scolded me for digging up old ghosts, and he had my mother's things packed up here. We never discussed her or my father again."

She pulled out an album, brittle with age, and gingerly flipped through its black, memory-filled pages. "She was so beautiful. Here's a picture of her with her favorite horse."

Eric looked over her shoulder at the images bringing Carrinne equal parts pain and joy.

"I think his name was Holiday," she continued in a far-away voice. "Because Oliver bought him for a Christmas present. He sold the horse after my mother died."

She grew silent as she leafed through the book.

"Any pictures of boyfriends?"

"No, but here's one of her senior prom. The inscription says she's with her friends Cindy and Theresa."

Carrinne reached the end and handed it to him. She almost succeeded in hiding her disappointment.

"We'll keep looking." He laid a reassuring hand on her shoulder as she dove back into the trunk.

She picked up a bedraggled stuffed dog. "Finding anything in all this stuff is a long shot, isn't it?"

"A long shot's better than no shot at all."

"Right." She cleared her throat and handed him the dog. Her face set, she pushed aside dolls and toys to dig to the bottom. "What we need is a sure thing."

He carefully stacked each item she handed him. "I thought you said you'd already been through all your mom's things."

"But this stuff is mostly from my mother's closet, and I never really got a chance to look through it. My nanny insisted there was another diary. She saw my mother writing in it just before I was born." The longer Carrinne looked, the less careful she became. She was pulling items from the trunk quicker than he could set them aside. "It has to be in here somewhere. It just has to."

Her desperation was painful to watch. It was as if she were digging for secrets in her mother's grave, rather than in a trunk full of musty old memories. Her breath became choppy. Her hands shook. She lifted an oversized porcelain doll from the trunk, and its hair caught on the latch. The delicate figure, clothed in satin the color of Carrinne's forest-green eyes, tumbled headfirst to the attic's wood floor. With a sickening thump, its angelic face broke into three large pieces.

"Oh, no." She scooped up the doll and the broken china, her voice breaking as she stood. "This was my mother's favorite."

"Maybe we can glue it back together." He tried to lift it from her hand. She jerked away, scratching her palm on a jagged porcelain edge.

"Ah!"

"Let me see, darlin'." He wiped at the trace of blood. Then he brought her palm to his mouth and feathered a kiss across the scrape, not realizing what he was doing until it was too late. Shock vibrated through him at the feel of her skin beneath his lips.

Carrinne froze.

He froze.

Her hand trembled under his lips, her breath catching on a feminine gasp that aroused him to the point of pain. Desire hammered through his resolve to keep his hands to himself. Threading his fingers through her hair, he clenched handfuls of golden curls. He drew her lips to his, capturing another of those lost sounds, letting his kiss communicate everything he'd never be able to say in words.

He needed her. He'd always needed her. Nothing in his life was real without her.

Carrinne had never in her life felt more lost.

She forgot to remember her reasons for keeping Eric at a distance. Forgot she shouldn't be reaching for him, molding the strength of his chest and shoulders with needy hands. She shouldn't be clinging to his lips, capturing his breath with her own. It was dangerous to want any of this. The taste of him, the feel of his mouth opening above hers, his tongue taking hers in a dance that had her quivering deep inside.

Losing herself in the feel of him, she fought for the discipline that had kept men from getting too close for years. But the secret place she'd locked away from others had always been Eric's for the taking. In other men's arms, she was in control. With Eric, she was lost in an instant. Only, the day was fast approaching when she'd have to tell him about Maggie. And this time when he turned away from her, it would be for good.

That inevitable reality gave her the strength she needed to pull back. The hands that had been urging him closer began to push. The moans of desire she hadn't been able to stem became protests.

"Eric…" She turned her face away, panting as his lips traveled across her cheek. "Please…don't do this anymore. Stop."

His teeth grazed her ear a moment before she felt him grow still. A curse hissed through his ragged breathing, and his hands captured hers, squeezing them tightly. He bowed his forehead to hers, the effort it was taking him to pull away almost as erotic as his kisses.

"I'm sorry." He nudged her forehead one last time, then inched away. "I'm so sorry, darlin'. I know I said I would keep my distance, but—"

"Hello," a booming voice called from the stairs leading to the attic. "Eric? You up there, son?"

"In here, Gus." Eric released her with a grimace, his thumb tracing her lower lip. "We'll finish this later," he murmured to her.

Sparks flew from the promise of his touch. Carrinne inhaled against a need so sharp, it took everything in her not to reach for him again.

A fifty-something man stomped up the last of the attic stairs. He wore a navy-blue knit shirt and jeans. His John Deere cap covered a full head of salt-and-pepper hair.

"Eric." The burly man gave Eric's hand a strong shake. "How the hell have you been?"

"Fine." Eric slapped the man's shoulder. "Just fine. How's retirement?"

"Don't know yet, haven't had much time for it." Gus tucked his hands in his back pockets. "Been doing some freelance work over at the Walker County Sheriff's Department. Seems they can always use a good detective."

"Well, that's exactly why I had Tony call you," Eric said. "We could use a little of that help ourselves."

Gus gave Carrinne a smile as he studied her from head to toe. He turned back to Eric. "Well you're in luck. I was in town this weekend doing some prep work for a potential client. You gonna introduce me to your lady friend?"

"Carrinne Wilmington." Carrinne reached to shake his hand, taking the initiative if for no other reason than to dispel the *lady friend* notion. "Sheriff Rivers said you might be able to help me. I appreciate you taking the time to stop by."

Gus's grasp was firm. "My pleasure. Always did wonder what this old place was like on the inside."

He glanced at her mother's trunk. "So what can I do for you people?"

"Someone's stalking Carrinne," Eric answered before she could. "He totaled her car yesterday while she was in it, and he made a threatening phone call this morning. The department's looking into it, but I'd feel better with you on board. Dad always said you could squeeze clues out of a bowl of nothing."

Gus chuckled, then sobered as he studied the scant distance between Carrinne and Eric. "Well, why don't we start with why you're back in town, Ms. Wilmington. Rumor has it, you're searching for someone."

"Yes, my father." She took a step away from Eric, trying to do it casually.

"Mind telling me why, after all this time? Seems to me I remember you leaving Oakwood back when you were a teenager. Heard you've been in New York all this time."

"Yes, I moved to New York. But it's critical that I locate my father now." She blinked at the steadying touch of Eric's hand on her arm.

"I heard around town that you were visiting your grandfather yesterday when the accident happened. How does he figure into all of this?"

"He's agreed to help me in my search. That's why we're here, looking through my mother's things for any information we can find."

"Looking for anything in particular?"

"A diary." Her shoulders slumped. "My mother never told anyone who my father was, but she may have kept a diary the last year of her life. It's about all we have to go on for now."

"So." Gus stepped past Carrinne and Eric, glancing again at the trunk and the memories spread around them on the floor. "You're trying to piece together your past. And at the same time, some nut wants you out of Oakwood yesterday. Any chance the two are connected?"

"You mean that her father might not want to be found?" Eric asked. "It's a possibility."

"My father?" It was a grotesquely logical possibility. One she should have thought of herself. "You mean he might be trying to scare me out of town?"

"That would certainly put a different slant on your search." Gus scratched his head. "But it's also possible this person has no idea why you're back, and something totally unrelated's got him spooked. Tony said the caller this morning wanted you to get out of town. Get out and don't come back, he said. Not stop snooping or stop digging up the past."

"Either way, Carrinne's better off if we find her father as soon as possible," Eric said. "If for no other reason than to rule him out as a suspect."

Gus stood. He pulled a handkerchief from his back pocket and wiped at the beads of moisture dotting his forehead. "I guess it's worth checking into. Any chance there's someone closer to home who's using your trip here as a cover for getting back at you?"

"Except for my business associates, no one from New York knows I'm here," she hedged.

"Could it be an ex, a disgruntled co-worker, maybe a client? Someone with an ax to grind who could have found out you'd be here for a while."

"No one I can think of."

"Tony's already running a full background check, just to be sure," Eric added.

"What?" She spun to look at him, her heart pounding in her ears. "Since when?"

"Since last night." Eric's eyes narrowed, the cop reasserting himself over the man who'd kissed her so tenderly just a few minutes ago. "I won't invade your privacy any more than I have to, but we can't afford to overlook anything."

"Well." Gus pulled off his hat, ran his fingers through his hair, and flipped the cap back onto his head. "How about I start by looking into everyone you've come in contact with since you arrived at Oakwood."

"I…I made a list for Eric before we came over here." It was difficult to reply when she couldn't breathe. Tony was checking into her life in New York at that very moment. He'd find out about Maggie before the end of the day. They all would.

"Tony has the list," Eric added.

"Good." Gus pulled a business card from his wallet and handed it to Eric. "Call me if you come up with something else."

Carrinne tried to keep track of their conversation.

Tried to think of something to stall Eric's momentum. But the words wouldn't come.

"When you get to the station," Eric was saying, "start with running down any information you can find on Carrinne's mother and the Wilmington family around the time she would have gotten pregnant."

Gus nodded. "That scamp brother of yours said you had him working on a Sunday."

"His shift starts in a few hours anyway. He didn't seem to mind going in early."

"No, I don't suppose he did." The detective gave Carrinne an understanding wink and headed for the stairs.

"We're going to find this guy." Eric drew her in front of him, his hands on her hips. "Gus is a bloodhound. He never misses. We'll nail whoever's after you in no time."

She couldn't process his words. Couldn't think past the realization that she'd run out of time. She either let Tony or Gus uncover Maggie's existence, or she told Eric about their daughter herself. The best she could hope for now was to control the damage.

A part of her felt absurdly relieved.

Once Eric learned she'd kept Maggie from him, this growing attraction building between them would disappear. Her weakness for him, the dangerous dreams of family and home that he made her want to dream, would cease to be a threat because once Eric learned what she'd done, he'd never touch her again. And then she'd be safe.

She looked up into his beautiful, troubled eyes and let herself sink into his embrace one last time. Then she pushed away and locked her hands in front of her.

"Eric. There's something I have to tell you."

CHAPTER EIGHT

ERIC WATCHED the color drain from Carrinne's face. A reaction, he had no doubt, to how aggressively he and Tony were digging into her personal life.

He grabbed her purse and turned her toward the stairs. "Let's find some place cooler to talk."

"But I have to tell you—"

"Downstairs first." He led her through the attic door. "We can talk while we're getting something to drink. One more minute up here, and I'm going to have a heat stroke."

The hair rose on his neck at the mixture of dread and determination in her eyes. Just minutes ago, she'd been so soft and sweet, melting into him, dropping all her defenses and humbling him to his soul. Now, she'd never seemed more distant.

Calvin met them on the second floor. He was cleaning a display case filled with crystal so fragile, Eric instinctively lightened his step. The elderly gentleman laid his dust cloth aside and smiled. "Ms. Wilmington, I hope you found what you were looking for."

"No." Carrinne's complexion was on the pasty side of gray. "Not yet."

"We were hoping there'd be something cold to drink in the kitchen," Eric added.

"Why sure." Calvin's cheerful demeanor sobered. "You two must have been roasting up there. Nina makes the best iced tea in Oakwood. There's always a pitcher in the refrigerator."

"Thanks." Eric led Carrinne down the hall to the spiral staircase that dominated the center of the mansion.

"Why don't I have whatever Ms. Wilmington wants to look through brought down to her grandfather's study?" Calvin offered from behind them. "No reason why you two should be sweating the day away up there."

"Thanks." Eric nodded. "That might not be a bad idea. We'll come find you when we're ready to start again."

At the bottom of the stairs, the first floor stretched out before them. They headed toward the back of the house, through an enormous formal dining room the size of an entire floor of Eric's house. Each perfectly refinished antique they passed was likely worth a year's salary.

All those times he'd met Carrinne in the garden, he mused, and he'd never stepped foot inside the Wilmington mansion until now. His father had been here once. It was the day Gerald Rivers discovered Oliver was backing his opponent in his reelection campaign for sheriff. Eric's dad had refused to bend to Oliver's will during his first term, and the old curmudgeon had been determined to use his influence to push Gerald out of office. Eric's dad had confronted Wilmington, telling him he didn't give a damn about the Wilmington name or money, and neither did the people who were going to reelect him. He was the hardest-working sheriff Oakwood had ever had, and that's all that mattered.

And he'd been right, getting himself reelected by a landslide. For the first time since his mother had left, Eric had been able to look at his dad and feel something more than anger and resentment for all that the man hadn't been able to keep from happening. He'd finally understood the calling that had kept his father at the office morning, noon and night, leaving Eric at home to watch his baby brother. For a fleeting moment, he'd been proud of being Gerald Rivers' son.

And when Wilmington had tried to keep Eric out of the same office, he'd considered it a compliment.

The kitchen was in proportion with the rest of the house, which was to say it was huge. An eighteen-foot ceiling topped the state-of-the-art cabinetry and appliances. The granite counters and an industrial-grade refrigerator were not exactly what Eric had expected.

"Wow." Carrinne stood in the middle of the room, her jaw agape. "Look at this place."

"Hard to believe the difference, isn't it?" A plump black woman sidled over from a pantry that looked to be the size of Eric's bedroom. "I had to badger your grandfather for years, threatened to quit, before he agreed to bring us into the twenty-first century."

"Nina." Carrinne launched herself into the woman's hug. "It's good to see you."

Nina squeezed, then stood back. "You're just as beautiful as your momma."

"Thank you." Carrinne's smile wobbled. "It's been so long. It's wonderful to see you. You and Calvin both."

"You look like a good breeze would send you flying, girl." Nina pushed her toward one of the cane-bottomed kitchen chairs. "You sit right there and let me make you some lunch."

"Now, Nina. Don't fuss." Carrinne eased into the chair. "The sheriff and I just wanted something cool to drink."

Nina glanced at Eric as he stepped behind Carrinne. "You gonna make sure she eats something?"

"Yes, ma'am." Eric squeezed Carrinne's shoulder and felt her stiffen.

"Well, all right then." The cook crossed to the stainless-steel refrigerator and took out a pitcher of iced tea. She poured two tall crystal glasses full and placed them on the table. "I've got some ironing to do in the washroom. Holler if you need anything."

Her apron flapped loosely as she left, its ties hanging down her khaki-clad legs. Calvin had been wearing casual pants, too, and a golf shirt. So had Robert, the butler who'd let them in the front door.

"The staff wears interesting uniforms." Eric sipped his tea, taking in the elevated lifestyle on display around him. "Your grandfather doesn't exactly stand on ceremony at home, does he?"

"Never did." Carrinne pushed her glass away and picked at the lace covering the mahogany pedestal table. "For all of his pretence and throwing his weight around town, he always said things like uniformed servants were just putting on airs. He knew how much money he had, so why make the staff wear fancy costumes just to impress other people? It's more important that they be comfortable enough to do their jobs."

"And he's sent their kids to school?" Eric asked, remembering her conversation with Calvin earlier. Philanthropy wasn't a concept you generally heard in conjunction with the old man's name.

Her smile was rueful. "Another Wilmington philosophy. Make sure the staff's families are secure, and you've got guaranteed job retention. He's not much on love and shameless displays like encouragement, and when you're in the way of what he wants, he doesn't mind steamrolling right over you. But everyone depending on him can count on the best money can buy."

Eric shook his head. "Pretty profound reasoning, if it weren't so diabolically manipulative."

"Believe it or not, I think he really does care in his own way." Carrinne's expression was far away for a moment. "One man's manipulation is another man's just cause."

"Another Oliver Wilmington saying?"

She shrugged. "Sometimes he's right."

Eric blinked at the sadness in her tone.

He took the chair next to her, turning it around so he

could straddle the seat and lean his forearms on the scrolled backrest. "What is it you wanted to tell me upstairs? If you want to lay into me for telling Tony and Gus to look into your life back in New York, have at it."

She grew even stiller, if that was possible. "I don't know exactly how to say this…"

"Don't worry about what we're going to find. You've got to know that there's nothing in your life that's going to change our…" Our what? What was the word he'd used earlier? "Our friendship."

Because not touching her was impossible, he smoothed her bangs out of her eyes. His thumb traced the worry lines that cropped up between her eyebrows every time she thought really hard.

"You're tough, and you've survived," he continued when she still hadn't said anything. "You did what you had to do to get by. I know a little bit about that, and I admire how much grit it must have taken to make what you have out of your life. Hell, a few ghosts in the closet are good for the character."

"Ghost."

"What?"

"Just one ghost." She swallowed, then turned those forest-green eyes on him. There was fear there. Fear and a strength that took his breath away. "A living, breathing teenage variety."

His mind totally blanked, then skipped forward. He smiled his relief. "You mean you have a child? I think that's great."

"A daughter…she…I…" She tripped over her words, then stopped altogether.

She reached into her purse, pulling out her wallet and leafing through the pictures inside. Silently she removed a photo from its protective sleeve and handed it to him.

Eric looked at the smiling face of a teenage girl. Her bright eyes and the determined set of her jaw gave her prettiness a tough edge. There was something familiar about her, even though her coloring was nothing like Carrinne's. Dark hair. Dark eyes. Her face was more angular than her mother's. In fact, she reminded him of Tony as a teenager, before his features had matured—

In a stunned instant, Eric was out of his chair, the truth he held in his hands ripping a shout—a denial— from his throat.

"What's her name?" he managed to say, dropping the picture on the table between them. The guilt overwhelming Carrinne's delicate features made him want to howl, because his instincts told him to comfort her. He braced his hands on the arms of her chair. A distant part of his brain registered that his size and body language were scaring her, but he didn't care. "How old is she? What's her name?"

"Her name is Maggie, and she's sixteen." Carrinne pushed herself to her feet and took several steps back. "I—"

"Shut up." He raised a hand to run it through his hair. When she flinched away, he ground his teeth. "Damn it. How is this possible? I…I have a…"

"Daughter," Carrinne said.

"Maggie." His child's name was barely a whisper on his lips. He sat again, but being in the chair didn't curb the sensation that he was falling. Details began to piece themselves together. "She's the one who called you last night."

Carrinne nodded and reached to comfort him.

He shot her a look that stalled her hand in midair. "She's the ace up your sleeve that's insured your grandfather's cooperation all this time."

"I'm sorry I never told you," she said, still nodding. "I know now I should have given you a chance to be a part of her life. But you said you didn't want me. You didn't even want Tony. You said you didn't want to be responsible for anyone but yourself."

"You knew that night?" Unable to reconcile the amazing woman he'd thought Carrinne had become with the shaking, hand-wringing liar standing before him, he braced his elbows on the table and dropped his head to his hands. "That night by the side of the road. You knew you were pregnant, and you let me walk away. Then you left Oakwood with my child. Never once considering I had the right to know her."

"You didn't want to know *me*." Anger replaced her contrition. "I was a kid, remember. A silly, love-struck kid who was slowing you down. And when Oliver found out I was pregnant, he wanted me to have an abortion."

Eric's head snapped up.

With a shaky breath, she continued. "I had two

choices. I could tell you and beg you to take me back and become one more burden for you to hate. Or I could grow up and find a way to survive on my own. So I left."

"You ran." Her innocence was well practiced, he had to give her that. "You make yourself sound so noble. Hell, I still might buy it if I didn't know better. The lost Southern flower making her way in the big city. A single mother raising a child on her own, abandoned by everyone she wanted to trust. Changed by her experience, harder and less trusting. But still an innocent at heart, because her motives are forever selfless and pure."

Desperation he thought he'd banished years ago had him surging to his feet. The desperate need to hurt someone as badly as he'd been hurt. To hurt the person who'd betrayed him.

He grabbed Carrinne's arms, hauling her against him. "You took my child. The life I should have had a part in shaping. The family that should have been mine. Just like my mother. You ran like a coward, and you took everything with you."

"No, you pushed me away." She struggled only a second before becoming eerily still. "You gave up everything when you said you didn't care."

"Well I care now." His smile felt both cruel and satisfying. Carrinne's eyes flinched. The need to hurt her drove him on. "And you knew I'd care, didn't you? You knew I'd care, and you were banking on finding a way out of all this without telling me."

"No, Eric. I—"

"Shh." He softened his grip. Rubbed reassuring circles up and down her arm. She relaxed slightly, and he prepared to go in for the kill. He'd never felt more like the bastard she clearly thought he was.

When he leaned forward and softly kissed her cold lips, her mouth shook beneath his, just as it had upstairs when she'd melted into their embrace. Only now, her tremors were from fear.

Smart girl.

"No more lies, darlin'," he coaxed. "Just tell me where to find my daughter. I think it's about time we met."

"Eric, you can't." Her eyes begged.

"Can't?"

"Maggie won't understand." Her hand rose to his chest, resting above the heart she'd just ripped to shreds. "She's already going through so much because of my illness."

He shoved her away, cursing.

This woman he'd let himself fall for again, the only woman who'd ever had any claim on his heart, she'd done the unforgivable. "Tell me where to find Maggie."

Nina picked that moment to return. She stopped and stared, as if she could sense the dangerous emotions charging between the other two people in the room.

Eric lowered his voice and spoke directly into Carrinne's ear. "Tell me where she is, or I'll find her myself. Either way, you're not going to keep me from my daughter. Not another single day."

CHAPTER NINE

CARRINNE STOOD before Eric, shaking, watching her worst nightmare come to life. His anger, his outrage, were everything she'd expected. His determination to see Maggie a forgone conclusion.

"Is something wrong?" Nina asked as she stepped to Carrinne's side.

"No." Carrinne gave Eric a pointed stare, praying he wouldn't reveal Maggie's existence to Nina or anyone else until they'd settled things. "But the sheriff and I need to discuss something in private."

"Why don't you use your grandfather's study," Nina offered. "I'll have some lunch ready around noon."

Carrinne picked up their daughter's picture. Her stomach knotted as Eric's eyes burned holes straight through her.

"All right." He swept his arm in the direction of the kitchen door, waiting for her to lead the way.

Carrinne somehow got her legs moving. Eric was an angry presence behind her as they walked back through the dining room, toward the front of the house. Was it just a few hours ago that she'd begun to relax around him?

They'd discussed being friends. They'd kissed like lovers.

All that was over now. Forever.

They stepped inside her grandfather's study, and the grandeur of the room brought her to a halt. The ancient mahogany desk was still as solid and unbending as its owner. Large bay windows offered some of the best views of the property's magnificent gardens. And the walls. They were still lined with shelves, covered in books. It was the books that called to her more than anything else. They tempted her with escape. Reminded her of the worlds and dreams she'd left behind. Fantasies that had fed her when she was a child, and destroyed her when she'd finally grown up.

Eric shut the door behind them, leaning against it. "We have our privacy. Now what?"

"I don't want Nina or anyone else to overhear us." She walked around the desk and sat, running her hands over its gleaming surface. The chair's butter-soft leather surrounded her as she drew up her feet and curled them beneath her. "You have to understand. A revelation like this would destroy Maggie."

"Oh, I understand perfectly. You think our child would be traumatized by having me as a father." His clipped words were menacing in their softness. "I assume your grandfather's known I'm the father all this time. He knew when he demanded you terminate the pregnancy."

"Yes, he knew. After the way we flaunted our relationship, it's not like there was much doubt. And yes, I didn't tell you because back then I was afraid of what kind of father you'd be." No use avoiding the cold, hard facts at this point. She cleared her voice. "But I know differently now. I've seen what you sacrificed for Tony. How you stuck it out here and gave him everything he needed. You've been wonderful for him."

She could sense him processing her words. He remained at the door, his distrust more of a distance between them than the five feet separating them. She had to make him understand.

"You always wanted to be anywhere but here," she said. "You wanted to ride free, to find a life outside your family and this small town. Yet you stayed, doing everything your father would have wanted you to do. Becoming responsible and stable for Tony's sake, regardless of what it cost you. You even took a sheriff's position you didn't want, just so you could keep an eye on Tony. Am I right?"

He blinked. "What's your point?"

"I'm trying to make you see that my asking you not to reveal yourself to Maggie right now has nothing to do with my opinion of what kind of father you'd be to her."

He crossed his arms, his hard face giving no hint whether she was getting through.

She refused to break eye contact, refused to be the coward he thought she was. She wasn't giving up. This was too important. "Maggie thinks her father's dead. She's grown up believing that he loved her, that she would have been the apple of his eye. If she found out now that I ran because I didn't think you'd wanted her—"

"She'd hate you." He waited for her to deny it.

"Yes. She'll never forgive me for lying to her." That day was coming. Not today, but it was coming.

"So, this is about you."

"No, this is about Maggie, damn it." Anger seared through her guilt. "Do you care anything about her, or is this just about seeing how much you can hurt me back?"

"I've never met Maggie, and I already care more about my daughter than I do my own life." His conviction, the emotion lacing every word, hurt more than any curse he could have thrown at her.

Lord, what had she done?

"I'm so sorry," she managed to say. "More sorry than you can possibly know. I did what I thought was best, and I was wrong. But please, don't compound my mistakes by heaping your own on top of them."

"And contacting my daughter would be a mistake?"

The harsh angles of his face softened into a bewildered scowl. He stepped to one of the leather guest chairs and sat, leaning forward to brace his elbows on his thighs. "Believe it or not, I do see my part in all this. And I understand that meeting me now will be a huge adjustment for Maggie. But—"

"There is no but! She doesn't need one more thing in her life going to hell right now."

"Because you're sick." Pain and understanding dawned in his eyes.

"Because she knows I could be dying," Carrinne corrected. She never let herself think about dying, but she had to make Eric understand. "You know I'm right. Don't add more to the burden Maggie's already carrying."

Silence surrounded them, buffering the hostility of the last few minutes. Eric wanted to know his daughter, and he couldn't. Not now. Carrinne braced herself to absorb every hateful word to come.

"Were you ever going to tell me?" he asked instead, his voice rougher than she'd ever heard it. "What if you never found a donor? Would you have let someone else finish raising Maggie, just to keep her away from me?"

"No." But that wasn't the whole truth. She felt the fear, the hopelessness, pulling at her, and she fought the urge to end the conversation right then and there. Eric deserved an answer, no matter what it cost her. "I never thought that far ahead. The doctors said I have a few years, and I...I don't let myself think of the end, not while I still have options."

"And if your options had finally run out?" Emotions swirled in his eyes. Pain, concern, fury, fear.

"If I never found my father, and no other donor became available?"

"Yes," he replied softly.

Her mind played a brief flash of Maggie, crying in Kim's arms beside a flower-draped casket. "Then I'd have made the decision I thought was best for Maggie."

Precious, razor-edged images assailed her. Maggie's college graduation, her wedding, the children of her own she would one day have. All the things Carrinne might never see. Wincing, she fought not to torture herself with thoughts of all she'd be missing if her time ran out.

"You would have made the decision *you* thought was best." Eric shoved himself from the chair and walked to one of the bay windows. He looked out over what had once been her grandmother's sitting garden.

"What if I hadn't gone on call with Tony Friday night?" he asked the sheer curtains that muted the vivid green of the world beyond. "I might never have found out. You would have given my daughter to someone else and let her live the rest of her life thinking both her parents were dead."

Even though she was drowning in her own pain, her spirit heard Eric's suffering. He'd missed so much of Maggie's past, just as Carrinne might not have their daughter's future. Ignoring her useless self-pity, she pulled herself together.

"But you did find out, Eric. And I'm glad you know. Somehow we'll find a way to tell Maggie together, when the time's right."

"So now it's *we*." He rounded on her. "Now *we're* in this together."

"Please, don't—"

"Where the hell do you get *we* from? You tell me you might be dying, but only when you have no other choice. You fight me every step of the way, even though I'm try-ing to help you find the one thing you need to survive—"

"I didn't expect to find you here. And then all I knew

of you was from before. I couldn't risk telling you about Maggie, not knowing what kind of man you were." Her words echoed through the room. "But when I saw who you've become with my own eyes, I realized I had to tell you."

"But you didn't. Not until you knew Tony's background check would force your hand. And you still want to call the shots."

"It's for the best."

"Lying to someone you love is never for the best." Regret sparked in the dead brown of his eyes. "I lied to you seventeen years ago when I said I didn't want you. You lied when you took our child and left. Look where that's gotten us. If I don't go to Maggie now, now that I know, I'm lying to her right along with you. And she'll blame me the same way she's going to blame you when she finally finds out."

"I know it's not a good decision." Carrinne refused to give in to the luxury of regret. "But it's the only one we've got. Maggie can't take this right now."

She waited, holding her breath until her chest burned. Hoping. Dreading. "You have to believe me."

"I don't know what to believe." He headed for the door.

"Eric. Please don't leave. Not until we've talked this through."

"I have to think." He didn't look back. "And I need to see what Gus and Tony have dug up. I'll be back by four to take you in for your checkup with Dr. Burns."

"But what about Maggie? Please—"

"I won't contact her." His words were soulless. Empty. "Not yet."

"Thank you," she said to his back.

Halfway out the door, he stopped and cocked his head to the side. "You said only a blood relative can be a living donor?"

"Yes."

"So does that mean Maggie might be able to help you?"

"No. That's not a possibility." Her breath caught on her lie. But her decision about Maggie undergoing the donor procedure was not open for debate. "Finding my father's the only option."

"Then that's what we'll do. For our daughter's sake." He walked away, his stride stiff, his hands jammed in the pockets of his jeans.

It was good that he knew, Carrinne reminded herself. He couldn't stand being around her anymore, and that was for the best.

She couldn't face what she had to face unless her feelings were locked away and under control. And that's exactly where they'd stay now that he despised her for what she'd done.

But he did love their daughter. Tears shimmered, blocking Carrinne's vision. Love for Maggie had eclipsed the hurt in Eric's expression. If the worst happened, if Carrinne didn't make it, Maggie would have her father to help her through the loss.

Her beautiful daughter—*their* beautiful daughter— wouldn't have to face the future alone.

"NO LUCK with your mother's things?" Nina entered the solarium, startling Carrinne.

Carrinne had fled the study, unable to focus on searching through the dusty piles that had been transferred from the attic. She'd wandered out to the solarium, needing contact with some part of the past that didn't threaten to break her heart.

"Nothing yet." She trailed her hand over the pots of budding camellias set atop a low table. "No sign of my mother's last diary. After all these years, I don't know why I'm so surprised. For all I know, Oliver found it and threw it out."

"Your grandfather's never thrown a thing of your mother's away," Nina said with certainty. "He loved her so much, clung to her in an unhealthy way after Mrs. Wilmington died, if you ask me. He couldn't bear the thought of parting with anything that belonged to her."

"Just like he couldn't bear the thought of loving me."

"I know you've always believed that, honey." Nina hugged Carrinne's shoulders. "And there was many a time when I wanted to box the man's ears for the cold way he treated you. But he cared. I think something inside him just broke when he lost Ms. Angelica. You didn't know him before, so all you've seen is the after. But the difference in him was like day and night. He just stopped being able to show how he felt."

"Oh, he showed it all right. When I was here, I was

a Wilmington asset to be controlled. When I left, I wasn't even important enough to come looking for."

"The man's been grieving for over thirty years, honey. And the wrong kind of grief does terrible things to people." Nina squeezed again. "It's not too late for the two of you to work this out. Your grandfather's never been sick a day in his life before now. A few months in the hospital is enough to soften even a head as hard as his."

"I don't want to work things out. I don't have time." Carrinne could have told her old friend why, but why wasn't important. "I just want to find my mother's diary and get back to my life in New York."

"You can look some more after lunch." Nina pressed an embroidered handkerchief to her forehead. "Now come in out of all this heat and eat something. Sheriff Rivers said your doctor wanted you to have regular meals. No exceptions. As long as you're home, you're going to take care of yourself."

Home.

Carrinne surveyed the tidy rows of tables filled with seedlings and maturing bedding plants. This was the only place in Oakwood besides Eric's house that felt even remotely like home. Turning away from her childhood refuge, she walked with Nina through the mudroom that separated the solarium from the kitchen.

Something the housekeeper had said worked its way through her melancholy.

"You spoke with Eric?"

"He found me before he headed out. Wanted to make

sure Calvin was still here to have your mother's things brought down. Now that's one protective man."

"Protective?" Carrinne sat at the kitchen table. "Determined, maybe."

Nina ladled tomato soup into a rimmed china bowl. Carrinne smiled as the housekeeper placed her favorite lunch in front of her. It felt wonderful to be fussed over.

"He left some things for you to take after lunch." Nina pointed to the bag Carrinne thought she'd left behind at his house. It held her antibiotics.

Eric was taking care of her, even now.

In her mind, Carrinne stomped her foot. Damn him for being so considerate. He had no business caring about whether or not she ate, or took her medication, or stayed out of that suffocating attic. He had no business being such a wonderful, kind man. Not after what she'd told him. Not when she was counting on him to be distant and angry and wanting nothing more to do with her.

"The sheriff's just helping me for a few days," she told both herself and Nina. "Until his department closes the case on my accident, I'm official police business."

"He's a good sheriff, I'll give him that. Always been competent and thorough, just like his daddy." Nina placed a sandwich in front of Carrinne, then a linen napkin trimmed in a lace pattern that matched the tablecloth's design. "But if I don't miss my guess, the man's still head over heels in love with you."

Carrinne choked on her first spoonful of soup.

The older woman patted her shoulder, as if to make the truth easier to swallow. "After the way you two carried on when you were kids, it's no wonder."

"We dated over seventeen years ago, Nina. That's all it was."

"Girl, you're forgetting I used to live here. That tree you met under at night was outside my bedroom window. Dating doesn't exactly describe what I saw the two of you doing."

Heat rushed to Carrinne's cheeks, embarrassment no thirty-three-year-old single mother should still be able to feel. "We…we were just… It wasn't—"

"Wasn't what I thought?"

"I…we…"

"Were in love." Nina gave Carrinne a wink. "Or maybe it was teenage lust. All I know is there was enough heat coming from those late-night clinches to steam up my windows."

"That was a long time ago." Carrinne applied herself to her lunch. "I didn't even know Eric still lived here when I came back."

Nina simply smiled her don't-mind-me-I-just-understand-things-better-than-you smile.

Carrinne took her hand. "Please don't say anything about Sheriff Rivers and me to anyone else."

"I don't have to, honey." Nina stepped to the sink. "You two are the talk of the town. Have been since you checked out of your motel and moved in with him and his brother. You know, your grandfather's going to hit the roof, hearing the two of you are together again."

"We are *not* together." Carrinne closed her eyes and rubbed at the headache that had made a return appearance. "Besides, it's none of my grandfather's business who I'm with."

"Can't imagine he'll be too happy about it, considering how he's felt about the Riverses all these years. It was a good thing Gerald Rivers was so well liked around here. I don't know very many people who could have stood up to your grandfather and walked away unscathed. Your grandfather's one of Eric's biggest critics."

Carrinne pushed her soup away. As a teenager, she'd made a point of throwing her relationship with Eric in Oliver's face. She'd ridden around town on Eric's motorcycle, had baby-sat for his little brother. Every night she'd had dinner at the Rivers' house, Oliver had met her at the door when she returned, furious and demanding to know why she'd defied him yet again. Now, the news she was staying with Eric would reach her grandfather, and the man had a penchant for making trouble when he was unhappy.

Eric was already on the edge. If Oliver got it into his head to confront him, Eric's tenuous agreement not to approach Maggie might blow up in her face.

Maggie! She checked her watch. Even though there was nothing new to report, she couldn't miss calling again. Then, she had a meddlesome grandfather to deal with.

ERIC ENTERED the conference room where his brother and Gus were working. *Torn up* didn't begin to describe the condition of his insides at the moment.

"I've got the cell phone records." Tony held up a computer printout. "We'll have to wait until the banks open in the morning before we can get any financials."

"That's not good enough."

Tony's raised eyebrow questioned the sharp edge to Eric's voice.

"You want me to get Judge Hartley on the phone?" he asked.

"Yeah, give him a call at home." Eric reined in the fury still eating at him. Hartley and their dad had gone to grade school together. "Get him to sign a warrant out ASAP. We need to know now if anyone close to the Wilmingtons has a financial reason to want Carrinne out of town."

"You got it." Tony picked up the conference-room phone, his expression full of questions Eric wasn't ready to answer.

Eric's thoughts returned to his daughter. A daughter who didn't know he existed, because seventeen years ago he'd told her mother to get the hell out of his life. Because Carrinne hadn't trusted him to love her and their child enough to stick it out. Maggie was a frightened teenager, already trying to cope with her mother's newly diagnosed illness. And all he could do for her right now was stay away. That and keep her mother safe long enough to find a liver donor.

He walked over to where Gus sat in front of a computer

workstation. The detective had pulled up the Library Link Web page and was searching archived issues of the *Oakwood Gazette* and papers from surrounding counties.

"So far, nothing out of the ordinary about her mother from the late sixties," Gus said. "Nothing at all until her death in 1970."

"Keep looking. Cross-check with the people we already know Carrinne's come into contact with since she's been back."

"Eric." Tony was off the phone and once again searching through the listing of cell-phone numbers. "Take a look at this. The call this morning is definitely local. But twice in the last two days, Carrinne's received calls from a New York cell account set up in her name."

"Focus on the local number. Get me a location."

"What about the calls from New York? Did she ever tell you anything about them?"

"Yeah, she told me." Eric took the listing and studied the trail of cell calls he now knew were from Maggie. He'd been just two doors down last night when Carrinne had talked with their daughter. He blinked as his daughter's phone number burned itself into his brain.

"You know who it is?" Tony was studying his expression.

"Yeah. I know who it is. And it's a dead end. Let's focus on this morning's call." Eric noticed again his kid brother's resemblance to Maggie. And Tony looked like a younger reflection of Eric.

Hell, man. Just say it. Your daughter looks like you.

His daughter.

With a shake of his head, he handed back the listing and headed toward his office. "I'm going to take another look at the report on Carrinne's wreck."

When he reached his desk, he plucked the case file from the top of the scattered piles that had grown higher since he'd been slaving over them yesterday morning. He sat and stared blindly at the report, unable to focus.

Something inside him had been shifting slowly, ever since he'd heard Carrinne speak their daughter's name. Some hidden lock was working itself loose, no matter how hard he resisted. He had a daughter. There was a piece of him and Carrinne out there. Another life bound to him through blood, drawing him into something he'd never thought he wanted—commitment.

Responsibility for Tony had been a burden thrust upon him. But he refused to think of knowing his daughter as anything but a gift.

Maggie's cell number replayed itself in his mind.

He wanted to call her. He wanted to fly to New York and see her, hold her, try to explain the feelings surging inside him. He could. He could do anything he pleased. And yet he could do nothing at all.

Carrinne was right. Thrusting himself into their daughter's life right now would be cruel. And since he was being honest, he couldn't help but respect Carrinne's reasons for not telling him about Maggie in the first place. He'd given her every reason to doubt him, to be afraid of the kind of father he'd be. He'd compared her to his mother, but she was nothing like the woman who'd abandoned her family for a better life. Carrinne hadn't run from her family. She'd run to protect it.

But damn it, all he could think about was the years. All the stinking years he'd missed, years he'd had with Tony but not with his own daughter. It put things into perspective, all he'd taken for granted with his brother. Carrinne's reaction to the wall of photos trailing up the stairwell came to him again with piercing clarity.

You've been a wonderful father…

All this time, he'd been playing at being a dad. Raising Tony, telling himself he'd never have what it took to be a *real* father, but he sure as hell wasn't going to bail on his brother. All it had taken to make him feel like a father was four simple words.

Her name is Maggie.

He'd been a man determined to fulfill his obligations, then he was hitting the road to follow his dreams, leaving responsibility behind. Then one sentence had shown him what his dreams were really made of. He wanted Maggie in his life. Now, tomorrow, and always. There was no doubt in his mind. And what about the girl's mother? What about Carrinne?

A thrill of excitement spread from the center of his chest.

"How's it going?" Angie Carter stepped into his office, her deputy's uniform neatly pressed as always. "I heard Carrinne got a nasty phone call this morning. Any leads?"

"We're just getting started." He picked up the folder and began thumbing through the accident report.

"It figures Carrinne would be the one who'd get you in here on both a Saturday and a Sunday." Angie sat in one of the chairs on the other side of the desk.

"What?" Eric gave her his full, frazzled attention.

"Carrinne Wilmington. The woman from your past the whole town's saying has moved in with you. Tony and Gus are running background checks on her, her mother, and anyone who's ever worked for Oliver Wilmington. You're holed up in here poring over that case report, even though you know we've found nothing conclusive. We have collision marks on her rear bumper, a hazy video and a witness with a vague description of a man in a dark van. Nothing's changed, but you're still digging for some reason that you're not inclined to share. I figure by tomorrow, you'll have the entire department involved in some way or another."

"It's just another case." He threw the printout onto the desk. "Carrinne living with me is a precaution."

"So this is business, not personal. You don't have any feelings for her anymore."

Eric didn't move. He didn't blink.

"I was there, remember?" Angie settled deeper into her chair. "Carrinne and I were in the same homeroom and study hall in high school. I even covered for her a few times when you took her for those after-lunch rides on that Harley that's been collecting dust in your garage for the last two decades. The rebel and the goodygoodiest girl in town. I always thought your fascination with her was kinda sweet."

"Sweet?" Eric eyed his very competent, very attractive in her own tomboyish way, second-in-command. "You covered for us because you thought I was sweet?"

"You know." She smiled and propped her legs on his desk. Her perfectly creased uniform pants screaming 'regulation' at Eric's jeans and faded T-shirt. "The princess taming the bad boy. The daredevil falling for Oliver Wilmington's little angel. Carrinne was good for you, and that was good enough for me. So I covered for you two. Then you broke her heart."

The understanding censure in Angie's words made Eric chuckle. Small-town friendships were hell when the people you saw at work every day were the same ones who'd seen you pick your nose in grade school.

He'd guessed years ago that Angie had suffered from a teenage crush on him. Then they'd both gone through the academy and started in the force together, working their way up through the ranks, even partnering on patrol for a short time. They shared a healthy professional respect for one another now, and she was one of the few people in town he could talk straight with.

Angie smiled. "Kind of puts a kink into things, Carrinne showing up again after all these years."

"It's sure made for a hell of a mess." He leaned back in his squeaky chair, almost wishing the last forty-eight hours were nothing more than the result of bad Chinese takeout and a restless night. Almost.

"So you want to tell me what this is all about?" Angie's gaze fell to the accident report. "'Cause I've pretty much guessed that the accident and the prank phone call are just the beginning."

He sighed and ran a hand through his hair. "We think whoever we're looking for may have some connection to Carrinne's father."

Angie's feet dropped to the floor. "You think someone wants her to stop looking for him?"

"Until we find a lead that explains it otherwise, that's the theory that goes down best." The thought of someone getting to Carrinne, hurting her again, made his hands shake no matter how angry he still was at what she'd done. He pounded the desk with his fist. "We've got to have more to go on."

Angie nodded and rose. "I'll go see if I can help Tony and Gus. There's nothing much else doing around here today anyway."

"Thanks, Angie."

A smile softened her makeup-free features. "No sweat. What are friends for?"

Her words lingered as Eric watched her leave.

What are friends for?

Something his dad had tried to tell him years ago echoed right behind her words.

There's nothing better than working for the department, son. It's a brotherhood. Your fellow officers are your friends, your family. There's nothing better on this earth.

Maybe it was learning about Maggie. Maybe it was

his uncharacteristic introspection about commitment and family. But even his lousy job felt different now.

His relationships on the force had been a source of stability he'd come to depend on without even realizing it. He was part of a squad of colleagues who, like Angie, would always be there for him, and he for them. If that wasn't family, what was? And then there was the life he'd carved out with his brother. The life Carrinne had called wonderful. The life only days ago he'd been looking forward to leaving behind.

What he'd built for himself in Oakwood *was* light years away from the empty, independent life he'd told Carrinne he wanted when they were dating. And he was damn lucky for it, even if he'd been so blind along the way that it was a wonder he hadn't destroyed every good thing that had dropped into his lap. Carrinne had been right to run from him. She would have been crazy to stay. She'd made her own choices, but he'd pushed her into them.

So what exactly did a man do when he found himself right smack dab in the middle of wanting the family and commitment he'd spent his life trying to outrun?

CHAPTER TEN

MAGGIE WILMINGTON hefted her overstuffed backpack higher on her shoulder, turned and waved a careless goodbye to Kim, who stood on the apartment steps. She'd bought herself the rest of the day and into the evening, saying she and some friends needed to work on a history project at the Metropolitan Museum of Art. She turned the corner that led to the subway station. When she was sure she was out of Kim's sight, she ran to the next block and hailed a cab.

"La Guardia," she said to the driver as she pulled her mom's crumpled itinerary from her pack.

She'd called ahead and reserved her flights on the credit card her mom had left her for emergencies. She was catching the same flights her mom had taken just two days ago. A connection into Atlanta, then she'd board a small plane that would take her the rest of the way to Oakwood. She had her student ID to get her through security and a few days changes of clothes in her bag. Barring the unforeseen, she'd have touched down in Georgia before Kim even realized something was up.

Her mom had sounded terrible when she'd called at lunch. Tired and disappointed, no matter how hard she'd tried to hide it. She still hadn't found whatever or whomever she'd gone to Oakwood to look for, and she couldn't keep doing this on her own.

Chasing her mom to a tiny town in Georgia probably wasn't the smartest thing Maggie had ever done. She was going to catch it once she got there. But once her mom got over being angry, she would be happy to see her. Happy not to be facing whatever she was doing there alone. Maggie saw again the fear of going back to Oakwood that had filled her mom's eyes. What was wrong with this Oakwood place? Her mom wasn't afraid of anything.

Squaring her shoulders, Maggie watched the blur of buildings fly by. It would be after six before she arrived. She'd head to the motel first, and if her mom wasn't there she'd find another way to track her down. Her mom was following a lead on a donor, which meant she was looking for family. In a place as small as this Oakwood sounded, it shouldn't be hard to find whatever Wilmingtons still lived there.

At least she wouldn't be stuck here in New York anymore, with no way to help her mom and ready to bang her head against the wall.

ERIC WAS READY to bang his head against the conference-room wall. A deputy had found the van that had hit Carrinne, abandoned and banged up on the highway between town and the airport. They'd had it towed into the station, and Angie and another deputy had spent over an hour going over every inch of it for clues.

They'd found nothing. Not even a fingerprint.

On top of that, Tony had tracked this morning's threatening call to a pay phone clear across town. Which meant the caller could have been anybody. Someone was headed over there to dust for prints, but the caller had no doubt worn gloves. Two steps forward, one step back.

Giving up concentrating, his mind returning over and over to Carrinne, Eric left Tony and Gus to their paper trails and background checks and dialed the Wilmington mansion from the conference-room phone. Carrinne was in a house filled with servants, so she was fine. He was still mad as hell at her for keeping Maggie's existence from him. But a very big part of him wanted to be back at her side. Helping her with the painful process of sifting through her mother's things.

"Wilmington residence," Robert's deep voice answered.

"Robert, Sheriff Rivers here. Can I speak with Ms. Wilmington?"

"Afraid not, sir. She left about twenty minutes ago."

"What do you mean she left?"

"She wanted to see her grandfather, and she said something about a checkup with her doctor. Calvin took her on over to the hospital."

"Damn it." Eric slammed the phone into its wall unit.

"I think Gus has something here." Tony and Gus

were sitting at the conference table, poring over the financial records the bank manager had just faxed them. "Didn't I hear that Oliver Wilmington gave his lawyer legal power of attorney after his stroke?"

CARRINNE FROZE beside the half-closed door of her grandfather's hospital room. She'd sneaked past the nurses' station this time, not wanting to risk another lecture about visitation guidelines.

"She called me at the crack of dawn this morning," Brimsley said from inside, "and informed me that I had no choice but to help her, because she was your granddaughter."

"Well, that's true enough." She couldn't see Oliver's face, but she'd heard that self-satisfied tone enough times to picture the expression that went along with it. Smug. Barely interested enough to give you the benefit of a response.

"You mean to tell me I'm supposed to be at that woman's beck and call? I'm more family to you than she is. Where's she been for the last seventeen years? And why is she back now? 'Cause I'm not buying this lame search for her father. She says she didn't even know you'd had a stroke. But it's quite a coincidence, her showing up just as you're no longer in a position to take care of your own affairs. If you ask me, the piece of her past she's searching for is your money, not her father. I don't trust a word she says, and neither should you. I'm the one who's been here for you all these years."

"And you've been paid handsomely for your service," Oliver responded. "Carrinne's my family. You're my lawyer. Don't make the mistake of confusing the two."

"So, either I help her," Brimsley continued, "or—"

"Or I'll find myself an attorney who will do his job and keep his nose out of my personal affairs."

Carrinne reached to push the door completely open. From out of nowhere, a large hand covered her mouth, muffling her squeal as she was pulled backward. She blinked, focusing on Eric's hard eyes as he leaned her against the wall on the other side of the hall. Tony, in full uniform, joined them. Eric's hand prevented her from making a sound.

"Wait out here," he whispered, slowly gentling the pressure on her mouth.

"Wha—"

His hand pressed again, cutting off her words. His eyes were flat with barely controlled anger, but his touch was gentle.

"Not a sound," he whispered. Ribbons of heat sparked from every inch of flesh he touched. "Or I'll have Tony take you downstairs."

She managed a tiny nod.

He released her, his gaze skipping from her eyes to her mouth before he turned to his brother.

"Keep an eye on her," he said.

Eric stepped to her grandfather's door, just as Brimsley appeared on the other side, heading out. The lawyer skidded to a stop. Then he spotted Carrinne and Tony waiting in the hall.

"Get out of my way." He made the mistake of trying to step around Eric.

"Not so fast." In a blur, Eric pinned the older man against the wall. His forearm, muscles bulging beneath his faded T-shirt, pressed against Brimsley's throat. "Let's talk first."

"What do you think you're doing?" Brimsley struggled, gasping for air.

Eric's nose was a mere inch away from Brimsley's. "I'm trying to decide if I can get away with taking you apart in a public place," he said, his voice deadly calm. "It'll be a little hard to counter a harassment claim with a charge of resisting arrest, since you've got Wilmington here as a witness. But I'm wondering what his story will be once I show him evidence that you've been robbing him blind and threatening his granddaughter."

"What?" Carrinne stepped closer. Tony pulled her back.

"What are you talking about?" her grandfather wheezed from his bed inside. Carrinne could just make out his frail form as he shifted against his pillows. "Brimsley, what is going on?"

"I don't know what evidence your granddaughter's lover thinks he has, but that little bitch—agh!"

Eric flipped Brimsley until the man's face was smashed against the wall. Tony pulled a pair of cuffs from his belt and handed them to his brother.

"You're under arrest for embezzlement, and we're

working up a case for attempted murder," Eric grated as he fastened the cuffs around the lawyer's wrists. "We traced Carrinne's threatening phone call to a pay phone a block from your house. One of my men is over there now dusting for prints. I'm betting we'll find yours. It's only a matter of time before we link you to the van that pushed Carrinne into that intersection yesterday. Did I mention we have it in the impound yard now?"

He turned Brimsley from the wall. "You have the right to remain silent. I suggest you do. You have the right to an attorney…"

"Tony, what's going on?" Carrinne fought the need to sit on the floor and catch her breath as Eric read the sputtering lawyer his rights.

"We had the bank fax over the financial records of everyone close to your family," Tony explained. "Anyone we know you've come into contact with the last two days. It was a long shot, but we didn't have much else to go on. And we hit pay dirt with your grandfather's lawyer."

"I don't understand—"

"So I made that stupid phone call this morning!" Brimsley winced as Eric yanked him away from the door. "But I had nothing to do with her accident, you have to believe me."

"Take him in." Eric passed Brimsley to Tony. "I'll be there as soon as I can. I want the pleasure of questioning the good lawyer here myself."

"You got it." Tony dragged Brimsley away.

"You have to believe me…" the lawyer continued to plead.

"Eric—" Carrinne started to ask.

"Sheriff Rivers," Oliver said in a brittle voice. "I demand an explanation!"

Eric sighed and took Carrinne's elbow. "I'm sorry. I wanted to tell you alone first. But by the time I found out, you were already on your way over here—"

"Rivers!" Oliver bellowed.

"Come on." He drew her to his side, where she fit with excruciating perfection. She leaned against him, letting him support her weight as they walked into her grandfather's room.

Oliver Wilmington took one look at Carrinne tucked against Eric's side, and his eyes hardened. "So the rumors are true. Brimsley's right. You are sleeping with this—"

"That's none of your business." Carrinne stepped away from Eric, forcing back the weakness and fatigue sucking her under. She shut the door to secure their privacy. "I came over here to make sure you didn't do anything stupid when you found out I was staying with Eric for a few days. Beyond that, I don't care what you think about anything I do. Now, would someone please tell me what's going on with Brimsley?"

Eric fought not to smile at the look of outraged shock on Oliver Wilmington's face. Carrinne was a force to reckon with.

He turned to Oliver. The only other person who'd known about their child. Maggie wouldn't exist if this bastard had had his way. The man's mission to keep Eric out of office took on a whole new light now. Eric wanted to throttle the old goat, but he reached instead for the professional bearing he'd watched his father wear like armor.

"We have evidence that Brimsley's been funneling large sums from your accounts for the last six weeks. Virtually from the day you granted him legal power of attorney. If you're lucky, you'll be able to track the funds down and get most of it back. You heard him admit to making a threatening phone call this morning to try and scare Carrinne out of town. Our assumption is that he's the one who caused her wreck yesterday. We're waiting for the evidence we need, but it's only a matter of time."

"Her collision wasn't an accident?" Oliver rasped. "What threatening phone call?"

"Someone's been trying to scare Carrinne out of town, Mr. Wilmington," Eric responded. "And until now we were assuming it had something to do with her search for her father."

"But Brimsley?" Wrinkles crisscrossed Carrinne's brow. "I know he's always disliked me, and he's been just as rude as ever since I came back—"

"He must have thought your return risked your grandfather changing his designation of power of attorney," Eric answered. "You're an accountant, you'd have discovered the money he'd stolen in no time."

"Why wasn't I told that someone's threatening my granddaughter?" Oliver demanded.

"Because it doesn't concern you." Carrinne's spine stiffened. "I don't want you involved."

Oliver sized Eric up. "But the sheriff here is involved up to his neck, is that it? Why are you living with him?"

"Until we found the person responsible for her collision," Eric said, "it seemed wise for her to stay under the protection of my brother and myself. Besides, she needed to recuperate from the accident."

Oliver's nod dismissed Eric. He turned his attention to Carrinne. "You really don't want to have anything to do with me past looking for your mother's diary, do you? You won't even let me help you when you're in danger. You don't trust me to see my…" He gave Eric a quick glance, then fell silent.

Carrinne's laugh was a faint tremble. "I guess I should thank you for keeping your word, but you don't have to worry about spilling the beans. That's part of what I came to tell you. Eric knows about Maggie."

"You told him?"

"That Maggie's my daughter, yes." Eric's heart skidded, then galloped forward as he said the words. "And you knew all along. Particularly when you demanded Carrinne have an abortion."

"Yes," Wilmington said. Their eyes met in mutual dislike. "I've made my share of mistakes."

"I've asked Eric not to approach Maggie." Carrinne stepped between them. "Not until the time is right to tell her about her father. Give me your word you won't contact her either."

"Of course." Oliver said absently, staring at Eric as if two decades later he still couldn't process the fact that a Rivers had been his granddaughter's lover, was his great-grandchild's father. Then he pinned his attention on Carrinne. "If that's what it takes to get you to let an old man see his great-granddaughter, so be it."

"Stop it, Oliver." Carrinne crossed her arms. "Whatever guilt you're trying to play on doesn't exist anymore. You've had years to get to know Maggie. Finding us would have been as easy as having one of your lackeys track me down. I'm in the phone book. I run a very public business."

"Yes, I wasted a lot of years. But now I'm old and dying. Facing one's mortality can change your perspective. But you already know that, don't you, my dear?" His smile was oddly sympathetic as he looked between Carrinne and Eric. "Perhaps we have more in common than either one of us thought."

Carrinne shook her head, her mouth opening in mute silence. She turned from them both. Yanking the door open, she rushed into the hall.

"Has she found her mother's diary?" The old man's everyday scowl deepened. "Any leads on her father?"

"No, not yet." Eric headed to the door to follow Carrinne. "But we're still looking."

"She's kept your daughter from you for sixteen years. Why are you still helping her?" Oliver's question stopped Eric at the door. "Because you love her?"

Eric shook his head, wishing everyone including himself would stop asking that question.

"Because I don't want my daughter to have to watch her mother die," he replied, knowing he was lying. No way was it as simple as that.

Wilmington's chuckle kicked into a coughing spasm. He gazed out the room's tinted window. "You sound like me all these years. I've done my best to convince myself that I didn't need love in my life anymore. I didn't need my daughter. My granddaughter. That losing my family didn't destroy me."

"You don't know what you're talking about." Eric headed toward the bank of elevators, the truth in Wilmington's words resonating too deep to shake.

Love. A man like Oliver Wilmington didn't know the first thing about love and family. But then again, Eric had thought the same thing about himself as little as two days ago. He wasn't the sticking kind, he'd reasoned. Losing first his mother and father, then destroying his relationship with Carrinne had taught Eric that loving and losing went hand-in-hand. So he didn't play the game anymore, because losing just hurt too damn much.

So why did every minute with Carrinne, every step she took away from him, feel like he was watching the one thing he needed most in the world slip right through his fingers?

CHAPTER ELEVEN

AFTER SEARCHING the hallways near Oliver Wilmington's room, Eric remembered Carrinne's checkup with Dr. Burns. He needed to get to the station to interrogate Brimsley, but he couldn't leave. Not until he was sure Carrinne was okay.

He found her huddled alone in the corner of the half-empty ER waiting area. She should have been elated. They had Brimsley in custody. She was safe now, and they were free to focus all their efforts on finding her father. But instead, she sat with her hands clenched in her lap, confusion and pain swimming in her eyes.

He sat on the small couch beside her chair, regretting each bitter word he'd said to her that morning.

"Oliver's right," she said, sensing him even though she didn't look up. "I'm no better than he is."

"You're nothing like that empty shell of a man upstairs."

"How can you say that after what I've done to you and Maggie?"

"You were frightened." He grasped her hand.

"I was a coward."

Carrinne felt cold from the inside out. She drew her legs beneath her and curled her arms around her chest.

It was almost overwhelming, her need to collapse into Eric's arms.

Facing one's mortality can change your perspective... Perhaps we have more in common than either one of us thought.

She looked up to see Eric's eyes fill with a concern she didn't deserve. "I've always prided myself on being an honest person. But when push came to shove, I was all too willing to manipulate you and the situation, even our daughter's future happiness. And I've used the fact that I might be...that I might be dying to rationalize every lie I've told you. All I really wanted was to have my own way. Just like my grandfather."

"Carrinne, don't—"

"How can you keep defending me?"

"Because I won't let you take the blame for everything that's happened, just because your grandfather fights dirty. I had a part in this, too."

"It was my choice to make—"

"Carrinne—"

"We have to tell her." This ended now. All the lies ended now.

"Who?" Eric blinked.

"Maggie. We have to tell her. Before this goes any further. Before any more damage is done."

"But what about your illness?" Carrinne's incredible

green eyes glazed with moisture. "She's already dealing with a lot, without throwing me into the mix."

Carrinne fumbled inside her bag for her wallet. She removed the picture of Maggie and placed it in his palm, their shared concern for their daughter a beautiful thing in her very dark world. "You're not something to deal with, Eric. You're her father. You're the best father I could have imagined for Maggie, and she's going to need you so very much. We can't damage that by waiting to tell her. You wanted her from the moment you found out about her, and she needs to know that. Before long, she may need you even more."

"Carrinne, don't talk like that."

Her rebel with a heart of gold.

He'd never let himself have love, had denied the power of his own feelings for so long and refused to risk his heart. It was going to be amazing, watching that magnificent heart thrive and shower their daughter with more happiness than she'd ever known.

"It's okay. I can say it now." She smiled through the fear. "I couldn't think of dying before. I couldn't bear the thought of leaving Maggie alone the way my mother left me after I killed her."

"You didn't kill your mother." His angry certainty was as immediate and uncompromising as it had been the one other time she'd said the truth out loud. He'd found her crying beside her mother's grave. It had been her sixteenth birthday.

She smiled again, knowing he was wrong. Loving

him for trying to spare her the truth. "I couldn't think of dying before, but now I can. Because you'll still be here loving Maggie, no matter what happens. Even if we don't find my father, I'm so glad I came back and found you."

In the blink of an eye, he'd pulled her into his arms. She clung as he locked her against him, his hand cradling her head to his chest. He lifted her into his lap, and she melted into the rightness of being in his arms.

His mouth covered hers, his need and hers sweeping her past, the pain of not knowing what the future held, into a world that existed only with Eric. His passion was her anchor, his strength calling her own. Being in his arms was the miracle she'd been missing, the promise that she was forever complete.

"Carrinne." His husky voice flamed straight through her.

She felt him shudder, felt him gathering himself to pull away. "No."

With a groan, he set her away from him, somehow managing to create distance while he still cradled her in his lap. His hands shook. His breath labored as if he'd run a mile.

"I need to get to the station and question Brimsley," he said.

Nodding, she mentally kicked herself. Forcing her arms to uncling themselves from around his neck, she inched away until she once again sat beside him. His hand rested on her knee as she smoothed the hair from her face and checked to see that, mercifully, no one seemed to have noticed them. "I need to finish looking through my mother's trunk."

Eric's expression hardened. "You have a checkup with Dr. Burns."

"I'm fine. I—"

"I have to go, but I'll pull a deputy over here if I need to. You're going to see your doctor."

Her brain revved up for a battle. But the concern etched across his troubled face stopped her. His bullying had never seemed so dear. "Why do you have to keep being so nice to me?"

"I can't seem to help myself."

She couldn't help herself either. She gave him a soft, lingering kiss. "I'll see the doctor. I promise."

They stood together, his hand supporting her lower back. He tried to hand the picture back.

"Keep it." She smoothed a wrinkle from his shirt. "It's yours."

"I'll pick you up later at Oliver's." He put the picture in his pocket, then drew her hand from his chest and kissed it.

"And tonight," she replied against a surge of longing, "we'll call our daughter together."

MAGGIE WILMINGTON stepped off the small commuter plane at the Oakwood municipal airport and pushed her bangs from her eyes. Early afternoon heat rolled off the paved runway, blasting her with more Southern welcome than she'd bargained for.

Nowhere, she thought to herself as she dropped her backpack to the ground. Her mom had grown up in south Georgia nowhere. The view from the plane had revealed an area so rural, it amazed her there was an airstrip within a hundred miles of the place.

She followed the two other passengers as they trudged through the sweltering heat toward the only building in sight. The small building turned out to be the terminal. The other passengers had people waiting to pick them up, and soon Maggie found herself alone, except for an elderly woman behind the counter and a man napping in a nearby chair. He had a newspaper thrown over his head to block out the sunshine that streamed through the grime-covered windows.

She made her way to the counter. "Can you tell me where I can get a cab to take me into Oakwood?"

The woman eyed Maggie from behind silver-rimmed glasses studded with rhinestones and other fake jewels. "Where are your parents, honey?"

Maggie raised an eyebrow—the one pierced with three silver rings. "My mom's waiting for me in Oakwood. Is there a cab, or should I walk?"

"Gordon Willis's taxi service runs out here. But it'll take him thirty minutes, if he's not out doin' something else. Then another thirty to drive you back in. We could get you there quicker, but I reckon a ride into Oakwood'll cost you around twenty dollars. You got that kind of money?"

"Yes." Maggie waited, wondering if she was expected to cower beneath the woman's obvious skepticism. She took two different trains to get to and from high school each day. And if the traffic and weather were bad enough, cab rides in New York could hit twenty bucks before you'd gone five blocks.

The only thing that worried her at the moment was that she was melting in the black leather pants she'd thrown on with her tank top that morning. It must be over ninety degrees outside. And whatever they were using for air-conditioning in the terminal had probably gasped its last breath years before she was born.

"Harlen," the woman called out. "Got you a ride into Oakwood."

The sleeping man half falling out of his chair startled awake. He shoved aside the newspaper, revealing a face full of whiskers. "Huh…what the heck are you doing waking me up, woman?"

"Get on up out of that chair, Harlen, and give this girl a ride into town. She's supposed to be meeting her momma." She peered closer through her fifties rock-and-roll glasses. "What did you say your name was, honey?"

"I didn't." Maggie lifted her backpack and turned to the driver, who was now on his feet and wiping sleep from eyes that, thank goodness, didn't look hungover. He was mumbling something about God cursing men when he invented the institution of marriage.

"Where's your cab?" she asked.

"No cab. Just a station wagon we use for errands every now and again." He looked to the floor behind her. "Where's your suitcase?"

"I only have one bag." She jostled the backpack and headed for the front of the tiny building. "And I'm in a hurry."

"Anything you want from town?" the man asked the woman at the counter, who must have been his wife. He passed Maggie and held open the less than sturdy door leading outside.

"You could stop by the cleaners," the woman replied.

Outside, breathing the heavy, too-hot air once more, Maggie waited by the only car in sight, automatically assuming it was locked. Harlen opened her door without a key, shutting it behind her after she'd settled onto the cracked vinyl seat. He slipped behind the wheel, started the ignition and blasted the rattling air conditioner. To her happy surprise, waves of cold air washed through the car as they pulled onto the rural highway beside the airstrip.

"Where to?" He eyed her through the rearview mirror.

"The Econo Lodge on Route 60. And if my mom's not there, I'll need you to take me somewhere else. Would you mind waiting?"

"No problem. It's your money. You do have money, right?"

She gave him a disbelieving look, shook her head, and pulled her wallet from her backpack. She handed him the twenty dollars his wife had mentioned. "So can you wait a few minutes once we get there or not?"

"Sure, I can wait." He tucked the bill in his shirt pocket, peering even harder into the mirror.

Maggie ignored him, content to count the cows lounging in every sun-scorched field they passed.

"Any idea where you're going next?" he asked.

"I need to find someone named Wilmington. My mom's visiting family down here, but I don't know much more than that."

"Oliver Wilmington?"

She shrugged. "Maybe."

"No other Wilmingtons in these parts. You say you're family?"

Another shrug. "It's my last name, too. And my mom grew up here."

"Well, I'll be."

Maggie looked up to see his eyes widen, flick to the highway, then back to her reflection.

"Is there a problem?" Her mom had said that Oakwood was the kind of small town where everyone thought they had the right to know everyone else's business. Unlike New York City, where the wall-to-wall people and buildings made keeping up with your own stuff more time consuming than most people could handle.

"No, no problem." His attention returned to the road. "It'll be about fifteen minutes before we get to the motel."

"Fine." Maggie dug her sunglasses and a stick of chewing gum from her backpack. Slipping on the glasses, which were the same shade of magenta as the streaks in her hair, she popped the gum into her mouth and focused on the miles of green farmland rolling by.

Her mom loved green things. Had always kept enough plants in their tiny East Village apartment to fill a hothouse. She'd learned to grow things as a little girl, she'd said, because the climate in the South was almost seasonless. Seasonless evidently meant blazing hot.

Maggie tried to picture her stylish, city-smart mother growing up in a place like this. In spite of the argument she knew awaited her, she was actually looking forward to witnessing her mom's flashback to her small-town, *Gone With the Wind* roots.

CHAPTER TWELVE

CARRINNE STRUGGLED to focus, to pay attention as she shifted through the few remaining things in her mother's trunk.

She'd gotten the go-ahead on her concussion from Dr. Burns, and the doctor's assurance that her enzyme levels were fine. The antibiotic he'd prescribed was definitely tackling the infection, because her body temperature was completely normal. Calvin had driven her back here, so she could get to work—not that sitting around in a stupor was doing a darned bit of good. She'd phoned Eric with the good news about her condition, and the relief in his voice, the sincerity of his "Thank God," had addled her to a state of uselessness.

He cared about her. Despite everything, Eric still cared. And tonight they'd call Maggie together. Carrinne wasn't looking forward to facing her daughter's anger and confusion. But it would be a beginning for Maggie and Eric. Maybe for them all.

When she reached the bottom of the trunk, panic started building in earnest. She'd found several diaries, their entries poignant and hopeful, a young girl's private thoughts and dreams. But no sign of the diary from her mother's sixteenth year. She was at the end of her search with nothing to show for it.

Eric and his team would keep digging, she reminded herself. She wasn't facing this alone anymore. If her father was alive, if there was any way to find him, together she and Eric would make sure it happened.

Together.

Never a warm and fuzzy concept for her in the past, that simple word had become a dream she hadn't realized she could still dream. But seeing how much Eric cared about their daughter, about her, tempted Carrinne with thoughts of a future together. Shivering, she sidestepped the jumble of questions surrounding Eric and Maggie, and where they went from here. She had to focus on finding her mother's diary. Where could it be?

There wasn't a stick of furniture in this house she hadn't scoured as a child, nothing that had escaped her scrutiny except the contents of her mother's closet, now in this trunk. The diary had to be here somewhere. Her attention was drawn to the doll she'd dropped that morning. She lifted it, rubbing her fingertips across the shattered face.

"Calvin and I are ready to head out," Nina said from the doorway. "It's after six, and we have choir rehearsal at the church. Robert offered to stay on until you're done."

Carrinne looked up from the pieces of her mother's favorite doll. "Thanks Nina. I won't be much longer."

"Oh, you found Annie." Nina knelt on the floor, taking the doll from Carrinne's hands. "How your momma loved this doll. I believe it belonged to her mother, but that was before my time."

"Maybe if it can be repaired, I can give it to…to my daughter some day." Emotions rushed Carrinne. She was so tired of fighting them back.

"I'd like to think of you having a child of your own, a family. And your momma would have loved the thought of Annie going to her granddaughter. When she was a child, she dragged that doll with her everywhere she went. It was almost as big as she was. And she kept her by her bedside even when she was grown."

Everywhere she went.

Carrinne smoothed the emerald satin fabric of the doll's dress. Surely the face could be repaired. It was just a doll, but it had meant so much to her mother. Just like her diaries, she'd always had Annie by her side. Carrinne wanted to keep her close, too.

Just like her diaries.

Everywhere she went.

A harsh sound of hope was all she could muster as she took the doll from Nina and turned her over.

It couldn't be.

Her fingers made quick work of the dress's delicate fastenings. Patience born only of knowing how much Annie had meant to her mother kept her movements soft and deliberate. Finally, she eased the material free of the doll's arms and shoulders and inched it down her back.

Please, she prayed. Let her be right.

And there it was. A secret compartment, latched with a tiny gold hook. Large enough, because of the doll's size, to hold a small book.

"Oh my God." She smiled at Nina, then hugged her. "Do you know what this could mean?"

Nina's face was a study in surprise and hope. "It don't mean nothing until you open it up, girl. Go ahead. You've waited for this moment your whole life."

Laughing, she stared at the half-dressed doll. Finally this close, and she was almost afraid to look. She stopped breathing altogether as she reached for the clasp. It slid loose as if it had just been latched, and Carrinne carefully pulled open the delicately hinged door.

"I'M TELLING YOU, I don't know anything about her accident." Brimsley glowered at Eric.

They were sitting in the same interview room where he and Tony had met with Carrinne just two days ago. Eric had changed into his uniform as soon as he returned to the station. A subtle but effective reminder that this was business, not personal.

"The charge nurse on Oliver Wilmington's floor says you and Carrinne had an altercation when Carrinne arrived at the hospital yesterday."

"Yes, she picked a fight with me. That doesn't prove a thing."

Eric glanced at Tony. He'd asked his brother to sit in. He was relatively confident he could keep his hands off Brimsley, but the man was as slimy as low-country attorneys came. This interview was going to be by the book.

"We have the nurse's statement that you stormed away from Carrinne no more than fifteen minutes before someone plowed into her. We have a videotape of a man your size, hiding behind dark glasses and a hat, following Carrinne's car in a van we've now recovered. And we have your testimony that you threatened her this morning. You told her to, 'Get out now, or next time I'll do more than wreck your car.'"

"Yes, I said that to try and scare her out of town. But as soon as I left Ms. Wilmington yesterday, I made a long-distance conference call. I sat in the hospital lobby, on my cell phone, for over an hour. In fact, I watched Ms. Wilmington leave."

"We're already running your phone records." Eric didn't like the man's relaxed certainty. If he was lying, he was smoother than even Eric gave him credit for.

"Be my guest."

"You could very easily have left your phone on an open line while you followed Carrinne. You're smart enough to create an alibi like that for yourself."

"I suppose." Brimsley smiled with mock helpfulness. "But I didn't. I'd advise you to take my word for it."

"You're a smug bastard."

"And you're behind the eight ball. The most you've got me on is a harassment charge, and you're about eighty percent sure I'm telling you the truth. That means you're back to square one." He gave Eric a solemn nod. "Tough break, son."

Eric had lifted Brimsley from his chair before he even realized he'd moved. "You're going away for embezzlement. And if I find you lifted a finger to hurt Carrinne, you'll get the chance to see just how tough a break it is."

Brimsley blanched. "Take your hands off me, Rivers. You're on thin ice already, after that display at the hospital. I'll hit you with police brutality charges so fast—"

"What display?" Tony didn't move a muscle. "I saw a textbook arrest."

Eric smiled as sweat trickled down Brimsley's face. He released the man slowly, letting him drop back into his chair. Leaning forward, he got as far into the man's face as he could stomach. "You better pray I don't find anything to tie you to Carrinne's accident."

He left Tony to handle returning Brimsley to his cell. A disturbing voice in his head whispered not to completely discount what the lawyer had said. What if Brimsley was telling the truth?

Angie was waiting for him in the hall. "The prints we lifted from the pay phone match the ones we took when we booked the lawyer for embezzlement."

"We already know he made the call," Eric responded with more sarcasm than he'd intended.

"Yeah, but it doesn't figure." Angie worried her bottom lip between her teeth.

"What?"

"That he's the one who hit Carrinne's car. Brimsley's a sneak and he's a coward. It was a stupid move, calling her from a local phone. A rookie mistake. But we've got nothing from the van. No fiber, no prints, nothing. Why would the man do such a thorough job of covering his tracks yesterday, then blow it on that phone call this morning?"

"Well, hell," Eric muttered, brushing past her and heading outside.

"There's a message for you." She held up a slip of paper.

"Leave it on my desk. I need a few minutes."

"It's from Carrinne." Angie smiled when he skidded to a halt and returned to her side in two quick steps. "She said something about a diary. She's on her way over."

"THIS IS THE PLACE," the driver announced as he parked the station wagon in front of a gray brick mansion.

Maggie chewed on her thumbnail. She'd been nervous but cool during the flight down here. No big deal. She'd flown with her mom to business conferences for years. And even though she had to face the music once she found her mom, she hadn't worried too much about that either. But arriving at the motel to discover that her mother had checked out last night, leaving no word as to where she was going or if she planned on staying in Oakwood, had given Maggie plenty to worry about.

The so-friendly-he-was-weird clerk had said something about her mom wrecking her rental car, and that

Maggie should check with the local sheriff, of all people. She'd tried calling her mother's cell, but all she got was voice mail.

Now Wilber, or Harlen, or whatever his name was had driven her to some kind of mansion that was supposed to belong to someone in her family. She and her mom had scraped by for years on an ultra-tight budget, clipping coupons and cutting every corner imaginable. Only recently had they been able to relax a bit and not count every penny they spent. No way did her mother come from money like this.

"If this is your stop," the driver prompted. "I've got to run by the cleaners before they close. It's clear on the other side of town."

Maggie stifled her unfriendly grunt. Clear on the other side of town must be all of half a mile. "Are you sure this is the only Wilmington in Oakwood?"

"The Wilmingtons have lived here since the town was started. Old man Wilmington's the last of them, I guess. His daughter died over thirty years ago, and his granddaughter ran away when she was just a teenager. I hear tell he had a stroke not too long back."

Maggie opened the door and stepped onto the curb. Her mom had left Oakwood when she was a teenager. This place had been her mother's home?

The lawn surrounding the house went on forever. And the trees. All different kinds. Unlimited shades of green. It was like staring at one of the entrances to Central Park.

"You sure you don't want me to wait?" The driver checked his watch, then peered at the house through his open window. "Doesn't look much like anyone's home."

"No, I'll be fine." She pulled her backpack from the seat and shut the door. "Worst case, I'll just walk to the sheriff's office. Which way is it?"

He scratched his head and pointed his thumb down the street. "Take your first two lefts, and when you hit Crabapple go right a quarter mile or so. You sure you want to walk all that way?"

"Sure, no sweat." She walked longer than that to change from the seven train to the four in Grand Central Station. She reached into her pack for her wallet. "How much more do I owe you for the extra ride?"

"Ah. No problem. It's all part of the service." He smiled, looking beyond her to the quiet house. "You just take good care of yourself. Hope you find your momma real soon."

She watched him pull away, then headed up the long driveway. A winding sidewalk took her to a porch that was almost as wide as her entire apartment. She rang the doorbell and peered through the frosted glass that made up the top half of the door. She saw no movement, not a single light. She rang a few more times, finally giving up and stepping back to the edge of the porch.

How could her mom have lived in a place like this and never said a word? And if she had this kind of money, why run away to a strange city to have a baby on her own, all for the privilege of living month-to-month and never being sure she could make the rent? And what had that guy said about a grandfather, Maggie's great-grandfather?

Half worried, more than half pissed off, she tried her mom's cell again and was once more rolled to the voice mail. What the hell was going on?

CHAPTER THIRTEEN

WHEN CARRINNE hadn't been able to reach Eric on the phone, Calvin and Nina had offered to drop her at the Sheriff's Department on their way to church. Sitting in the back seat of their Buick, she thumbed through the pages of her mother's last diary. Excitement and a craving to read everything at once glued her to each word. She was so absorbed, she didn't realize they'd arrived at the station until Nina turned from the front seat and patted her knee.

"Thank you so much for the ride." She reached for her purse, only to realize it wasn't there. She must have left it in the study in her hurry to get the diary to Eric. "I hope I haven't made you late."

"Don't you worry about it, honey." Nina smiled, and so did her husband. "Watching you find what you were looking for has done our hearts good. We'll be singing like the angels tonight. Do you think you have what you need to find your father now?"

"I hope so." She squeezed Nina's hand, grateful for her help and a lifetime of friendship. "I hope so."

She hugged the diary close, making sure not to lose her place as she stepped out of the car. She'd only looked at the earlier entries so far, hadn't let herself delve into the ones toward the end. The ones right before her death, when her mother was pregnant. As precious as they would be, Carrinne knew she didn't want to be alone when she read them.

She could handle reading through the diary without Eric. She'd proven to herself and the world she could handle anything. But she didn't want just to *handle* this. This chance for healing, this opportunity for closure, was too precious. She wanted Eric's solid strength beside her as she read each bittersweet word and put the shadows of her past to rest.

The station door swung open as she reached for it, and Eric materialized before her. He smiled and opened his arms, and she rushed straight into them without a second's hesitation. Snuggling into the solid feel of him, she felt laughter bubble up and tumble free. Tears misted her eyes as he tilted her chin and brought his mouth to hers in a quick kiss.

"You found it?" he asked.

"In the doll." She wiped her eyes, smiling like an idiot and still laughing. "It was in my mother's doll all this time."

"Have you read any of it yet?"

"Only some of the beginning. I wanted to wait until we were together before looking at the rest." She felt his arms tighten at her words. Caressing his cheek, losing her soul in the tenderness swirling in his eyes, she kissed him softly. "I wanted to read it with you."

He pulled her against his side, and they walked into the station. She realized he'd changed into his uniform since she'd seen him at the hospital.

"How did it go with Brimsley?" she asked as they entered a large conference room.

"He's admitted to making the call this morning, but he has a flimsy alibi for yesterday." Eric guided her to a chair. Gus waved from where he sat behind a computer.

"What does that mean?" she asked, not sure she'd heard Eric right.

"It means we're looking into his story. And until we know more, he's still our chief suspect in your accident."

"But he may not have done it?"

Eric sat beside her. "No. It may not have been Brimsley."

He was worried, she could tell. She took a deep breath, telling herself not to panic. If Eric was on top of it, she was in good hands. She had to stay focused on finding her father.

"Here it is." She placed the diary on the table, sliding it in front of him.

He rubbed his fingers over the cracked cover and gave her a hesitant look. He opened to the first page. She scooted her chair closer.

"Mind if I look over your shoulder?" Gus said from behind them.

Actually she did. She asked Eric with her eyes if it was necessary.

"He's been researching your mom all day," Eric explained. "He might see something we don't."

She held onto a moment's hesitation, then surrendered to his logic.

"Of course." She hoped her smile to Gus was more welcoming than she felt. "I appreciate your help."

Her mother's private thoughts seemed too personal, somehow. Too intimate to share. But this was business, she reminded herself. Later she would reread each word for pleasure.

Eric scanned the first few pages filled with soft, girlish handwriting. All curls and gentle arcs. It was a one-year, pre-dated diary, and the entries began when her mother started her senior year in high school.

"Here we go," he said.

September 10, 1969.
My senior year began today…

Together, they scanned the wandering descriptions of dances and parties. Boyfriends and crushes. No one steady, nothing out of the ordinary. In January, she won first place at the county horse show and penned a rough sketch of Holiday to commemorate the moment.

Father was so proud. We celebrated at Buddy's on the way home. We devoured milk shakes and fries until I thought we'd pop!

Carrinne tried to imagine it. Her grandfather as a younger man, celebrating at the local hangout. Beaming with pride while he ate junk food with his sixteen-year-old daughter. Spending time with her. Giving her a piece of himself that had nothing to do with money and control. The man described in these pages had stopped living after Angelica's death, after Carrinne was born.

Eric was no longer thumbing through the pages. His stillness pulled Carrinne from her thoughts.

"The entries stop in early February," he said. He skipped forward through the blank, pre-dated pages.

"They start up again in March." Gus pointed over Eric's shoulder to the next entry.

But rather than the date, Carrinne couldn't tear her eyes away from the change in her mother's handwriting. In place of the happy swirls and dips were jagged, stark lines, written by a shaking, hesitant hand that before had been smooth and certain.

March 17, 1970.
My worst nightmares are true. He swore he'd kill me and my father if I told, but my secret won't be mine to keep much longer. Dr. Hamilton confirmed it today. I'm seven weeks pregnant.

Carrinne snatched the book from Eric, frantically re-reading the entry, desperate for it to say something other than what it did. *My worst nightmares are true...he'd kill me and my father...I'm seven weeks pregnant.*

"What...what does this mean?" She flipped forward, scanning, searching for the handwriting of the happy girl who'd dreamed of boys and horses. Instead, each harshly penned word reflected fear and despair. Until finally...

April 26, 1970.
Starting to show. Can't keep anything in my stomach. Father's threatening to take me to the hospital. I have to tell him. But how? I have to protect him and my precious baby from the man who raped me.

Raped me.
Raped me.
The words echoed through Carrinne's mind. She staggered out of her chair, barely hearing Eric's shout. She was already running out the door. Dizzy, disoriented, she searched for the bathroom, the contents of her stomach rolling and lurching upward.

Raped me.
Raped me.
Waiting no longer an option, she dropped to the floor beside a trashcan in a blessedly empty room and retched up everything she'd eaten since that morning. She wished the earth would open up and swallow her to its core.

Her poor mother. Raped. At sixteen. A hand cradled

her head. Her hair was pulled back from her face. Dimly, she became aware that it was Eric leaning over her, supporting her as she continued to heave, even though her stomach had long since emptied itself.

She was the product of rape. The father she was searching for, the man she'd thought might be her savior, had violated her mother, and ultimately was responsible for Angelica Wilmington's death and Carrinne's life.

"Drink this," Eric said as her stomach quieted, her brain going numb rather than facing the truth. He sat on the floor behind her and pulled her into his lap.

She couldn't stop shaking. The water he fed her choked going down and dribbled from her chin. Sputtering, gasping for air and a way out of the nightmare closing in on her, she shoved against his chest.

"Let me go," she cried when she wanted to scream. "Don't touch me."

She tried to stand, to run, but she couldn't stumble to her feet.

"Shh," Eric murmured. He curled Carrinne against him once more and prayed it was enough. He kissed her temple and held her as she sobbed. He might never let her go again.

Sitting with her on the floor of the break room, he searched for the right words to say. But there was nothing. Nothing on earth that could ease the crushing reality of what Carrinne had just read. She'd been overjoyed, thinking she was close to her miracle. She'd brought the diary to him, so they could be together when they read the truth that would mean so much to her and their daughter. He'd seen the first shining rays of hope on her face, then he'd watched the horror of her mother's secret reduce every last flicker to agony.

As her quiet sobs continued, he fought back his own fear. Fear for what this would do to the determination and grit that kept her going. Fear for what this meant about the person who'd tried to hurt her yesterday. He couldn't move past the thought that whoever had raped and threatened her mother was the one now threatening Carrinne. She was looking for her father, and he didn't want to be found.

It could be a bizarre coincidence. But he knew it wasn't. If only it could be that simple. His hands fisted against Carrinne's back. When he found the bastard responsible for this, he was going to rip his head off.

He looked over the top of her head to find Tony and Gus in the break room's open doorway. Gus was quietly filling Tony in on what they'd discovered. Tony looked to where Eric cradled Carrinne, his eyes blazing with both anger and the kind of protective tenderness that made Eric prouder of his brother than he'd ever been.

Carrinne's body grew limp in his lap, even though tremors still shook her, tears still rained down her cheeks. He lifted her face so he could look into her eyes, flinching as he gazed into their lost, terrified depths. Her skin was cold with shock, despite the station's constant eighty-degree temperature. He felt her wrist—her pulse was too fast and erratic.

"What can I do?" Tony crouched beside them.

Eric soothed his hand over Carrinne's back, torn between instinct and responsibility. He wanted to take her home and hold her, to be there for her all night as she assimilated the kind of news no one deserved to hear. But for her sake, he needed to get back to the diary. Needed to dig for answers in the few entries after the ones Carrinne had read. They had to find out who her father was, now more than ever.

"Pull your car around," he said to Tony. "I need you to take Carrinne back to the house and stay with her while I figure out what the hell's going on. She's supposed to be taking it easy. This kind of shock can't be good for her."

Tony gave Carrinne's arm a gentle pat, then he headed to get his car.

"Gus, go find me a blanket." Eric picked Carrinne up as he stood.

She clung to his shoulders. Her eyes were open and unfocused, blinking slowly every now and then. Gus handed him a blanket as they reached the front of the almost-empty building. Thankfully by this time of night on a Sunday, everyone who wasn't on watch had left for home hours ago.

Tony pulled to a stop next to the entrance. He jogged around the car and opened the passenger door to the back seat. Carrinne stirred and struggled when Eric settled her against the seat cushions.

"Shh." He soothed the hair from her face, waiting for

her eyes to focus on him before he continued. She didn't utter a word. "Tony's taking you home for a little while. You won't be alone. I'll be there as soon as I can."

He tucked the blanket around her as she leaned back, wishing he was still holding her in his arms.

"Call me and let me know how she's doing," he said as Tony shut the door and headed back around the car. If she didn't snap out of this soon, he'd have Tony take her back to the hospital.

He watched until the squad car disappeared around the corner, then turned to head back in. Gus was standing beside him.

"Hell of a way for her to find out something like that," the detective said.

Eric grunted as he stepped around the man. "Is there a good way to find out that you're the product of your mother's rape?"

"Excuse me," a voice called from the other side of the parking lot. "Can you tell me where I can find the sheriff?"

Eric, who already had the door open, looked over his shoulder to see who had spoken. Gus was in the way, so he waved the other man inside. He stepped forward to dispense with whatever small-town problem he didn't have time to deal with.

Before him stood the kind of tough teenager you saw in movies about urban America. She was a natural beauty in leather pants and a skin-tight top, with purple-streaked hair and a pierced eyebrow. She carried a canvas backpack over one shoulder, and he could have sworn the other boasted a tattoo in the shape of a cartoon character. She was smacking gum, and she was the most beautiful sight he had ever seen.

"Are you the sheriff?" his daughter asked, peeling off her purple sunglasses to look back at him with his own eyes.

Her bored expression sharpened the longer she looked, then her mouthed dropped open. Purple, his brain registered. Her gum was purple, too. Then her can't-touch-me expression crumbled into the face of a frightened, confused sixteen-year-old.

"Oh my God," she said, a split second before she turned and bolted back across the parking lot.

Eric sprinted after her, grabbing her as gently as he could considering she was fighting like a heavyweight to get away from him.

"Let me go, you son of a bitch." She squirmed and kicked, jabbing him with an elbow, then, when Eric managed to turn her to face him, an impressive right hook.

"That's enough," he growled, locking his daughter's hands behind her, then anchoring her to his side so the army boots she was using as lethal weapons wouldn't do as much damage. But that didn't stop her from trying. "Hold still for a minute, will you."

"Good afternoon, Sheriff," Mrs. Miller said. She and Mrs. Davis stood staring from the sidewalk just a few feet away.

"Afternoon, ladies." He smiled, then turned and marched Maggie toward the station.

"Let go of me, or I'm going to scream bloody murder." Just like her mom, Maggie was as tough as they came. But each angry word was laced with the sound of tears. A sound that made Eric want to scream himself.

"I'll let you go." He loosened his grasp only slightly, testing her. He looked behind them, gratified to find his nosy neighbor and her friend had moved on. "If you promise not to run again, and if you promise to keep it down."

A quick nod of her head was the only answer Maggie gave. But it was good enough. Eric let go of her completely. She stepped away, rubbing her arms where he'd held her. He raised his hand to his jaw, gingerly feeling where her fist had connected with bone.

"You…you're my…" She swallowed instead of finishing.

"Yes, I am," he answered, holding back every instinct that demanded he pull her close again. He didn't think his chin, or his shins, could take round two. "How did you know?"

Her eyes narrowed, betrayal eating away at the sheen of tears. She dropped the backpack that looked as if it must weigh thirty pounds and rummaged inside the front pocket. She withdrew a plastic-covered photograph, almost shoving it into his hand.

"This is the only picture I have. My mom told me you were dead."

Eric looked down at a photo of himself when he was

a teenager. His scowl said he hated the small town he'd grown up in, the bike he was sitting on said he was getting the hell out as fast as he possibly could. It was the same bike that had stood untouched in his garage since that last ride with Carrinne seventeen years ago. The picture's laminated covering was worn and wrinkled. It had clearly been handled often, carried from place to place by someone who treasured it. Someone who was clinging to the only tangible link she had to a father she'd never known.

He looked at his daughter, understanding too late all that Carrinne had feared. There was no easy way to explain how things had gotten so mixed up. This wasn't something that a quick hug and a so-glad-to-finally-meet-you could fix. The truth was the only thing he had to give Maggie, even if he should probably wait until he and Carrinne were together. He reached into the shirt pocket of his uniform and pulled out his daughter's picture.

"Your mom gave me this earlier today." He handed her the photo, watching for every nuance of reaction. "I had no idea…I never knew."

Maggie looked at the photo, then back to him, something in her manner subtly shifting. She took a step closer, then stopped and pulled herself upright.

"Why? Why the lies?" She crumpled the picture in her hand, making him wince. "Why would she do something like this?"

"That's something I think you ought to let your mom explain." Instincts told him to tread carefully. "What I *can* tell you is that she had a lot of good reasons, a lot of them dealing with me."

"What did you do?"

"Nothing." He jammed his hands in his pockets and shrugged. "That's the problem."

"I don't understand." Her forehead crinkled exactly the way Carrinne's did when she was concentrating.

"I know." He reached to pat her shoulder, and when she didn't flinch away, he completed the motion. She was solid, and sturdy, and all girl, all at the same time. How could anything that looked so much like him and Tony be so beautiful? "It's too complicated for me to explain by myself. All you need to know right now is that from the moment I found out about you, I've wanted to talk to you, to get to know you, to find out everything I've missed. God, you have no idea how sorry I am I missed it all."

She gazed up at him, her eyes searching. "Are you married? Do you have other kids?"

"No, on both counts." He forced himself to keep the surreal conversation going. Picking up her backpack, he started toward the building, grateful when she fell hesitantly in step beside him. "But I did raise my kid brother. He's twenty-three now. He still lives with me."

"Where's my mom?" Maggie asked when they stopped outside the entrance. "Is she all right? The creep at the motel said something about an accident with her rental car."

Eric hesitated, knowing the details should come from

Carrinne. "Yes, there was an accident, but she's fine. Although she's pretty upset right now. Something tells me she's going to be really glad to see you. I'll take you over to her as soon as I wrap up a few things here."

"She's sick you know." Maggie picked at her thumbnail, then brought her hand to her mouth so she could chew on the jagged edge. "That's why she came back here. At least that's the story she gave me."

"Yeah, she told me." He cupped his daughter's cheek, his touch tentative, testing. "I know how sick your mom is. I'm trying to help her find the donor she needs."

Maggie stood there, looking up at him, giving him the best present anyone had ever given him when she didn't move away from his touch. She blinked, and the tough-kid act disappeared into a sixteen-year-old vulnerability that made his knees shake.

"Did you love her?" she asked. "Did you love my mom?"

Looking down at his daughter, at the personification of everything he'd thought he would never want, could never have, Eric found himself on the edge of a cliff. Calmly, without even wanting to look back, he stepped off.

"Yeah," he said, squeezing her shoulder again when what he really wanted was to pull her into a hug that would most likely scare her to death. "I really think I did."

CHAPTER FOURTEEN

"I'VE ALREADY LOOKED through the last of the entries, son." Gus pushed his hands in his back pockets and shook his head at Eric. "She never names the man who raped her. Probably worried someone might find the diary and read it. She must have really believed the man would come back and hurt her or her family. You say Ms. Wilmington found it hidden in a doll?"

"Yeah. One Angelica Wilmington supposedly kept by her bed." Eric cast a quick glance to the other end of the conference room. Maggie was sitting there, just as she had been since they came inside ten minutes ago. The bored look on her face threatened to become a permanent fixture. He needed to get her to Carrinne.

"Well, if you ask me," Gus continued, "your lady friend's lucky to have found this out now."

"She's not my lady friend." Eric shot another pointed look at Maggie. When they'd walked into the conference room, he'd introduced her to Gus as Carrinne's daughter. "And I wouldn't call what just happened to Carrinne lucky."

"Hell, I know it was a blow." Gus glanced at Maggie and lowered his voice. "But at least she can head on back to New York and put this whole business about finding her daddy behind her. Can't imagine she'd still want to meet the man. She's better off letting us look for him and forgetting the whole thing. This guy could very likely be the one who tried to hurt her yesterday."

"Don't you think I've thought of that?" Eric lowered his voice even more, in the unlikely event Maggie was actually listening. "But Carrinne can't forget about finding him. She needs a blood relative to be a living organ donor. It's a matter of life or death."

"What? Is the kid sick?" Gus's expression darkened.

"No. Carrinne is. She needs part of her dad's liver."

"Hell, man, do you have any idea how unlikely it is he would consent to helping her, assuming we did find him?"

"I know."

"And we don't have a whole lot to go on in the first place. Just a general idea of the time frame the assault happened and whatever we can piece together from our archives. I went over the diary entries pretty carefully. We ain't got squat."

"I know, but we have to keep looking." Eric refused to give up.

"You know," Gus said. His detective's gaze studied Eric. "I never could figure you tangling with old man Wilmington's granddaughter. Messing with people who have that kind of money, you're bound to get burned in the end."

Eric picked up the diary. "Trust me, Gus. Her money and her grandfather are the least of my worries."

With a grunt, Gus pointed to the diary. "Why don't you let me take another crack at that? I've got nowhere to be tonight."

Eric shook his head. "Carrinne may want to look at it once she calms down. I'll bring it back with me later tonight. In the meantime, check for any rapes or violent crimes in the area during the early seventies."

"Already in the works." Gus pointed his thumb toward the computer.

MAGGIE HAD BEEN SITTING in the cramped conference room for almost twenty minutes, watching Oakwood's sheriff—her dad—talk with some old guy.

What choice did she have? The man still had her backpack, and she wasn't stupid enough to think she could wrestle it away from him. Besides, he'd said he'd take her to her mom. Saving her temper tantrum for her mother was at least some consolation.

A part of her was too worried to be really mad. Her mom had been in a car accident, and it didn't sound like she was doing well. But there was another part of Maggie that couldn't forget the lies. All these years, she'd thought she had no father, that she and her mom were all alone in the world. Jeez, less than two hours in this nowhere town and she'd already stumbled across a great-grandfather and a father. What was next, an identical twin separated from her at birth and given to a hick cousin to raise?

And this trip. More lies. It was supposed to be about finding a liver donor. And maybe part of it was. But the first thing her mom had done was track down Maggie's dad and tell him she was sick, that he had a daughter he might have to take on one day soon, whether he wanted her or not.

Her mom made a lot of noise, always pretending to be optimistic about their chances of finding a donor. But Maggie had read the medical reports her mother hid in the bookcase. She could see the truth behind every one of her mom's hollow smiles. They were running out of options. Yet her mother refused to let Maggie do the one thing that could end the whole ordeal. And now she'd sneaked away to manufacture an eleventh-hour father, just in case things didn't work out.

"Ready to go?" The sheriff walked toward her, a weak-ass smile he no doubt thought would put her at ease creeping across his face.

Or maybe, the quiet, less pissed-off voice inside her reasoned, he's actually glad to see you. Maybe that goofy grin is the way fathers are supposed to look at teenage daughters who drop into their lives out of the blue. Or maybe, she beat the reasonable voice back into its box, he was panicking. Because he has no frickin' clue what to do, and he's trying to figure out the quickest way to get her and her mom on the next plane back to New York.

"Yeah." She slumped out of the chair and grabbed her backpack away from him. "I'm ready."

Carrinne huddled deeper into the corner of Eric's couch, cradling a steaming cup of tea. Tea that must have been part of Mrs. Davis's emergency rations. She couldn't picture Eric or Tony drinking the stuff. Tony had sweetly made it for her and had sat with her until the first wave of shock wore off. When she hadn't wanted to talk, he'd slipped back into the kitchen to see about dinner.

Grateful for the privacy, Carrinne held her untouched tea and listened to the pendulum clock on the wall tick the minutes away. On the outside she was still, unmoving. But nothing could quiet the screaming in her mind. Her dreams about her mother, her hopes of finding the father she'd never known, of him giving her and Maggie a second chance at life, all of it was gone. Not only was she responsible for her mother's death, she had been conceived in a violent act that had shattered the final months of her mother's life.

And still she couldn't stop searching for the rapist... Her father. If there was any chance he was alive... The thought of the man's liver growing inside her had her stomach rebelling again. But if it meant protecting Maggie from the agony of losing a parent, what choice did Carrinne have?

She needed to talk to her daughter. She'd planned to call with Eric tonight, to find some way to let Maggie know about her father, but she needed to hear Maggie's voice too badly to wait. Her cell was in her purse at

Oliver's, so she reached for the phone beside the couch.
The sound of a car pulling up the driveway stopped her.

"Eric's back," Tony called from the kitchen.

Her relief was so strong, she was dizzy with it. Eric
had needed to stay at the station to follow up on what
they'd found. She understood that. But that didn't change
how desperately she needed his arms around her again.

She pushed herself from the couch and told her legs
to take her to the kitchen. She made it to the kitchen
table in time to see Eric walking up the steps from the
driveway. She drank in the sight of his broad shoulders,
his troubled face. Then movement behind him signaled
he wasn't alone. A flash of purple and the sight of an
all-too-familiar backpack slung across Eric's shoulder
were her only warning before their daughter pushed
past him and came to a halt a few feet away.

"Maggie?" She flew to her daughter, nothing registering except the instinct to pull her baby close. But the
rigid body in Carrinne's arms communicated reality
with shocking speed.

She released her, and Maggie stepped stiffly away.
It was the first time Carrinne had seen betrayal and distrust in her daughter's eyes. She deserved every bit of
it, but it still broke her heart.

"How did you get here?" she asked, because it was
the first thing that came to her mind. "Does Kim know
you're here?"

"Kim thinks I'm working late at the Met on a history
project."

"But how—"

"I took two planes and a cab, all right? That's how." Maggie stood with her hands on her hips. "Who the hell cares *how* I got here, Mom?"

Carrinne couldn't find the words. Her glance begged Eric for help.

"Why don't we all sit down." He set the backpack in the corner. Laying her mother's diary on the kitchen table, he pulled out two chairs, sitting in a third. Tony, who'd been at the stove making what smelled like grilled cheese sandwiches, stepped to the table, silently staring between Maggie, Eric and Carrinne.

"Tony," Eric said. "This is Carrinne's daughter, Maggie."

Carrinne watched Tony study Maggie's features and coloring, her striking resemblance to both him and his brother.

"Carrinne's daughter?" he asked.

"Yes." Carrinne sat in one of the chairs while Maggie leaned against the refrigerator with a thump. "And she's Eric's daughter as well."

Tony let loose a low whistle and settled into a chair himself. He flashed Maggie a charming smile. "I guess that makes me your uncle Anthony."

Maggie gave him a smirk full of *Who cares?* and returned to staring holes through Carrinne.

"Honey, I don't want you to think badly of Eric—"

"He told me. At the station," Maggie said. "You've been lying to him all this time, too."

"Yes. I told him today. And as soon as he found out, he wanted to meet you. We were going to call you tonight."

"Right." Maggie nodded with overdone understanding. "Why put it off any longer."

"Maggie—"

"What, Mom?" The understanding disappeared. White-hot rage took its place. "Don't be upset? Don't make you feel bad for what you've done? Or are you going to tell me again how it's going to be okay?"

"No, I—"

"Because you're not honestly expecting me to buy all this, are you?" Maggie shoved away from the refrigerator, pain dripping from each angry word. "I mean, I'm a big girl. You can say whatever you want, but I see what's going on. You've lied to everyone for years. And now you think you can fly down here, tell this guy he's a father, put a happy face on everything, and somehow manufacture an instant family for me now that you're dying? Wake up, Mom. It's too late! Do you honestly expect him to turn handsprings because he's saddled with a teenage daughter he doesn't want?"

"No. That's not how it happened—"

"You're dying?" Tony croaked.

Eric's warning glance silenced his younger brother.

"Eric does want you." Carrinne stood and tried to pull her daughter into her arms. Maggie jerked away. Her elbow raked the refrigerator door, sending magnets flying. Carrinne eased away. "I'm sorry. I never planned for any of this to happen the way it has. Please let me explain."

"No. No more explanations. No more lies." Her daughter's eyes narrowed. She looked from Carrinne to Eric. "I hate you both."

She rushed out of the kitchen. Carrinne started to follow.

"Let me go." Eric stopped her with a touch on her arm. "She needs to hear this from me."

Nodding, even though everything in Carrinne ached to go herself, she watched Eric walk away. He deserved the chance to make this right with their daughter.

"He'll get through to her." Tony stepped to Carrinne's side. "He's a hell of a father, whether he wants to believe it or not."

The admiration and pride in Tony's voice earned him a fierce hug.

"Yes, he is," she agreed.

Busy. She needed to keep busy. She needed not to have to answer the swirl of questions in Tony's warm, concerned eyes. She glanced at her mother's diary, then looked away. She couldn't deal with that again tonight either.

"I need to let my friend Kim know Maggie's here," she finally said, reaching for the phone.

ERIC FOUND his daughter halfway up the stairs, mesmerized by the same pictures that had shocked her mother less than twenty-four hours ago.

"In case you were hoping there'd been some kind of mistake, this should pretty much seal the deal." He pulled a framed photo off the wall. In the picture, a fifteen-year-old Tony was holding a skateboard, grinning and giving the camera a thumbs-up. Eric hadn't seen his daughter smile yet, but he had a pretty good idea what it would look like. "You guys could be brother and sister, you look so much alike."

Maggie shrugged and started up the stairs. "So you're stuck with me. So what."

Eric followed, biding his time. Letting her be angry, because he'd learned with Tony that there was no use talking with kids until some of the anger had burned itself out. She kept glancing at the pictures as she passed, trying not to let him see she was looking.

"Your mom's room is on the right," he said when they reached the top. "We've got another bedroom down the hall, if you want one of your own."

"What is she doing here, anyway?" Maggie asked. At least she was still talking. "Why did she check out of her motel?"

"The doctor wanted someone to keep an eye on her for a few days. The accident banged her up pretty badly, and there were some side effects from her liver condition. I had to just about hog-tie her to get her out of that motel. Your mom doesn't like it when she can't have her own way."

"Tell me about it." The sound Maggie made was classic teenage scorn. Then he got a suspicious glance. "But why here? I've seen my great-grandfather's house. Why didn't she stay there?"

"Because she couldn't be left alone last night, and because she and your great-grandfather have never exactly gotten along. Tony and I are the only other people in Oakwood she knows very well."

Maggie glanced down the hall. "You and your brother live here alone?"

"Yeah, ever since my dad died when I was just about your age."

Bright, intelligent eyes swung back his way. "You were around my age when my mom got pregnant with me."

"So it would seem." Eric ran a hand through his hair, wishing he'd found some cozy, fatherly place to have this conversation. "I was pretty much a screwup back then, ready to hit the road once I graduated from high school, ready to blow this small town and get out on my own. Your mom, she was the only thing tying me here until my dad died."

Maggie was chewing her thumbnail again, still gazing around. Every few seconds her attention skirted back to him before bouncing away to study something else. Each time her eyes settled on his face, they stayed a little longer than before. It wasn't much, but he'd take whatever he could get.

Tired of standing at the top of the stairs, towering over his daughter and feeling like a jackass, he sat and stretched his feet down the steps, leaning back on his elbows.

"Then, all of a sudden, I was stuck," he continued, intentionally using her words. "Tony was only six, but he was mine to raise, unless I wanted to turn him over to the system."

"You didn't want him?" She looked down at him, and he realized for the first time just how long her legs were. His daughter was going to be a knockout, once she stopped dying her hair the color of cartoon characters.

"That wasn't it." He studied the less than perfect creases in his uniform pants. "It wasn't Tony I didn't want as much as this town, this house and all the things tying me to a place I didn't want to be part of." He shrugged. "I didn't want any ties. Leaving here meant freedom."

"But you stayed." She settled on the step beside him, leaning her arms on her thighs and staring at her scuffed boots.

"Yeah, I stayed." His heart hammered in his throat, making it tough to get the words out. Please, God, don't let him screw this up. "Tony was all the family I had left." He felt her flinch. "At least I thought he was."

"Because my mom lied to you," Maggie added, an angry teenager again, who wanted to be told she was wrong.

"No, because I pushed your mom away." He sat straighter, bracing his arms on his knees like she had. He glanced at Maggie to make sure she was listening. "I was so torn up about my dad, about the future I'd thought I wanted going to hell, I needed to take it out on someone. That's where your mom came in."

"But she should have told you she was pregnant."

"She never had the chance. I pushed her away and told her to stay out of my life." He clenched his fists, then released them with a sigh. "I've never been very good at long-term relationships, Maggie. I never thought I had what it took to make them work. Your mom was a reminder of that, and I didn't want to be reminded."

"You didn't want her," Maggie clarified.

"That's what I told myself. What I told her."

Silence filled the stairwell. It seemed as if it filled the entire house, as if they were the only people there. As if his first real conversation with his child was happening at the very center of the universe.

"But there's something else you should know." He couldn't risk never getting another chance to say everything she needed to hear. "Your mom's right. From the very first moment I knew about you, there was no doubt in my mind what I wanted. I was angry at her for all the years I've missed with you. It took me a little while to accept my part in the decisions she'd made. But it didn't take me a second to decide that I was going to be there for you every day of the rest of your life."

He laid a hand on her knee, close to her hand but not touching it. He was sliding on thin ice, and he didn't have the first clue how to skate. "Not because I have to, but because I'm damn lucky to have a second chance. I don't feel stuck, and I don't want an out. And if you do get on that plane and head back to New York, I'm going to be right behind you."

She sat as still as stone, her lower lip trembling as she stared at her lap. It was suddenly too much. He dragged her into the hug he'd longed to give her since the moment Carrinne had laid her picture in his hand. She didn't hug him back, but she didn't pull away either.

He squeezed her close one last time before making himself rise to his feet.

"Welcome to the family," he said, brushing her bangs back from her eyes before heading down to the kitchen.

Maggie needed to be told about Carrinne's mother, about the rape and the chance that the rapist was trying to hurt Carrinne. But Eric figured the girl had enough to puzzle through already. Carrinne could fill her in on everything when she thought it was the right time.

Welcome to the family.

The words filled him with a sense of rightness totally out of place with the desperate situation facing them all. He had his family with him, all together. A family that he hadn't had a clue he needed so badly. For tonight at least, they were safe and sound under one roof. His roof.

Whatever it took, whatever he had to do, he was going to keep them safe and make sure they had the future they deserved.

CHAPTER FIFTEEN

TONY WAS GRILLING the last of the sandwiches when Eric returned to the kitchen. Carrinne sat at the table talking on the phone.

"No, she's going to be staying here with me for a few days," she said. Her eyes lifted to Eric's, communicating a mother's concern and a million questions. "I'm sorry about all this, but could you do me one more favor? Call the school and let them know. Tell them it's a family emergency. That I'll be in touch when we get back in town. Oh, and I left my cell phone somewhere else. Let me give you the number where we'll be staying."

"Who's she talking to?" Eric asked Tony as he bit off the corner of a sandwich, then quickly took another, larger bite. Mrs. Davis's English muffins were the last thing he'd eaten, and they'd had the staying power of cotton candy.

"She called the friend in New York Maggie was staying with." Tony flipped a sandwich in the pan, browning the second side. He glanced to where Carrinne continued to talk on the phone.

"How sick is she?" he asked.

"Pretty sick." Eric forced away the panic swallowing him from the inside out. Carrinne and Maggie needed him. Falling apart was a luxury that would have to wait. "That's why we have to find her father. He may be able to help."

Tony nodded, letting the topic drop, even though he must have a million questions.

"I didn't have time to tell you after Carrinne showed up at the station," he said. "We traced the van to an auto-theft report over in Pineview. And Brimsley's cell records are back. His alibi checks out. Just like he said, he was on the phone for over an hour around the time Carrinne was in her grandfather's room at the hospital."

"He could have been following her in the van at the same time."

"Yeah, he could have."

But they both knew he hadn't. "We've got to find her father."

His brother nodded. "Assuming he didn't hightail it yesterday, as soon as he heard we were involved. How's the kid?"

"Confused as hell."

"I know how she feels." Tony shot him a sideways glance. "You've been holding out on me, big brother. About a lot of things."

"Carrinne wanted to keep her condition under wraps," Eric explained. "And I just found out about Maggie this morning."

"And?" Tony flipped the toasted sandwich on top of the stack beside the stove.

"And?"

"What's next? Last time I checked, you were champing at the bit to get out of Oakwood and on your own. What's your plan now?"

Eric sighed. How could he possibly make plans?

"I guess…" he began, an image condensing in his mind of his entire family—Tony, him, Carrinne and their daughter—gathered together year after year in his father's house. Celebrating birthdays and holidays. Enjoying each other's company over dinners in the kitchen. Goofing around playing board games in the den. The family growing over the years, adding new spouses and children into the mix. Sticking together through thick and thin, because they belonged together. Because they loved each other.

"I guess we'd better get a bigger tree at Christmas this year," he finally said. "Because there's going to be an awful lot more presents under it."

"That's kinda the way I figured it, too." Tony grinned and nodded in approval.

He turned the burner off and moved the pan to cool on the stovetop. A look of understanding passed between them, an awareness of how much had gone unsaid. Of what was riding on finding Carrinne the donor she needed.

"You want me to get back to the station?" Tony asked.

Eric shook his head as he finished his last bite of sandwich. "Gus is still there, plowing through our case records from the early seventies. I'm going back later, and I don't want to leave Carrinne and Maggie alone. Just in case someone's stupid enough to come after them here."

"How's Maggie?" Carrinne's eyes were haunted as she joined them. "Where is she?"

Tony walked to Maggie's backpack. "Why don't I take this up and get her settled in the other bedroom?"

"Maggie's fine." Eric squeezed Carrinne's hand as Tony left. "I left her wandering around upstairs."

"Where... How did you find her in town?"

"She found me." He pulled plates from the cabinet. "She flew in this afternoon and found a ride to your motel. She evidently got to your grandfather's after you left, so she followed a rumor that said you were with me. She walked right up to me at the station. Took a good ten years off my life."

"She must have been... I can't even imagine how she felt."

"She's pretty shaken, but I think talking with you will make a world of difference."

"I wish I could believe you." Carrinne rubbed her bruised temple. "She's always thought she could trust me. Now that she knows I lied about you—"

"Why don't you take her something to eat? Food was always a good start to smoothing things over with Tony at this age."

"What do I say to her?" Carrinne asked. "What on earth can I possibly say to make all this right?"

Eric soothed a finger over the lines of worry wrinkling her forehead. "Why not start with what I told her?"

"What…what was that?" Hope flickered across her face, an afraid kind of hope he was intimately familiar with at the moment.

"That we're a family, and nothing's going to change that. Nothing's going to come between us ever again."

He was claiming everything he'd never believed could be his. And he was giving Carrinne the power to destroy him with just a single word. All she had to do was say no.

Instead, the answering dream in her eyes became his lifeline.

His hand feathered around her delicate neck, drawing her mouth to his. When she erased the final few inches separating them, her kiss was the sweetest he'd ever known. Giving and firm at the same time, her lips opened beneath his. His other hand found her cheek, holding her as he deepened the kiss, his tongue dipping into unbelievable softness for a taste.

Carrinne. The essence of her.

She tasted like she had when they were kids. Only the woman in his arms was so much more than the teenage crush he'd once known. This Carrinne was edgy and sweet, strong yet vulnerable. A no-nonsense woman, she was a walking contradiction who made him want to pull his hair out half the time. But her heart was so full of love, there was even a place in it for a skeptical hardass like him. Thank God.

She responded like living fire beneath his touch, and his memories merged with reality. Blood roared to his sex in a knee-weakening flood, the thrill of it making him groan and crush her even closer. Somehow, he registered her trying to inch away. From somewhere came the realization that this wasn't the time or the place. That there was something else they needed to be taking care of instead.

Your daughter, you idiot. Your daughter's upstairs falling apart. And she needs her mother.

It cost him, but he softened his hold, preparing to let Carrinne go. The final lingering kiss she gave him promised this was only a beginning, not an end.

"I…I need to talk to Maggie." She licked her lips, the innocent reflex sucking him back in. "Did—" She moaned as his lips found hers again, then she pulled away. "Did you and Gus find anything more in my mother's diary?"

"We're still looking." He forced his hands to his side. "But Gus is sniffing out whatever leads he can find. I brought the diary home in case you wanted to look through it some more. I need to take it back to the station with me later, once things settle down here."

She glanced to the book lying on the table and shuddered.

Eric handed her two plates of sandwiches, blocking her view of the table and the past she wasn't ready to deal with yet. "Go talk to Maggie. Take care of her first. Everything else can wait."

"SOMEONE TRIED to hurt you?" Maggie sat up from where she'd been lounging on her bed in a pile of teenage disinterest. "Why?"

"To scare me away. We're pretty sure it's because I'm looking for my father." Carrinne struggled to find a way to say the rest. "We just learned why my mother never told anyone who he was, and the answer…well, it's not anything like I expected."

"How could you grow up without a dad and not tell me about mine?" Maggie picked at the quilt beneath her, mentioning Eric for the first time.

Carrinne moved aside the plates of untouched grilled cheese and scooted closer. "Maggie, I know it's impossible for you to believe, but I thought I was doing what was best for you."

"You told me he was dead."

"Because I was certain he wouldn't want you. I know what living with that kind of rejection is like, and I didn't want it for you."

"You're talking about your grandfather, aren't you? The one who lives in that mansion you never told me you grew up in."

"Yes, I grew up there, and yes, we had plenty of money and a big house. But I knew every day of my life that your great-grandfather didn't want me."

"And that's why you ran away?"

"I left because I didn't have a choice." Carrinne would never reveal Oliver's ultimatum about terminating her pregnancy. She'd never let him hurt Maggie the way he'd hurt her. "Leaving your father and great-grandfather behind was the only way I could give you the life you deserved."

"Because they didn't want us?"

Carrinne sighed. "Yes. At the time, I was sure neither one of them wanted us in their lives."

"He…the sheriff… He said he wants us now." Maggie's glare dared Carrinne to contradict her.

"I truly believe he does." Certainty worked its magic on Carrinne. She smiled, the tension inside her softening at the memory of their last kiss. His touch. "But he was a different person when we were kids."

"Don't blame him. You're the one who ran away."

"That's not the way it happened, and Eric would be the first to agree with me." Carrinne covered her daughter's hand. "But I'm not making excuses. My reasons don't change how wrong I was to keep you two apart all these years. I should have come back once I'd made a life for us. I should have given him a chance to make his own choice. He's been a wonderful father to Tony, and you've missed so much together. I'm so sorry, honey."

Maggie slid her hand from Carrinne's and resumed toying with the spread. When she looked up, a frown of confusion clouded her anger. "But what does any of this have to do with someone wrecking your car and threatening you?"

"It's looking like my father doesn't want to be found. The accident may have been his way of trying to stop me."

"Do you know who he is?"

"Not exactly."

"Then how do you know it's him?"

"We found a diary today. The last one my mother kept the year she died. That's what I came back to look for."

"So?"

"Well." The truth tasted like poison. Carrinne swallowed and forced the words out. She had to come clean about everything, if she and Maggie were going to get through this okay. "Inside, we found entries that said my mother was raped. That the man who did it had threatened to kill her and my grandfather if she ever told anyone what happened."

Maggie's eyes rounded as the words sunk in. Fear crawled up Carrinne's spine, then fury. Her innocent daughter shouldn't have to hear something like this.

"Your father…" Her daughter stuttered, then inched closer.

"Raped my mother."

"But you needed him to be your donor."

"That may not happen now."

Maggie shook her head. She didn't want to hear another word.

This had to be a mistake, even though one look at her mom's sad, worried face was enough to confirm that it wasn't. She threw her arms around her mother's neck, fear obliterating the last of her hurt and anger.

Her mother wasn't crying. Carrinne Wilmington never cried. But the tears were there in the way she'd barely been able to say what she'd discovered. In the way she cradled Maggie now, rocking slightly. Soothing them both with the motion.

Maggie tried to imagine how it must feel, to know something like that about your own father, to know what the creep had done to your mother. And he'd been one of her mom's only chances for a liver transplant. Maggie's own tears spilled over.

"You have to let me be your donor now." She wiped at her nose.

"Maggie—"

"Mom." She pushed away. "How can you ask me to sit back and do nothing, to watch you die?"

"I'm not going to die, Maggie. There are other options."

"Yeah, options with odds that suck. I've read everything the doctors gave you and more. You need a blood relative, an immediate family member."

"And you could die on the table during the donor procedure. This is major surgery. Any postoperative complications might be life-threatening."

"Could…might." Maggie leapt off the bed, crazy mad, crazy scared. "The chances of that happening are minuscule."

"I won't ask you to risk your life."

"You're not asking. I'm telling you, I want to do this."

"I couldn't bear being responsible for something happening to you." The tears Maggie had been so sure wouldn't come filled her mom's eyes. Her mother brushed them away with an annoyed swish of her hand.

Maggie walked back to the bed, wishing she understood. Determined not to give up. "Nothing's going to happen to me, Mom. The doctors said I'd be fine. And we don't even know if I'm a match. Just promise me you'll keep an open mind."

"I can't promise anything right now, honey." Her mom fingered the slash of purple Maggie had dyed into her bangs just hours after her mom left to come down here.

"Please think about it. I'd die if I lost you."

"I know exactly how you feel," her mom whispered as she hugged her close. "That's why we have to find my father."

ERIC WAS WAITING in the hall when Carrinne left Maggie's room.

She flipped off the light and gently shut the door. "Maggie's sleeping. I got her to eat something, but she didn't even change out of her clothes before she dozed off."

He stepped to her side, pulling her into his arms. "Did you tell her?"

"Everything." Carrinne nodded against his chest, loving the solid feel of him. "I can't stand hearing her so scared."

"She needed to see you. That's why she came. Even as angry as she was at the station, she was worried about you."

"She tries to take care of me." A smile broke through her worry.

"That's my girl."

Carrinne looked up, warming all over at the tender possessiveness of his words. "She's so much like you. Sometimes too much. I watch her fearlessly not give a damn what the people around her think, her directness and her honesty, and I don't know whether to applaud or to be afraid for her."

Eric chuckled. "She sounds just fine to me."

"She's all the things that drew me to you." Entranced, finally able to share the wonder of her child with the man who'd helped create her, Carrinne caressed his cheek. "She's amazed me every day of her life."

Eric trapped her hand against his face. "Sounds like she takes after you."

Her tears made an unwelcome reappearance. He wiped each one away, then kissed her cheeks.

"I'm so sorry," she said as his lips trailed to her ear. His kisses found the delicate skin of her neck, and she struggled to hold on to the words she needed to say. "For everything."

He lifted his head, the understanding in his eyes all the forgiveness she'd ever need. "I have you both now, Carrinne. I don't deserve you, but you've tumbled back into my life anyway, giving it a meaning I never thought I'd have. For that, I'll love you for the rest of my life."

"What?" Her instincts screamed to pull away, but his hand settled on her hip and anchored their lower bodies together. The ridge of his arousal shot sparks to the deepest part of her.

"I said I love you, and I will for the rest of my life."

"I…" She struggled to return the priceless promise, to say all her heart felt. But lessons learned too hard and too long ago retained their tenacious hold. She shook her head. "I can't—"

"Shh." Eric lowered his mouth to hers. "I don't care whether you can say it or not. I don't need the words. Show me."

His voice was an erotic temptation, setting every nerve in her body on fire. She raised her mouth to his lips, whimpering when his arms crushed around her to mold their bodies together. Worries and fear scattered as his tongue mated with hers. Pleasure and urgency swept away the ability to think. She was alive, her soul free of the moment. Called to life by his.

Eric gentled his touch, not sure he could stop but determined to make himself do just that if that's what Carrinne needed.

"Are you all right with this?" he asked. "Is this too fast after everything that's happened?"

"No…I mean, yes," she said between kisses. "I need…I need…"

"This?" He deepened the kiss, inhaling the sweetness of her.

He couldn't get enough. His body recognized its mate and refused to be denied a moment longer. A final flicker of sanity said to end this. He should head back to the station and help Gus. But he held the world in his hands, and his heart knew it. And his world was soft and yielding, needing him with a fierceness that ended all further thought.

Eric filled his hands with the soft perfection of her bottom, lifting and pressing her against the wall. He settled between her thighs, nudging the very center of her heat. He put a hand to her breast, his thumb caressing the delicate point her nipple had become.

"I need you, too, darlin'," he whispered between kisses.

"Yes," she panted and ran her hands under his shirt. Up his back. "Yes."

He buried his face in the golden hair at her neck and stumbled toward her bedroom. It was the one farthest from their daughter's. When Carrinne wrapped her legs around his waist, rubbing against him with each step he took, he almost pinned her to the floor right there in the hall. He had to be inside her, as deep as he could get.

Finally in her room, the door closed behind them, he eased her onto the quilt-covered bed.

"I don't have any protection," he somehow managed to say.

She ran her hand down his neck, his chest. Her eyes held mysteries he'd give his life to know the answers to.

"I've been on the Pill for years," she said. "My hormones have been a mess since I had Maggie."

"Thank goodness."

"I've never seen it as much of a blessing myself." Her husky laugh shot straight through him. "Not until now."

He devoured her mouth, drinking in her delighted

sighs. Her legs retained their vicelike grip as he leaned into her, her hands making fast work of his uniform shirt. He peeled off her sweatshirt and bra and pressed her to the feather mattress, electricity sparking as they connected skin to skin.

He thought of taking it slow. Struggled to hold back. To make this new first time special for her. Then her body arched, her need feeding the furious storm raging through his soul. And he lost the ability to think at all.

She fumbled at his waist, making him aware he still wore his gun belt.

Groaning with the effort it took to pull away, he rid himself of the belt and the rest of his clothes.

When he turned back, Carrinne sat at the edge of the bed, gloriously naked herself, her gaze roaming over him without apology. And all he could do was stare back at what he'd dreamed of for seventeen long years.

"Please." She opened her arms and made room for him where he needed to be or die.

"Anything." He covered her, his hardness finding her softness, their joining exquisite, hotter than even his hottest memories. "Everything."

CARRINNE HELD TIGHT to Eric, her heart still racing, her mind free of everything but the amazing magic of being in his arms again. His weight crushed her to the mattress, but she didn't care. He shuddered, the lingering pulse of his release stroking her deep inside. How could she have forgotten?

"That was…" He groaned when she lifted her hips.

"Amazing," she finished for him.

"Mmmm." His lips grazed her breast. He took her nipple between his teeth, pulling gently. Her hips lifted again, jolting them both with renewed pleasure.

She threaded her fingers through his hair, pulling his face to hers, kissing him with every ounce of love she couldn't give voice to. He pulled her lower lip between his teeth and groaned, even as his lower body pulled away.

"Eric?" She tried to keep him close, but his hand on her hip stayed her.

"Trust me, darlin'. Nothing would make me happier than to spend the night relearning every single place you like to be kissed." He settled beside her, pulling her against him and wrapping her in the quilt as best he could while they were still lying on top of it. "But we need to talk."

"I don't want to talk." She snuggled in, liking her arms around his neck. "I don't want to think. I just want to feel."

He cradled her head to his chest and kissed her temple. "I know, but I have to get back to the station. We only have a few minutes."

Shadows of all she didn't want to face closed around them. Pushing reality away, she snaked a hand down his body. He was already growing hard again.

His strained chuckle rumbled between them as he disengaged her hand. He turned on the lamp beside the bed. "We need to talk about you and Maggie."

"We're fine. Everything's fine now."

"No, it's not. I want you two on a plane in the morning, heading back to New York."

"What? Why?" She struggled to sit up.

"Because you found what you came for. We have the diary, and my people can take it from here. Stay, and you'll continue to be a target for whoever tried to hurt you."

"But I'm no threat now. We've found the diary, and you said yourself there's nothing in it. Everyone in town knows you're involved. Why would he try to hurt me now?"

"You're assuming he's thinking logically. If it is your father, we're dealing with a violent predator who's cornered after believing he got away clean for over thirty years. For all we know, he may think getting rid of you will solve all his problems. He could be out there right now, waiting for us to let our guard down so he can get to you."

"But you won't do that."

He tucked her hair behind her ear, his eyes both tender and fierce. "I'm not willing to take the chance. You and Maggie can't be here until we've solved this thing."

She lay back down and pulled his arm around her. "I just found you again."

He cuddled closer. "And I'm not going anywhere. Once we catch the bastard, I'm pulling my Harley out of the garage, cleaning it up, and coming after you both."

She stared at the pattern on the quilt, his determination to keep her and Maggie safe, and to keep them in his life, warming her to her toes. Leaves were rustling in the summer breeze just outside the window, and suddenly nothing had ever felt as good as being back in Oakwood.

"You still have that old motorcycle after all these years?" she teased.

"I couldn't let it go, even though I had nowhere for it to take me."

Her heart hurt for the dreams he had denied himself, even as it swelled at the thought of Eric riding up to her East Village apartment on his motorcycle. "And you have somewhere to go now?"

"Damn straight." Her pulled her closer. "Isn't that what you want?"

"If you don't come, we'll track you down. Maggie needs her family."

"So do I," he replied. "Like I told her. There's no way you're getting rid of me."

Carrinne closed her eyes, Eric's breath and his solid strength comforting her. Her most secret dream burned bright and true, deep inside where it was still safe to dream. She'd searched for a home her entire life, had always thought of home as a place. Somewhere like Oakwood, where she would finally belong. But she would forever be home, she realized, as long as she had Eric and Maggie with her. If she could only believe that forever was something she deserved to have.

She'd give anything to be able to tell Eric she loved him, to know it would last longer than the year or two the doctors had promised. But no matter what happened, she was here in this moment, falling asleep in his arms. One perfect moment was enough. It had to be.

It was everything.

CHAPTER SIXTEEN

ERIC SLID from the bed, careful not to wake Carrinne. He tucked the quilt around her, brushing his hand over the satin of her shoulder, almost crawling back in. Even though it was seventy-five degrees in the house, he knew she'd wake up chilled. And he wanted to be there to keep her warm.

She looked so small, curled up with her head on the pillow, drained from the shock of the last two days. Yet when he'd covered her with his strength, her spirit had soared to life beneath him.

Carrinne needed rest, and he needed to get back to the station. He yanked on his pants, grabbed his shirt and his holster, and with one last look, forced himself to walk away.

He pulled her bedroom door shut behind him. Maggie's door was still closed, the light off. He checked his watch, wincing at the time. It was after ten, and Gus was expecting him back at the station. One look at his wrinkled uniform, and he ducked into his own bedroom to throw on jeans and a fresh shirt.

Once downstairs, the flickering light of the TV led

him to the otherwise dark den. Tony was sprawled on the couch, drinking coffee and watching a Clint Eastwood spaghetti Western they had both seen at least fifty times. His gun lay on the coffee table beside his legs.

"I'm heading back in to meet with Gus," Eric said.

"I've got things covered here. I double-checked all the windows and doors. We should be fine." Tony took a sip of his coffee, a knowing smile spreading across his face as he studied Eric's change of clothes.

Eric headed to the kitchen, ignoring his brother's amusement at his expense. The nearly full pot of coffee told him Tony had planned an all-nighter if Eric needed him. He poured himself a cup of steaming caffeine, then took a seat at the kitchen table, staring at Angelica Wilmington's diary.

How long would it take to find Carrinne's father? Assuming they ever did. He grabbed the portable phone and dialed the station as he thumbed through the diary. Maybe Gus had come up with something.

"Oakwood Sheriff's Department."

"Hey, Marge," he said to the night receptionist as he found the entry in March, Angelica's first heart-wrenching mention of her pregnancy. "Can you get me Gus Crain on the phone? He should be back in the conference room."

"Just a sec."

He scanned the few entries after Angelica had recorded her rape. She mentioned the rapist only once, and then only to say that he'd grabbed her one night as she'd walked home alone after a basketball game. That was it. No other details someone could have traced back to the man. She'd clearly been too terrified to write more.

Damn it. Gus was right. They had nothing.

"Sheriff Rivers," Marge said over the phone. "I can't find Mr. Crain anywhere. The duty sergeant said he thought he saw him leave several hours ago, right after you did."

"Are you sure?"

"I checked the conference room myself. All I can tell you is he's not here now."

"Thanks, Marge." He'd probably given up waiting and headed home. "If you see him, have him call me at the house."

Eric ended the call and stared at the diary pages without seeing them. Maybe Gus had found something to follow up on. He dug the detective's business card from his wallet and dialed his cell number. As the phone rang, Eric flipped through Angelica's earlier entries. Maybe there was something there. Rapists often know their victims.

The call transferred to voice mail. "Leave a message after the beep."

"Gus, where the hell did you go, man? Call me if you found something."

Eric hung up, dialing the home number on the card. He continued to flip backward through Angelica Wilmington's senior year in high school, delving further and

further into the past. A name caught his eye several
times. He pulled the diary closer.

January 24, 1970.
Wendel got angry when I didn't want to sit with
him at lunch…Cindy said I should tell Father, but
I don't want to get Wendel in trouble…

January 16.
Cindy and Theresa and I walked a different way
today, but Wendel still managed to find me and ask
to carry my books…the girls laughed at him…I
think they hurt his feelings…

The answering machine at Gus's picked up. Eric kept
reading as he waited for the beep.

"Give me a call at home when you get in, Gus. I'll
be up most of the night going over the diary." He ended
the call and laid the portable phone on the table.

January 6.
Wendel walked me home again today…don't know
how to tell him no when he's being so sweet…

December 16.
The last day of school before break…Wendel gave
me a Christmas present and asked if he could
carry my books home…he's so shy…

December 10.
Theresa said Billy said Wendel told him he likes
me…isn't that funny…he's never even talked to
me…

Eric returned to the January entries and beyond, his
stomach clenching. Perhaps he was jumping to conclu-
sions, but maybe…

February 1, 1970.
Wendel insisted I sit with him at lunch today. Theresa and Billy and everyone found some place
else. He asked me to go steady. Just like that, can
you believe it? Of course I told him no. I tried to
be nice about it, but he got so angry. He said I'd
been leading him on the whole time, that I was a
tease, and I thought because I had money and my
last name was Wilmington that I was better than
everybody else. It was awful. I started crying and
I told him I didn't ever want to talk to him again.
He was still screaming at me when I ran out of the
cafeteria. And I thought he was so sweet.

It was the only entry Angelica had made in February. And there was nothing else until the first disturbing entry in March—when she'd learned she was seven
weeks pregnant.
My God. This was it.
Wendel. Wendel who?

His hands shook as he located the entries from the beginning of the school year. He scanned each one, looking for the name. Where was the damn name? Finally...

September 25, 1969.
A new boy in homeroom today. His family moved here from Pineview for his dad's job. He seems shy but sweet. We sit next to each other in American History. I think Wendel Crain will be a funny new friend.

Crain?
Pineview?
Gus Crain's family was from Pineview.
Where the van that ran Carrinne down had been stolen.
The puzzle started piecing itself together, a crazy image forming out of bits and scraps of nothing. Eric snatched the phone and dialed Gus's cell again. He reread Angelica Wilmington's words, telling himself he was crazy. Voice mail answered again. He hung up and with a curse and tried the home number, getting the same response.

Gus had said he'd stay at the station and start digging through old cases. Only he'd disappeared almost as soon as they'd found the diary.

No, denial reasoned back. The detective had been a decorated member of the force. He was one of Dad's best friends.

And the only other person who'd had time alone with the diary since they discovered the rape. He'd even been in town the day of Carrinne's wreck. Doing prep work for another case, he'd said. But conveniently on the spot at the exact moment they needed him.

Eric's mind kept circling, zeroing in, making the circumstantial case that made no sense at all. Gus was a nickname the man had gotten at the academy, Eric's dad had said. And, in his midfifties, he was the right age to have gone to school with Angelica Wilmington. That little voice Eric didn't want to hear told him to make one more call.

He dialed and waited, hoping he was wrong.

"Oakwood Sheriff's Department."

"Marge, look something up for me."

"What you got?"

"I need you to pull up a personnel record." He swallowed. "Look up Gus Crain for me. He was a detective for the department about fifteen, twenty years ago."

He could hear her typing.

"Got it," she said, way sooner than Eric was ready.

"I need to know his full name."

"Looks like it's Wendel Grover Crain," she said, solving a mystery without even realizing it. And destroying so much more.

Eric hung up in silence.

Gus Crain was Carrinne's father.

CARRINNE WOKE SLOWLY, exhausted but floating in a sea of peace that made it hard to care.

Exhausted felt good. Everything felt good. Feeling anything but good was inconceivable, because Eric loved her.

Different layers of awake pulled at her. The chill of the sheets, the softness of the lightweight blanket as she snuggled deeper. Summer-night sounds chanted outside the window, ringing in her ears like nursery rhymes from childhood, their simple cadence and lyrics teasing, resonating of home.

She blinked into the darkness, confused when she realized it wasn't morning. Disappointed but not surprised that she was alone. Eric would have headed back to the station by now.

Hunger growled in a stomach no longer satisfied with Tony's deluxe cheese sandwich. She checked the bedside clock. Midnight wasn't a bad time for a snack. Actually, anytime was a good time considering she hadn't been interested in food for weeks.

She wrestled out of the covers, flipped on the light, and crawled into leggings and another sweatshirt from her suitcase. She stopped in front of the mirror that hung over the bureau, expecting… Expecting what? That Eric's love had stamped her with some visible mark confirming just how much tonight had changed her?

She felt strong for the first time since hearing her condition diagnosed. Finding Eric again, finding what she'd thought they'd lost forever, made facing the future possible, whatever happened. Surely, she must look different somehow. But all she saw was the same Carrinne as before, the only difference perhaps the softness in her eyes. The satisfied smile she couldn't quite hide.

Her hand covering her heart, she stepped into the hallway and tiptoed to Maggie's room. Tonight of all nights, she needed to check on her baby, just as she had when Maggie was an infant. She opened the door a crack, the light from the hall spilling over where her *baby* was sprawled diagonally across the still-made bed. She hadn't moved since Carrinne was last there.

The least she could do was take off those boots.

Carrinne smiled as she bent to her motherly task, even as a secret pain burned through her chest. One day soon, Maggie might not have a mom to check on her when she wasn't looking. But Carrinne refused to let the sadness in, refused to be so selfish as to want more when tonight, right now, she'd been blessed with so much.

She quietly finished with Maggie's shoes. Then, left with no other reason to stand there staring at her beautiful daughter, she turned to leave.

"Mom?" The bed squeaked as Maggie shifted and sat up. She squinted into the light streaming in from the hall. "What's going on?"

"It's late, honey. I was on my way down to the kitchen. You want something to eat?"

Maggie bounded off the bed, awake in an instant as only a teenager motivated by food could be. "I'm starved."

Carrinne giggled and pulled her daughter's sleep-warmed body close. They headed downstairs.

"What's with the purple?" she asked, feathering her fingers through Maggie's ever-changing highlights.

"I thought it'd be fun."

"Yeah, what's not fun about coordinating your hair color with your sunglasses?" Carrinne elbowed her daughter in the ribs.

They entered the kitchen to find Tony sitting at the table, drinking coffee and reading the paper.

"I didn't know you two were up," he said. He laid the paper beside a lethal-looking handgun.

"What's happened?" Carrinne stumbled to a halt. "Is Eric back at the station?"

"Uh, no." Tony stood and tucked the gun into his belt. He wouldn't meet her eyes. "Eric's out on a call. He wanted me to hang out down here until he got back."

"With a gun?"

"Carrinne—"

"What call?" She knew before she asked, but asking gave her a few minutes more to hope she was wrong. "When was the last time something happened in Oakwood important enough for the sheriff to take a call in the middle of the night?"

"Well, he rode along with me when you broke into the mansion," Tony offered with a charming smile that she returned with a blank stare.

He rubbed his jaw and glanced at Maggie, as if he were weighing his words carefully.

"Eric thinks he's found your father," he said.

"Who is he?"

"Carrinne—"

"Who?" She felt Maggie's arm link with hers. She squeezed her daughter's hand with fingers that no longer had any feeling.

"It's Gus," Tony said with a sigh and a worried look for both of them.

"Gus?" She realized her head was shaking. "But... How? No! He didn't know anything about any of this until he met with Eric and me at my grandfather's house."

"He was already in town for the weekend when you broke into your grandfather's place." Tony spread his fingers before him on the table. "Best we can figure, Gus heard the rumors that you were back, that you were looking for something to help you find your father... He put two and two together, and decided to stop you before you got too close to the truth. When that didn't work, he agreed to work with us, most likely to keep an eye on the investigation."

"He... He's my father?" Carrinne clung to her daughter's hand. "You think he's the one who caused my car to spin out at the hospital?"

Tony nodded.

Carrinne fought to breathe.

"Where?" She finally made herself ask. "Where are they?"

"Eric has him cornered in Pineview."

CHAPTER SEVENTEEN

ERIC KNELT BEHIND a cluster of trees, twenty yards from Gus Crain's front door. He ducked as a shotgun fired from one of the downstairs windows.

Ringed around the house were four squad cars, an ambulance and six other officers—what must be half of the Pineview Sheriff's Department—who, like Eric, were crouching behind the protection of trees and cars. Blue and red lights flashed through the night, casting their nerve-tingling spell.

As soon as Eric realized Gus was running, he'd gambled that the detective would go home first. Gus had a head start, but Pineview was over an hour outside of Oakwood. A few emergency calls to the Pineview Sheriff's Department shortened Gus's window of opportunity, and a patrol car had arrived in time to trap him inside the house.

An exchange of gunfire had injured one of the responding officers, and from the deterioration of Gus's response, they were pretty sure he'd been hit as well. But with his injuries had come escalating barrages of gunfire. Eric and the other personnel had arrived during the last hour, and each time they'd tried to advance they'd been forced back by Gus's uncanny aim with the shotgun.

They were at a stand-off. The former detective had to know that continuing to resist was pointless. It would most likely get him killed, because the local law enforcement would eventually have no choice but to return fire. And Gus wasn't stupid. That's what worried Eric the most.

"We've got him on the line." An officer passed a field phone to Dillan Reed, the Pineview sheriff. "He's asking for Sheriff Rivers."

Reed handed the device to Eric. "I know you want him back in Oakwood alive," he said, having already gotten a sketchy version of the story from Eric. "But the bastard doesn't seem very inclined to oblige, and I want this done without any more of my men getting hurt. You've got five minutes to talk him out."

Eric almost didn't take the handset. He didn't want it. All the way over here, he'd tried to reconcile the tough, honest man he'd admired for years with the monster who'd raped a girl, terrorized her until her death, then had gone after his own daughter to cover his ass. If it weren't for Carrinne needing part of the man's liver, Eric would be home with her and Maggie right now, waiting for Reed to call when it was all over.

But Gus was no good to Carrinne if he didn't make it out of that house in one piece. Eric took the phone.

"Rivers here."

"How's it going out there, son?" the detective asked in a shaky voice.

"About like you'd expect, Gus. Or should I say Wendel?"

"Yeah, I figured it wouldn't take you long to put it all together. I found those entries in just a couple of minutes myself." Gus chuckled and coughed. "I was kinda banking on you taking your time. Maybe waiting until morning."

"Time isn't something Carrinne can afford." Eric ground his teeth. "Don't you even care? She's your daughter."

"She…she was a mistake. If it weren't for her, Angelica wouldn't have died…" Another wheezing cough. "I never meant to hurt Angelica. She'd have understood that eventually…if it weren't for the baby…."

"You met your granddaughter tonight. Is she a mistake, too?"

"She never should have come here…. Carrinne should have stayed away. I tried to run her off that day at the hospital. Kinda hoped that accident would send her packing. It's her fault…should have stayed away… Angelica would have learned to love me…."

Gus was talking in circles, his confusion brought on by either blood loss or years of rationalizing what he'd done. Eric didn't care which. All he could think about was stopping the situation from escalating.

Static crackled across the line. Seconds crept by. Then there was the sound of the shotgun being reloaded. Gus fired a fresh round into the squad car parked beside Eric's tree. Sheriff Reed gave a command over his radio, and an officer slipped along the roof's second-floor shadows, disappearing through an open window.

Eric held up his hand, asking Reed for another minute. "What are you doing, Gus? What's it going to take to end this? You're hurt, and you know there's no good way out of this but surrendering."

"I know there's no way I'm going to jail," Gus ground out in a voice that was determined and resigned at the same time. "Do you have any idea what they do to ex-cops and rapists in south Georgia prisons? I've already done my time. Thirty-two years of living with what I did...trying to make it right. I helped people...saved more lives than I can count..."

"You were a good cop and a better detective."

The officer inside the house would be in position by now, waiting on his sheriff's signal. Reed's eyes said time was up.

"One of the best," Eric pressed on. "That'll go a long way with a judge and jury. It doesn't have to end this way."

"Sure it does...it's over..."

More coughing. Another shot, this time taking out the ambulance window. More reloading. The man knew what he was doing. He wanted what was about to happen.

"Does Reed have his sniper in place yet?" Gus asked.

"Stop it, you sick bastard," Eric bit out. Every sound, every heartbeat seemed suspended in time. "You don't want to go out this way. To hurt anyone else. Give your-self up, and let us get you to the hospital."

"It's not going to happen that way, son. I just wanted you to know, I didn't mean to hurt her.... I didn't mean to—"

"No, you didn't. Just like you don't want to hurt any-one now. Put the gun down. I'm coming in." Eric stood. The next shotgun blast blew a chunk out of the tree just a few inches from his head.

"Go," Reed said into the radio.

Two quick shots fired inside the house, echoing through the phone in Eric's hand. Then there was nothing but static.

THE SOUND of a car pulling up the drive lured Carrinne awake. She'd dozed off on the couch, Maggie's head resting in her lap. She glanced at the mantel clock. It was almost four.

Tony had finished filling them in on what they'd found in her mother's diary. Details she still couldn't quite believe, about a brutal man who'd terrorized her mother and had turned his sights on Carrinne. And Eric had gone after him hours ago.

She'd been too worried to go upstairs and pretend to sleep. Worried, not about what would happen to her horror of a father, or whether he'd agree to be a liver donor. None of that mattered. She could lose Eric, she'd realized, if Gus was the monster they thought he was. And the fear that had consumed her from that moment on was an emptiness she didn't think she could bear. At some point while she sat waiting, as the hours slowly slipped away, she'd started praying. There had to be a miracle out there, somewhere, which could see the people she loved safely through this latest nightmare.

The side door to the kitchen creaked opened. Hushed masculine voices drifted through the silent house. She heard someone head up the stairs as she eased Maggie's head from her lap and slid off the couch. What seemed like cotton-covered pins needled up and down the left side of her body as she moved.

She teetered into the kitchen and found Eric alone. His back to her, both hands braced against the counter. He was staring down at a steaming cup of Tony's coffee. His head came up as the hardwood creaked beneath her, but he didn't turn around.

"I've been so worried." She hugged his waist, needing to feel him safe in her arms. He turned then, drawing her into his embrace. And as he held her, everything not right in her world—her mother's rape, learning about Gus, her fears for the future—all faded away.

"What happened?" Maggie stumbled through the door, her clothes rumpled, her eyes huge.

Eric tightened his hold, then he released Carrinne. His features rearranged themselves into an empty canvas. The eyes that said so much when he chose to give her a glimpse into his soul grew remote and bottomless. Carrinne watched him create the same practiced distance that had masked his worry and concern when she'd first come back to Oakwood.

"Did Gus get away?" She took a hesitant step back.

"No, we caught him." Eric pulled chairs away from the table. "Let's sit down."

Maggie took a seat. Carrinne didn't budge.

"I don't need to sit," she said. "As long as Gus is taken care of, and you're safe, I can handle the rest."

Without a word, Eric took her by the shoulders and gently eased her to sit beside Maggie.

"Gus was already injured when I got there," he said as he joined them at the table. "He'd shot at the first officers on the scene and was wounded when they returned fire. Pineview sheriff deputies were all over the place."

"Did he… Did you talk to him?" A piece of her needed to know if Gus had acknowledged her. A piece of her still cared what her father thought, even though he was her mother's rapist. The realization made her want to gag. A slash of her hand erased her question. "Never mind. Just tell me what happened next."

"He kept shooting at us." Eric took a fortifying breath. "He said he wouldn't go to prison."

"He tried to shoot his way out?"

"He didn't want out, darlin'." Strong hands covered hers. "And he made sure the Pineview sheriff didn't have a choice. They sent someone in to stop him."

"Stop him?" Tears rushed to her eyes. For her father. For a man she'd both hate and mourn every day for the rest of her life. "They killed him, didn't they?"

Eric's eyes filled with anguish.

"No!" Maggie gasped. "But what about Mom's liver? Can he still be tested to be a donor?"

Carrinne couldn't move. She couldn't utter a sound. Grief was consuming her, unwelcomed, but too real to ignore. Grief for a man who'd never wanted to know her, a man whose passing should be a relief. Instead, it was one more regret she'd never have the chance to make right. And with him had gone her fragile new dream's only chance to survive.

Gus couldn't have planned a better way to destroy her. He'd given up, with no thought to anyone but himself. And his cowardice had demolished Carrinne's only chance to start over with Maggie and Eric. Through the panic and denial, she found the strength to stand.

"Where did they take him?" She needed her purse. Her electronic organizer. "My doctors in New York may know a way to save his liver. Maybe it's not too late."

Eric took her hand. "Gus took four bullets, Carrinne. By the time we got to him, he'd been bleeding out for hours. I followed the ambulance to the county hospital." Tears filled his eyes. He looked from her to their daughter. "One of the bullets destroyed his liver. There's nothing they could do to save it."

She felt it sink in. The knowing. The acceptance that this was the way it had to be. This whole trip, searching for her father, had been a gamble at best. And she'd lost. But as she sat numbly beside Eric once more, the love shining in his eyes reminded her of just how much she'd won after all.

"Mom?" Maggie found Carrinne's other hand. "Are you okay?"

"Yeah." Carrinne clung to them both. "Of course I am. I didn't even know him, and we have no idea whether his liver could have helped me in the first place."

"And there are other donor options, right?" Eric asked. "There's a national registry."

"Yeah." She tried to make her smile believable. "We have plenty of time."

"But we may not need time," Maggie added. "My tests should be back today."

"What tests?" Eric's eyes narrowed.

"I had myself tested to be a living donor," Maggie explained.

Eric's grip loosened as he stared at Carrinne. "You told me she wasn't a viable donor."

"I said her being my donor wasn't a possibility. And it's not." Carrinne winced at the accusation spreading across his face. "Maggie has her own life to lead, Eric. And the donor procedure comes with a mile-long list of potential complications."

"Mom, the doctors said the risks are minimal. I'm young, and I'm healthy, and—"

"And they'll have to saw you in half, Maggie. There's nothing minimal about it."

"What kind of risks are we talking about?" Eric asked.

"It doesn't matter. Any risk is too great." Carrinne stood and moved away from them both. Lord, why did they have to do this now? "This is not open for discussion."

"Why, for God's sake?" Eric's frustration, his desperation, was rolling off him in waves.

"How can you ask me that? How can you ask me to risk Maggie's life to save my own? Just like…my…my—"

"Your mother?" he finished for her, his tone incredulous. "You're not responsible for what happened then, any more than you are for the choices you have to make now."

"There is no choice to make." Carrinne glanced at Maggie, then shot Eric a look she hoped would end this line of conversation before it began. She wasn't discussing her mother in front of Maggie.

"If the doctors are recommending the procedure," he reasoned, "and Maggie's a match, we should at least consider—"

"There is no *we,*" Carrinne interrupted. "Not about this."

"Mom—"

"That's right, I'm your mother. And I won't endanger my only child's life because it's a shortcut to protecting my own. I couldn't live with that. I won't allow it."

"Allow it? God, Mom. You think you can control everything!"

Bitter memories assailed Carrinne. How many times had she said the same thing to Oliver? She'd despised her grandfather for dictating every choice she'd made in her own life, never once asking her what she wanted.

"That's not true," she said in little more than a whisper.

"Isn't it?" Eric looked up from drumming his fingers on the table. "You came back here, on some impossible search to find your father. Insisted on doing it on your own, until you were so sick and in so much danger you had no choice but to let me help. Then you lied to me about Maggie being a donor, because you knew I'd have your butt on the next plane back to New York if I knew finding your father wasn't your only answer. You've been controlling things from the start. And where has it gotten you?"

"Nowhere." She raised her chin, ready to face the reality of her situation even if they weren't. "But that doesn't change the facts. I've learned not to dream after something that's not going to happen. I know better. I stopped wishing for the impossible a long time ago. So what if I'm right back where I started? That's something I can accept."

She went to Maggie, smoothed her hand through her daughter's hair, smiled into her soft brown eyes. "I don't regret a single thing that's happened, because you and your father have found each other. No matter what happens now, you're going to be okay."

"And isn't that convenient for you?" Eric was looking at her the way she'd once looked at him—that day on the side of a country road, when he'd broken her heart and said he no longer wanted her in his life. "What a deal. You get to be a coward without the guilt."

"What?"

"You're caving, because you've got an out. Maggie was right from the start. Now that I'm in the picture, you're off the hook, no matter how much it costs the rest of us. You talk about refusing to dream the impossible, but what you're really doing is refusing to try."

"That's not true. I'm still looking for a donor. I'm going to do everything the doctors say. They make medical breakthroughs every day."

"And all along, you'll never have to make the tough choice." Love mixed with disappointment made for an awful expression on his face. "You don't have to risk giving your heart completely or committing to our family. You don't have to risk having someone you love put themselves on the line for you. You just get to bow out gracefully, consoling yourself that Maggie and I will live happily ever after once you're gone. It's the ultimate control."

"That's not what I'm doing." He was twisting everything.

"Sure it is." He stood, hesitating at her side for only a second on his way out of the kitchen. "Who would have thought that dying was easier than letting us love you?"

CHAPTER EIGHTEEN

ERIC LOOKED UP from his paperwork to find Angie lounging in the doorway.

"Not now," he said, not caring if the whole town was burning down around them. He'd been at his desk since dawn, trying to work himself into an exhausted heap incapable of thinking or feeling. "Whatever it is, just handle it."

"I'm sorry about Gus." She didn't come in and sit as she normally did, but she didn't seem inclined to leave either. "He was a good cop and a good detective. I know how much he meant to you and your dad."

Eric grunted, turning to the computer to log his notes from last night's events in Pineview. Gus wasn't a topic he was ready to discuss, not even with Angie. The sordid details could wait until another day.

"I heard a rumor that he was Carrinne Wilmington's father."

Eric's fingers stalled on the keyboard. Damn. It hadn't taken twenty-four hours for the sketchy information he'd given the doctors at the county hospital about Carrinne's need for Gus's liver to make its way back to Oakwood.

"How're Carrinne and her daughter taking it?"

"Maggie's my child, too," he corrected. His daughter's identity was one rumor he was more than happy to start himself. Angie's eyes widened. He was glad she'd heard it from him. "They're both handling things about like you'd expect."

Only that wasn't true. Carrinne wasn't handling anything.

...I won't endanger my only child's life because it's a shortcut to protecting my own. I won't allow it.

"...Eric?" Angie stepped into the office. "You okay?"

"Not even close." He pushed away from the computer and used the palms of his hands to rub at the hours of sleeplessness burning behind his eyes.

He understood where Carrinne was coming from. They'd discussed her feelings of responsibility for her own mother's death only once, but he knew enough. His chances of changing her mind about Maggie were slim to none.

The family he'd known about for less than twenty-four hours, the woman he'd loved his entire life, their future, were all slipping through his fingers. And the only shot they had at a miracle hinged on Carrinne realizing that when you're playing for keeps, playing it safe is just about the worst kind of giving up.

CARRINNE SAT WATCHING her grandfather sleep in his hospital bed. What on earth was she was doing here?

It wasn't even noon yet, but her body longed to be

back at Eric's, napping like their daughter. The only real sleep she'd gotten in the last thirty-six hours had been those few priceless hours after she'd drifted off in Eric's arms. Every time she'd closed her eyes since, the events of the night had swamped her, refusing to let go, the images running together.

The moment when she'd read those horrible entries in her mother's diary. How she'd found, then lost, her father, all in the same few hours. The guilt of both needing him and hating him for what he'd done to everyone she loved. Maggie's expression, still clouded with worry and anger, as she'd headed up to bed just as dawn had started to pinken the sky outside. The resigned acceptance on Eric's face when he'd showered and left for the station, avoiding Carrinne and any further discussion about Maggie.

A walk and some fresh air had seemed the only thing standing between her and insanity. Tony offered to hang out in case Maggie woke, so Carrinne had walked first one block, then another. Before she knew it, she'd caught the bus at the corner of Crabapple and Juniper. And then she'd gotten off at the stop beside the hospital. She still had no idea why.

Did she honestly think seeing her grandfather was going to help her somehow make sense out of the confusion closing in around her?

It's the ultimate control.

Eric would never forgive her. To him, she was a quitter. She was caving.

God, Mom. You think you can control everything.

Carrinne watched Oliver sleep. What was it she'd said to him just two days ago?

You don't know how to do anything but control people, do you?

Not a speck of fight left in her, she stopped denying their shared instinct to reshape the world around them to suit their needs. It was the very skill that had helped her survive since she'd started over in New York.

But her decisions for Maggie came from love, not control. That's what made her different from Oliver. She wouldn't take risks with her daughter's life. *It's all going to work out fine, trust me,* was a nice concept, until you found yourself responsible for whether someone else lived or died. When reality kicks you in the pants, you learn to protect your own.

Her grandfather stirred, blinking awake without noticing Carrinne sitting beside him.

"Why couldn't you love me?" she asked softly. Finally, after all these years, it was time to hear the ugly truth. Perhaps because it no longer mattered. Or maybe because it mattered too much.

"Carrinne." His expression was a cross between *glad you came back* and *oh my God, it's you again.* "How long have you been sitting there?"

"I have no idea." She leaned forward, needing to understand what she'd never been ready to face before. "Why didn't you even try to love me?"

When he didn't answer, she stood and paced to the

window, frustrated with him for never changing, and with herself for still needing something he couldn't give. "I mean, what was it that made you so determined to ignore me? You provided for me and controlled the hell out of my life, so on some level you must have cared. But you held your approval and love back like I wasn't good enough for it. Like I didn't deserve the effort."

"You deserved everything," he finally said, his eyes closing above sunken cheeks. Nurse Able had said he'd spent a restless night, shocked first by the business with Brimsley, then rattled again upon hearing the gossip flying about what Gus had done to Carrinne and her mother. "But I couldn't…"

"Couldn't what? Couldn't love me? It's the same tragic story, isn't it? You losing first your wife, then your angel of a daughter. You couldn't face giving your heart again, so you locked it away to keep yourself safe. Everyone in town has bought that excuse for years, but I know the truth. I was the child your daughter trusted you to love. Only you *couldn't*."

"I always cared about you, Carrinne. I always lo—"

"Don't you dare. Don't you say that to me now." She stepped to the bed, her palm itching to slap him. She was crossing way over the line, and she knew it. He was sick, and none of this mattered anyway. But she didn't care. "For years I pitied you, felt sorry for you and loved you despite it all. I kept looking for something behind that blank wall of nothing you gave me. Something that told me I was finally good enough for you."

She inched closer. She needed him to say it. He was the past that had shaped her, and she was tired of running from the truth. "But you pushed me away on purpose, didn't you? Because you blamed me for my mother's death. You made sure I spent my childhood paying for being alive, knowing that I could never make up for what I'd taken from you."

"You're wrong." His voice held a strength she hadn't heard since coming home. His eyes didn't waver from hers. "You couldn't be more wrong. I don't blame you for your mother's death. You were the one good thing in my life once Angelica was gone."

Carrinne rocked backward, his words anticlimactic, even as they blasted through what remained of what she'd thought she understood. "Then…why?"

"Because I'm the selfish bastard you always said I was. Because I was a coward." Regret transformed his features, too raw and too real for her to pretend not to see it. "Loving your mother and losing her almost killed me. My wife was gone, my child was gone. If it weren't for you, I think I would have put a bullet through my head. Somehow, I found a way to go on, but it couldn't be the same as before. I was convinced that the only way I would make it was if I did it alone. Building with you what I'd had with your mother… I couldn't risk it. So I made damn sure it never happened."

"You deliberately alienated me." His confirmation of

what she'd always suspected ran through her veins like ice water.

He nodded. "And in the end I got exactly what I wanted. I ran you off, and with you went the temptation to feel anything at all. I was finally safe. Completely alone in the world. But then you came back. And I realized how wrong I've been from the start. How much I've denied us both."

"Am I supposed to be flattered that you've finally decided I'm someone worth loving?"

"I don't expect you to believe that I've always loved you. I don't deserve that. But I do. I love you. And I won't let you think you're responsible for Angelica's death. You're not responsible for any of this."

Each time he said he loved her, it transformed his face a little more. It was as if light were shining on a dark, dusty corner for the first time in over thirty years.

And each time he said she wasn't the reason her mother died, Carrinne wanted to scream at him to stop lying. Because it couldn't be true.

Otherwise, there was nothing left to protect her from the choices *she'd* made. Nothing to gloss over the truth that she deserved to be alone, just as much as Oliver did.

"ERIC," Tony said from the doorway to Eric's office. "Do—"

"Do you know where my mom is?" Maggie pushed past him and stepped to the desk.

"No." Eric stood. "I thought she was home with you."

"Tony said she left to take a walk." Maggie looked behind her for confirmation.

"That was hours ago," Tony added.

Eric touched his daughter's arm, a selfish gesture that was more for his own comfort than hers. "Did she say anything to you after I left?"

"Not really." Maggie's shoulders gave a guilty shrug. "I didn't give her much of a chance. I was too angry to talk anymore."

"I was pretty angry myself." He rubbed Maggie's shoulder, giving her his best don't-beat-yourself-up-kid smile. Then it dawned on him that, unlike Tony, she might welcome a more affectionate kind of reassurance. He pulled her to his side and fought not to do a victory dance when she nestled her head on his shoulder.

"Don't worry," he said instead. "We'll find her together. And somehow, we'll find a way to change her mind about you being a donor."

He caught Tony's worried smile over the top of his daughter's head, and he had to smile himself. Holding Maggie, feeling her no longer fighting the bond forming between them, was the answer to a prayer he hadn't even realized was chanting inside him.

He only hoped heaven had one more miracle wedged up its sleeve for them.

"CARRINNE!"

Carrinne looked up as Eric and Maggie turned the corner around her grandfather's house. They headed toward her at a full-out sprint. The sight of Eric in his sheriff's uniform, his stride way too hurried for his James Dean persona, was every girlhood dream she'd ever had come true. Their daughter even ran like Eric, Carrinne realized.

Her heart swelled. Her pulse raced. Her soul sang with the whispering of the cypress limbs she sat beneath. She loved them both so much, it made her heart hurt to think of all they might never have together.

"What are you doing out here?" Eric knelt beside her. Perspiration trickled down his cheek.

"You've been gone all morning." Maggie dropped to the ground on her other side.

"Nina said you'd been sitting out here in this heat for over an hour," Eric added before Carrinne could respond.

She looked down at the first edition of *Wuthering Heights* she'd taken from the study.

"I've been reading." She lifted her eyes to watch the cloudless summer sky, framed by the cypress tree, stretching out above them as far as the eye could see. "And dreaming."

"But you don't dream anymore." Eric was close enough for her to see the pain darkening his deep brown eyes.

Their daughter's eyes.

"Call it research." She flipped the book closed and handed it to Maggie. Then she reached into her purse. "I'd stopped by the hospital to see Oliver, and Calvin brought over my cell phone. There was a message on it from Kim. Maggie's tests are back."

No one moved. No one spoke. Tension sparked the air.

"I had them fax the results to Oliver's study." She found the paper and pulled it out, handing it to Maggie. "You're a match."

Eric's gaze cut from the report to the book in their daughter's lap. "And your first instinct was hang out in the garden and catch up on your classics?"

Carrinne smiled, even as she struggled for some way to explain the confusion that had called her back to the place where she'd found sanctuary as a child.

"*Wuthering Heights* is a story about a woman who destroys what's most important to her because of the choices she makes for love," she said. "It's about lies and truth and the dreams we mangle when we distort one or the other or both."

Maggie's face filled with excitement as she read the report. Then every soft curve hardened into resignation. She handed the report back and crossed her arms over her chest. "So what? What does a book from my tenth-grade reading list have to do with me being a donor match for you?"

Carrinne took a deep breath, praying harder than she'd ever prayed in her life that she would get this right. "I thought my dream was to protect you, honey. To make sure I kept you safe, whatever the cost. But that was just a lie."

She thought of her grandfather, of the gift he'd finally given her without even knowing it. All her life, he'd used the past as an excuse to give up on the future. And he'd paid a terrible price.

"All along, the person I was really keeping safe was myself. I've felt responsible for my own mother's death for so long, Maggie, and—"

"What?" Maggie scooted closer. "Why—"

"It's a long story," Carrinne replied. "And the reasons don't really matter anymore. What I need you—" she took Maggie's hand and looked at Eric to make sure he was listening "—both of you, to understand is that my life's been one determined plan after another to make sure nothing like that ever happened again. You couldn't be a donor, honey. Not for me. Any risk to you, no matter how minimal, was out of the question. Because *I* couldn't handle it. Regardless of what I was doing to you or your father."

"What are you saying?" Eric's arm curled around her. His hand cupped Maggie's shoulder, pulling her closer into their group embrace.

"You were right." Carrinne lost herself in the hope and love she saw in his eyes. "I'd rather have died than live with the reality of Maggie risking her life for me. I was terrified of anyone loving me that much again. I didn't care that the choice wasn't mine alone to make. I just kept reasoning that I was doing the *right* thing. The safe thing. It was a lie, but it was easier to swallow than the truth—that I was running from my past and throwing away our family's chance for a future."

Eric smoothed his palm across her cheek, leaning in and kissing her with the softness of the warm July breeze stirring around them. The pride on his face was mixed with the deeper emotions he'd never been able to hide when they'd met beneath this old tree. "And now?"

"And now." She put her arms around her daughter and the only man she'd ever loved. "I want to fight for my dreams. I love you both. And I want it all. Forget about what happened forever ago. I want our family, and I want a lifetime of tomorrows with you both."

EPILOGUE

"CARRINNE," a Southern voice from her dreams whispered. "Carrinne. Wake up, darlin'."

"Maggie…" Carrinne mumbled. There was something she needed to know about Maggie. She snuggled into the warm hand caressing her cheek, the medication she somehow knew she'd been given lulling her under again. What was it she was saying? "…where's Ma—"

"Maggie's fine. She's in recovery." The voice belonged to the bad boy with a heart of gold who only moments ago had been whisking her down a dreamy highway on his motorcycle. He squeezed her hand, pulling her further from sleep's protective layers. "Now open those gorgeous eyes for me. You've left me here alone long enough."

He was alone. And there were tears in his voice. Eric never cried.

She squeezed the hand holding hers and fought to do what he asked. She should be in pain, a distant thought told her, but the cloud of nothing she was floating on refused to let her feel anything at all. Except urgency.

"…don't worry…" Her lips rasped together like

sandpaper. She struggled to lick them, and cool water appeared, trickling into her dry mouth. She swallowed, swimming closer to the pool of light on the other side of her closed eyelids. "…not alone anymore."

"That's it, darlin'." She felt his smile. "Wake up enough to hear the news about Maggie."

"Maggie?" Pushing against the weights on her eyes, she forced them open a crack and searched. "Where's Maggie?"

"Maggie's fine." The shadow beside her hovered closer, condensing into a fuzzy reflection of Eric. "She's recovering in a room of her own down the hall."

The operations.

Her transplant.

Her brain reengaged, opening the door to her memory. They were in Mount Sinai Hospital in New York. After months of waiting, today had been the day. She blinked, fighting to bring Eric's face into focus.

"Maggie's okay?"

His smile was the first clear thing she saw. He wiped tears of happiness from his eyes, then dabbed at the ones trickling down her own face.

"She's perfect. She's been awake for several hours. I just left her when they told me you were coming around. She made me promise to come back once I was sure you were okay."

"I'm…okay." She waited. "Aren't I?"

"You're amazing." His kiss feathered her forehead. "You'll both be in ICU until they've ruled out any complicatiòns, but the doctors said the transplant couldn't have gone better. Maggie should be able to go home early next week. You'll be ready to dance at our wedding in six months. I won't accept anything less."

He was being bossy again. And she loved it.

She turned until she could graze a kiss across his cheek. Some dandy narcotic seeped exhaustion to her through the IV.

"You've got a date," she said around a tiny yawn. "I love you."

She'd never be able to say that enough. Couldn't wait for their spring wedding in her grandmother's rose garden in Oakwood, so she could say it in front of God and everybody.

"I love you, too, darlin'," he whispered. "Rest. I'll be here when you wake up. Everything's going to be okay."

Images flashed behind lids that refused to stay open a moment longer. Maggie and Eric's joy when they learned Maggie was a match and that Carrinne had agreed to the living donor transplant. Oliver's earnest offer to pay for the transplant procedures, his request that they consider having the wedding at the mansion on Governor's Square. Eric trailing beside her as they wheeled her to surgery just that morning, telling her, as he had for the last two months, that everything was going to be okay.

There were still so many things to settle. Eric had taken a leave of absence until she and Maggie recovered from their surgeries, but he had a little over a year left in his term as sheriff. She was taking her own time off until after the wedding, and just last week, she'd signed a contract with a new partner. Something she'd never, ever, expected she'd want. But with someone holding down the fort in the city, she could commute back and forth between Georgia and New York until Eric's term was over. Then after that, maybe if there really was some kind of a relationship left to salvage with her grandfather… Who knew? Eric was even making noise about possibly running for another term.

A good accountant could always find work, wherever she lived. And having Eric back had reminded her of everything she'd forgotten she'd loved about Oakwood. Everything she wanted to share with her daughter before Maggie went away to college next year.

There were still so many maybes…. Still no guarantees. But Eric was right. Everything was going to be okay, no matter what they had to face from now on. Because they had each other. And they had Maggie, which made them the family she'd always wanted.

Together, for as long as they had left, their lives would never be anything less than a dream come true.

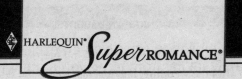

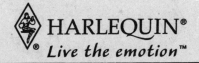

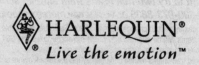

If you enjoyed what you just read,
then we've got an offer you can't resist!

Take 2 bestselling
love stories FREE!
Plus get a FREE surprise gift!

Christmas comes to

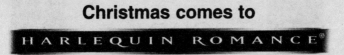

HARLEQUIN ROMANCE®

In November 2004, don't miss:

CHRISTMAS EVE MARRIAGE
(#3820)
by Jessica Hart

In this seasonal romance, the only thing Thea is looking for on her long-awaited holiday is a little R and R—she certainly doesn't expect to find herself roped into being Rhys Kingsford's pretend fiancée!

A SURPRISE CHRISTMAS PROPOSAL
(#3821)
by Liz Fielding

A much-needed job brings sassy Sophie Harrington up close and personal with rugged bachelor Gabriel York in this festive story. But how long before he realizes that Sophie isn't just for Christmas—but for life…?

Available wherever Harlequin books are sold.

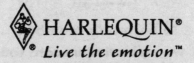

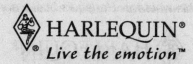

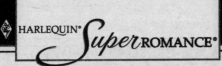

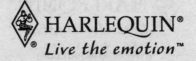

A baby to be always means something special!

COMING HOME TO TEXAS
by **Victoria Chancellor**
September 2004

A plus-size model with a plus-size secret comes to Ranger Springs, Texas, to find a temporary husband—who also happens to be the father of her baby to be.

SANTA BABY
by **Laura Marie Altom**
November 2004

Christmas Eve, Alaska. A small-plane crash—and nine months later, a baby. But Whitney and her pilot, Colby, are completely at odds about their son's future. Until the next Christmas!

And in December watch for *The Baby's Bodyguard* **by Jacqueline Diamond**

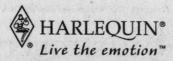

HARLEQUIN®
Live the emotion™

www.eHarlequin.com

HARBYTB